CHASING D. ..MS AT WAGGING TAILS DOGS' HOME

SARAH HOPE

Boldwood

First published in Great Britain in 2023 by Boldwood Books Ltd.

Copyright © Sarah Hope, 2023

Cover Design by Head Design Ltd

Cover Illustration: Head Design Ltd and Shutterstock

Every effort has been made to obtain the necessary permissions with reference to copyright material, both illustrative and quoted. We apologise for any omissions in this respect and will be pleased to make the appropriate acknowledgements in any future edition.

A CIP catalogue record for this book is available from the British Library.

Paperback ISBN 978-1-80549-060-9

Large Print ISBN 978-1-80549-061-6

Hardback ISBN 978-1-80549-059-3

Ebook ISBN 978-1-80549-062-3

Kindle ISBN 978-1-80549-063-0

Audio CD ISBN 978-1-80549-054-8

MP3 CD ISBN 978-1-80549-055-5

Digital audio download ISBN 978-1-80549-057-9

Boldwood Books Ltd
23 Bowerdean Street
London SW6 3TN
www.boldwoodbooks.com

For my children. Let's change our stars.

xXx

1

Poppy Hargraves watched as the taxi pulled away from the side of the road, a sheen of rainwater splashing her jeans as the car hit a puddle.

Shrugging, she turned towards the narrow lane behind her and listened as the metal sign swung in the wind, the creak slow and methodical as the wind blew inland. If it wasn't for the picture of the dog and the words 'Wagging Tails Dogs' Home' hand-painted on it, people would likely pass by without realising the dogs' home was situated a few short metres away.

She remembered Aunt Flora telling her that was why she and Uncle Arthur had fallen in love with the once ramshackle cottage. For one, it had enough land to realise their dream of building and opening up a dogs' rescue, but also, lying on the outskirts of the small village of West Par, it was close enough to socialise the dogs into the local community but far enough away as not to worry about any noise affecting close neighbours.

Taking hold of the handle of the suitcase, Poppy began the short walk towards the gates at the end of the lane. The taxi driver had offered to drop her closer, but she'd fancied the walk, a last moment to savour the time and space alone before seeing Aunt Flora.

It wasn't even Aunt Flora she was worried about seeing. Well, not worried. Apprehensive. She'd told Aunt Flora everything, right from the moment she'd had the conversation with Ben about ending their relationship to deciding to move out of their mutual home. She'd even rung her from the school toilets after running out of class, mid-teaching Year Six about the rainforest canopy, a topic she normally loved, crying down the phone that she couldn't face going back home and spending another evening sitting in silence with Ben knowing full well that he had arranged to take a work colleague for a lunch date the following week. And that was fine. It really was. They were separated. He was free to do what he wanted. See who he wanted. But did he have to tell her? Have to make it clear that he was ready to move on so soon? No, it wasn't seeing Aunt Flora that she was delaying, it was going in and acknowledging that she was running from a failed relationship.

She hated that phrase – failed relationship – yes, it had failed, but it wasn't just on her. She'd tried. She'd tried everything these last two years to keep their love alive, to win Ben back, to have him look at her as though she was the best thing in his life again, but nothing had worked.

She stepped in a puddle, the water seeping in through her trainers. She supposed she had failed. Maybe the phrase made sense after all. But he'd failed too.

Brushing the raindrops from her fringe, she yanked the suitcase up the kerb and onto the path, forcing her lips into a smile. She could do this. She was strong. Besides, this was just what she needed, being away from the mutual home, from Ben, a break from supply teaching. Yes. And how many times had she walked down this lane? At least four times a day every summer for three weeks. Wonderful weeks of the school holidays until she'd gone to uni and suddenly her summers had been filled with trying to earn money – jobs at the petting farm, at the corner shop, or filling freezers at the supermarket, anything she could find close to Durham – where she'd studied – to supplement her student loan. She'd had the best time here at the dogs' home, visiting Aunt Flora and the dogs. An escape from the relentless arguments between her parents at home and the bullying she'd endured at school. Particularly during her teenage years, the couple of years before her parents had finally decided to walk away from their unhappy marriage and when Gail Patterson, the worst of the school bullies, had really stepped up the vendetta against her.

Yes, Aunt Flora, Percy, Susan, and the numerous dogs in their care had been just what she'd needed – a chance to regain her confidence even if it had only been for those few glorious weeks each year. Even as an adult, she'd visited one weekend a month, staying longer during the summer, or tried to. Up until five years ago.

And now, after five years of not visiting, she was back. Once again, with her life in tatters. Once again in need of the comfort and security only her aunt could provide for her.

She set the suitcase back on its little wheels and just as she began to unlatch the gate, something caught her eye behind her, a flash of brilliant yellow against the dreary lane. It couldn't be, but with those little golden bees emblazoned across the yellow material, it must be. Turning, she slumped her shoulders. It was. The floaty blouse she'd packed for no other reason than it was her favourite was being carried on the breeze, dipping and dancing down the lane.

Abandoning her suitcase, she ran towards it, jumping up and catching it just before it was propelled into the brambles along the side of the road.

'Got you.' She folded it before smoothing the material down

with the pads of her fingers. She'd worn the blouse on her first date with Ben. Not that that was the reason she loved it so much. No. It was just her go-to top. The smart floaty piece was perfect for all occasions – interviews, dates, meeting Ben's parents for the first time, girls' nights out. Everything. And it looked as new as it had the day she'd bought it over six years ago.

Poppy picked at a loose thread on the collar. *Almost* as good as new. How had it even worked its way out of the suitcase? Hadn't she zipped it up properly? As she stepped forward, her trainer squelched into a puddle again, and she looked down. Great, she'd just stepped on one of her white vest tops.

She picked it up and held it at arm's length, the murky puddle water dripping to the ground. As she looked towards the suitcase, her heart sank. The zip had come undone at the bottom and an array of clothing now littered the lane – all wet and muddy.

Her friend, Melissa, had warned her the suitcase was old when she'd borrowed it, but Poppy would have remembered if she'd mentioned a fault with the zip. Wouldn't she?

She sighed. Maybe she wouldn't have. When she'd picked it up, she'd been in such a daze after a difficult week supplying at the most notorious school in her local vicinity and surviving on next to no sleep hunched on the sofa bed in the spare room. Melissa could have likely said anything and Poppy wouldn't have remembered.

Turning her face to the sky, she rolled her shoulders back as raindrops dribbled down her face. There was something about the rain she loved; the way it made her feel. It was almost freeing, especially here, so close to the ocean. The raindrops were laced with that unmistakable salty aroma of the sea. Salty rainwater washing her worries away.

She scoffed. If only it were that easy.

Poppy walked back to the suitcase, picking up underwear, tops and pyjamas as she did. She'd have to replace the suitcase when she went home. Whether the zip had already been dodgy or not, it hadn't been this bad.

Pushing open the door to the reception to Wagging Tails, Poppy scanned around, noting the empty reception desk. The gentle tunes of instrumental Christmas music, which was playing quietly from the radio behind the counter, immediately enveloped her.

'Aunt Flora?'

Nothing.

She set the suitcase next to the counter and heaped her muddy clothes on top before stepping around the reception desk and peering into the kitchen. That was empty, too. Shrugging out of her wet coat, she moved around to the back door which led to the kennels and quietly opened it.

As soon as she stepped inside, a raucous rally of barking and whining began. She winced. She'd forgotten how excited the dogs got when someone walked in. As a child, she'd loved running up and down the corridor next to the kennels, waving and petting the dogs one by one, trying to share her time equally between them.

She peered into each kennel, quietly approaching each dog, holding out her hand and letting the dogs get used to her before she fussed them.

Still no sign of Aunt Flora though, and with the excited barking there wouldn't be much point in calling out for her again. Still, it was nice to meet the dogs. There were two empty kennels, which she guessed meant they must have had some luck on the adoption front. That was probably down to Darren, the reporter her aunt had told her about. She'd said he was writing a weekly column in the local paper featuring dogs Wagging Tails had up for adoption.

Poppy frowned. Was his name Darren? Or Darryl, maybe? Whatever it was, according to her aunt, his columns had been having an enormous impact on the rate of adoptions.

As she approached the next kennel, she paused, a huge smile taking over her face.

'Ralph? Is it really you?'

Would he recognise her? After all these years? He'd been very young when he'd first been brought to Wagging Tails and then she'd only seen him a handful of times.

'Hello, Ralph. Oh, sweetheart, it's so lovely to see you.' Holding her palm flat against the bars of the door, she knelt down until she was level with the Staffie. 'Do you remember me?'

She watched as Ralph lifted his head from his bed of duvets and looked at her, his deep eyes holding memories that she, Aunt Flora, or anyone for that matter, would never find out. Standing up, he stretched before shaking his body, his eyes fixed on her. He sauntered over and leaned his head up against the door, his fur warm against the metal.

'You remember me.'

Sitting down, she leaned against the door too, her forehead against his, a lump forming in her throat.

'Is that you, Ginny, lovely?'

Poppy kissed Ralph's forehead and stood up before following her aunt's voice.

'It's me, Aunt Flora.'

She walked to the far kennel, where Poppy could see her aunt was sitting on the floor, surrounded by three small puppies, each one clambering onto her lap, vying for attention.

'Poppy! Poppy, oh, darling. How are you?' Flora grinned and held her arms out towards her.

How was she? Now, that was one question she actually didn't really know the answer to herself. Relieved? Angry? Overwhelmingly sad?

Shrugging, she pushed open the door and lowered herself next to her aunt.

Probably seeing the look on Poppy's face, her aunt quickly added, 'Oh, lovely. You don't need to answer that. It was daft of me to ask such a question. Come here.'

Leaning her head against Aunt Flora's shoulder, Poppy looked down at the puppies who had paused their game to cock their heads and peer at her, their dark eyes glistening with curiosity.

'Meet Sage, Basil and Thyme.'

Poppy shook her head, a small involuntary laugh escaping her lips. 'Susan named them?'

'You guessed it.' Flora picked up one of the wriggling pups and placed it in Poppy's arms. 'Here, Thyme is the calmer of the trio, believe it or not, and if there's one thing she loves more than running around like a headless chicken, it's snuggling in your arms.'

'Aw, she's such a cutie.' Poppy lowered her face to Thyme's head, breathing in that unmistakable biscuity aroma of puppy, and watched as she closed her eyes.

'She is. Don't go getting attached, though. I know how soppy you go over a spaniel, but these three are already reserved and will go to their forever homes just as soon as they've had their vaccinations.'

2

Stretching her arms above her head, Poppy squashed the mound of pillows away from her head and sat up. That was the best night's sleep she'd had in a long time. She looked out of the window, the dim light of a winter's morning filtering through the edges of the curtains. What time was it?

Nine thirty. She'd even slept through breakfast time. Pushing the duvet to the end of the bed, she stood up and slipped her feet into the fluffy grey slippers Aunt Flora had left for her. She walked across to the window, opened the curtains and looked out. She could see Susan and someone she didn't recognise exercising dogs in the paddocks and, beyond that, the kennels. A van had just pulled up into the courtyard.

She watched as a woman jumped out before going to the back of the van and lifting out tray after tray of dog food.

As a child, Poppy had always loved delivery day. The driver had always brought a bag of dog toys he'd collected from his colleagues, and it had been her job to share these fairly between the dogs. She'd taken this responsibility seriously, making sure each dog got the perfect gift – tennis balls for the energetic, cuddly teddies for the elder dogs and the ones missing the comfort of home, squeaky toys for those who liked to chew.

Closing the curtains again, she looked towards the suitcase by the door, a pile of clean dry clothes now balanced on top. Yesterday evening, Aunt Flora had taken the muddy clothes away and must have returned the freshly laundered items sometime. Picking them up, Poppy held them to her face. Aunt Flora was still using the same honeysuckle-fragranced fabric conditioner she had years before. In a way, it felt like home.

Poppy replaced the clothes before rolling her shoulders back and looking in the mirror which stood on the old dressing table Uncle Arthur had French polished. She pulled at the skin under her eyes, the dark circles deep and sunken. Well, with a few more nights' sleep as good as the one she'd just had, at least they should begin to improve.

It was Saturday. The day Ben was apparently going on his first date since they'd decided to separate. She swallowed. It may have been a mutual decision to separate – a difficult one but a mutual one – but it still stung to her core that he was seemingly moving on so quickly. They'd barely been apart four months. Four months of still living together. For three of those months Poppy had believed he'd tell her they'd made a mistake, tell her he still loved her and wanted to work on their relationship instead of walking away. But that hadn't happened, and as such, one month followed, with Poppy crying into her pillow in the spare bedroom as her new reality set in.

Standing up tall, she took a deep breath in. She needed to move on, too. Not in any romantic way. She shuddered. No, she wasn't ready for *that*. But emotionally. She needed to take this time out. Be kind to herself, as Melissa kept telling her, and begin to visualise a future as a single woman. A future without Ben. She sighed. After six years of having Ben in her life she knew it would be difficult, but if he could do it, she had to believe she could too.

* * *

Poppy pushed the door to the reception area of Wagging Tails open and stepped through, the heat from the small electric fire quickly warming her. She looked across at the counter, her eyes drawn to the flickering fairy lights strung across the front. She hadn't noticed them yesterday. Someone must have added them this morning.

'Poppy, lovely. How was your sleep?' Aunt Flora pushed her reading glasses to the top of her head and walked around the counter towards her.

'Good, thanks. And thank you for doing my washing. Sorry I've woken up so late.' She leaned her head against Aunt Flora's shoulder as she gave her a quick hug.

'No worries, lovely. You were lucky the mud came out. Especially on your white vest top.'

'Yes, I thought that would be ruined.' Poppy shrugged out of her coat and hung it on the hooks behind the counter. It was only a short walk from the cottage, but it was freezing outside and she'd likely need it again if she took any of the dogs for a walk. 'What can I do?'

Flora looked across at the clock on the shelf. 'I've got to pop out with Ginny in a couple of minutes to make a home visit to a local animal hoarder. We've been working with him for months now to try to encourage him to surrender some of his animals and we're hoping he'll let us take a few on today.'

'Oh, really? How many has he got?' Poppy frowned. She'd watched a documentary on TV last year about an animal hoarder who had literally had at least a hundred cats.

'He has twenty-eight dogs and fifteen cats. A lovely bloke,

elderly. His farm was repossessed a few years back now, and I think he just missed the animals. He squats in one of the old farm worker's cottages on the edge of his land and has just accumulated all these animals.' She shook her head. 'It's a really sad case. You can see he loves each and every one of them, but with his health going downhill, he's just not been able to give them the care and attention they need.'

Poppy grimaced. 'Wow, that many? Do you think he'll really give them up?'

'I hope so. We're working with a local cat rescue, too. He's giving the animals the basic care so they can't legally be taken away without his consent but the conditions they're living in, *he's* living in...' Flora shook her head.

'It sounds positive that you think he might let you rehome some today, though?'

'Yes, yes. Although we've been here before. Two weeks ago, he promised to let us take a couple and then wouldn't even let us into the property, but we'll see.' Flora crossed her fingers and held them up so Poppy could see. 'Anyway, Susan is at the supplier's today, Alex is up at the top paddock with Ralph, and Sally, our trainer, has taken Fluffles down to the village to do some on-lead training, so are you okay holding down the fort here for a bit? Sally should be back soon, and Alex's number is in the book if you need him.'

'Umm, okay.' Poppy nodded. She hadn't 'held down the fort' as her aunt put it for years, but as a teenager, she'd loved feeling as though she was in charge, even if the reality had been that there had always been other people on site.

'Talking of Ginny, here she comes now.' Flora grinned as a woman walked through the door, wiping her hands down her jeans, adding mud to the large splodges on her knees. Flora turned to her and said, 'Did Ronnie have you over again, Ginny, love?'

'His best one yet. He might not be huge but he's one strong dog.'

Ginny shook her head and laughed as she closed the door. When she noticed Poppy, she beamed. 'Hi, you must be Poppy? Flora said you were coming to stay for a while.'

'Hi, yes. Lovely to finally meet you, Ginny. I feel as though I know you already, the number of times Aunt Flora has mentioned you.'

'Oh, yes?' Ginny looked from Poppy to Flora and back again. 'Should I be worried?'

Poppy laughed. 'Nope, it's all been good. She's forever singing your praises.'

'Argh, that's a relief.' Ginny smiled and looked down at her hands, which were still smeared with mud. 'I'd give you a hug, but I don't think you'd want me to.'

'You get cleaned up while I grab my coat.' Flora turned to Poppy. 'And you're sure you don't mind me running out on you on your first morning here?'

'Of course not. Go and rescue those pups!' Waving them off, Poppy grinned. She'd go and see the dogs and then see if Aunt Flora had left any paperwork to do. She knew Flora liked to scribble down any new dog's details before writing them up for the website. Poppy had always enjoyed helping with that.

After Flora and Ginny had left, Poppy opened the door to the corridor that led to the kennels, grabbing a handful of treats on the way.

* * *

Tapping the top of the pen against her chin, Poppy looked down at what she'd written so far... 'Fluffles, a diva of a poodle-cross, had arrived at Wagging Tails looking forlorn'...

Nope. Forlorn? Really? She scribbled it out... Changed it to 'rather sorry for herself'. Better.

Poppy leaned back on the stool and looked across at the CCTV monitor her aunt had installed a few months earlier. Something had caught her eye – a flicker of movement at the front gate. She watched as a car pulled up and a woman jumped out, removing a box from the passenger seat before speeding off again.

She squinted at the small black and white screen. A box had definitely been left there. Odd. People normally popped in with donations instead of leaving them at the gate. She must have been in a hurry or perhaps Aunt Flora had been expecting whatever it was she'd been dropping off.

Stepping outside, Poppy pulled her cardie tighter around herself as the cold wind whipped around her. She looked up at the sky. Dense white clouds hung low, not even a sliver of blue could be seen. There'd be snow this year, she was sure of that.

She pulled the gate open, bent down and lifted the box, immediately lowering it again as the weight in it shifted to the side.

'What?'

Peering inside, Poppy opened her mouth in shock as a bedraggled dog looked up at her, his dark eyes sad and sunken.

'Oh, sweetheart.'

Gingerly, she lifted the dog into her arms and tucked him under her cardigan. He was so light she could hardly feel him at all. She looked down the lane and sighed. The car was long gone. The poor dog dumped and forgotten.

As she turned back to the gate, she glanced at the box again and reached down as she noticed an envelope taped to the side of it. She tugged it off before slipping it into her pocket.

'Let's get you inside and comfortable and then we can see what your so-called owner has to say.'

Once inside again, Poppy lowered the dog to the floor and leaned back on her haunches. She wasn't the best at determining different breeds, but she was certain this little one was a cockapoo.

Ben's parents had a cockapoo called Samuel, a sweet little thing. Although this one in front of her was a world away from being the happy, healthy dog Samuel was. No, something wasn't right. The way his eyes didn't meet hers, no interest in his new surroundings. He'd even let her, a complete stranger, pick him up and carry him without so much of a complaint or an attempt to jump down and walk.

The dog sank to the floor in front of her, his paws out in front of him, seemingly too tired to explore the reception area, sniff at all the new smells or cock an ear to listen to the sounds of the other dogs barking. She watched as he slowly lifted his head a centimetre before coughing a deep, rasping cough.

She glanced around the reception area, searching for where Aunt Flora kept the blankets before giving up. She shrugged out of her cardigan and laid it over the dog, covering his dull matted fur before pulling the envelope from her pocket. She read the short letter before laying it down and reaching for the phone.

'Alex? Is that Alex?'

'Hi, it certainly is.' Alex's cheerful voice wafted down the phone line. She'd never met him, but his voice oozed kindness.

'Hi, you don't know me but I'm Poppy, Flora's niece. I'm in the reception and she told me to ring you if I had any problems.' She could hear the urgency in her voice.

'Poppy. Hi, Flora said you were coming. What's up?'

'A dog has just been dumped at the gates, in a box, with a letter and the letter says...' she grabbed the piece of paper again '... it says "Please look after Dougal. He's poorly and I have no money for vet's bills." He's not well at all. Very skinny and coughing. Do you think it's kennel cough? What if the other dogs catch it?'

Poppy chewed her bottom lip and glanced towards the door to the kennels.

'Oh, bless him. He sounds in a bad way. All the dogs have had their vaccinations, but he probably needs to be taken straight to the vet if he's that bad. I haven't got my car today. Did Flora and Ginny take the van?'

She stood up and looked out of the window. 'Yes, they did.'

Alex sighed. 'I don't suppose you're insured for Flora's car, are you?'

'Yes, yes, I am. She said she'd put me on the insurance.'

'Great. Are you okay taking him and I'll make my way back with Ralph now? Just ask our vet, Gavin, to pop the charges on the tab. He only charges for medication at cost price anyway. He's good like that.'

Poppy nodded and grabbed her aunt's car keys from the bookshelf behind the counter.

'Which vet's is it?' She picked up a card from the counter. 'Don't worry, I've found it.'

'Great. Well, good luck and let me know if there're any problems.'

'Will do.' Ending the call, Poppy gently picked Dougal up and carried him to her aunt's car.

3

'Dougal?' the receptionist called.

Looking up, Poppy scooped Dougal from her lap and stood up, glad not to have to sit on the hard plastic chairs – which seem compulsory in every waiting room – a moment longer.

'Here,' she said.

'Come on through.'

Inside the small treatment room, the smell of antiseptic was strong, and the walls covered in glossy posters. Poppy gently lowered the small cockapoo onto the surface of the shiny black examining table and stroked Dougal's ears.

'Oh dear, oh dear, what have we got here then?' The vet stepped back to allow them through before closing the door behind them. The vet was tall and well-built and the way he held his shoulders back seeped confidence as his presence filled the room.

'This is Dougal. He was left at the gate of Wagging Tails Dogs' Home. I'm helping out there for my aunt.'

The vet nodded and as he held his stethoscope to Dougal's chest, he frowned, his eyes darkening with concern.

'Anyway, he had a note with him that said he was poorly, but his owner couldn't afford to take him to the vet.' She paused as Dougal began coughing, before taking a long shuddering breath. 'Do you think he's got kennel cough?'

Folding his arms, the vet frowned once more. 'I don't think so, although without further tests I wouldn't like to completely rule kennel cough out.'

'What else could it be?'

'Without even weighing him, it's obvious he's severely under-weight and undernourished. His ribs are visible, and his fur is in poor condition. It could be a simple case of neglect or one of a number of issues, from the easily treatable to the not so.'

Poppy stroked Dougal behind the ears. Why was life so cruel? This little pup had been born and likely bought with the best of intentions, and now he had been either neglected to the point he was barely surviving or allowed to get so ill he'd been given up. Whichever it was, the owner was responsible. She flared her nostrils and blinked as the sting of tears hit the back of her eyes.

'As I said, it may well be treatable, but we'll need to run some tests to determine what it is exactly. And you have no idea how long he's been living with this condition?'

'No, he was dropped off this morning.' She glanced at the clock on the wall. 'Just over an hour ago, actually. Everything I know is in this letter.' She reached into her pocket and passed him the scrunched-up piece of paper. 'Here you are.'

'Of course.' He laid his hand on her arm, his hand surprisingly warm despite the surgery being on the chilly side, before taking the letter and quickly skimming it. 'You've done the right thing, bringing him here.'

Nodding, Poppy looked across at him. His eyes were a deep shade of brown, the kind that drew you in, comforted you.

'Thank you.'

'Right, I'll go and get the necessary equipment and we'll draw some blood.' He looked at her, his eyes locking with hers, his mouth drawing into a quick smile.

She watched as he walked out of the room and then looked down to where he'd placed his hand on her arm. He knew how to reassure someone. That was obvious. And the way he'd looked at her? Was he flirting? She shook her head, a low grunt of a sarcastic laugh escaping. What was she even thinking?

Looking back down at Dougal, she whispered, 'You'll be fine, sweetheart. Just be a brave little boy and we'll get you feeling better.'

'Here we are,' The vet said, coming back into the room. 'Now just hold still, pup, and it will all be over soon.' He drew the blood before Dougal had a chance to realise what was going on. 'Right, I'll hurry these through and all being well, we'll contact you tomorrow with the results. In the meantime, I'd advise keeping him separated from the other dogs in your care. Just until we know what we're dealing with.'

'Great. Thank you.' She stepped back as he lowered Dougal to the floor. 'Come on, Dougal. Let's get you back to Wagging Tails and get you comfy.'

'Nice to meet you. And hopefully, we can get him healthy soon enough.'

Holding the door open for her, he smiled.

'And you.' She caught his eye before turning and focusing on Dougal.

Back out in the waiting area, she looked through the large windows towards Aunt Flora's car and paused. 'Do you want picking up?' she asked Dougal. 'It suddenly seems a long way to the car.'

She gently scooped up the small cockapoo who immediately flopped his body against her, his head laid against her shoulder. Nodding her thanks as a man holding a cat carrier held the door open for her, she stepped outside, shivering against the cold and immediately wishing she'd put her cardigan back on instead of leaving it on the car seat where she'd used it to wrap Dougal up. She'd been in such a hurry after talking to Alex on the phone that she hadn't even thought to throw her coat on. Her sole focus had been on getting Dougal here.

'Excuse me. You've not paid yet.'

Was that aimed at her? She turned around and looked at the receptionist who was hanging out of the doorway, her arms wrapped around her middle.

'Me?'

'That's right.' The woman held the door wide open, signalling Poppy to go back through.

'Oh, I'm from Wagging Tails Dogs' Home.' She shifted Dougal in her arms.

'That's nice.'

Smiling, Poppy began to make her way back towards the car again.

'I'm sorry. Excuse me, but payment needs to be made before you leave.' The woman's voice was apologetic but stern.

Poppy paused again and then retraced her steps. She was sure Alex had said they didn't have to pay for treatment and there was a tab for medication. And Dougal hadn't been given any medication. Not yet. And surely the blood test didn't count? That would be part of a treatment plan, she thought.

As Poppy reached the door, the receptionist disappeared inside and back behind her desk before she could explain, leaving her with no option but to follow. Letting the door swing shut behind her, she gently placed Dougal down onto the floor and waited at the desk as the woman clicked on her computer.

'That will be sixty-five pounds for today's appointment, please.' The woman tapped the computer screen.

'Sorry, I should have explained. I'm with The Wagging Tails Dogs' Home and they have an agreement with the vet to only pay for medication, not treatment. And I believe they have a tab to put medication charges on.'

Frowning, the woman looked back at her computer screen. 'It's just saying you owe sixty-five pounds. Nothing about getting it any cheaper or any tab.'

Poppy frowned. Something wasn't right. 'And you're sure it's under the right account? The dogs' home?'

'Yes. The Wagging Tails Dogs' Home.' The woman twisted the screen around to show her.

Poppy peered at the screen. Everything looked right. The correct address, telephone number.

'That's odd. Can you check with the vet please?'

'I can.' The receptionist leaned her head to the side and looked behind Poppy. 'I'll just serve this gentleman first, if you don't mind.'

'Of course not.' Shuffling to the side, Poppy looked at the receptionist's name tag. Kerry. She didn't recognise the name. Not that she probably would. She hadn't come to the vet with her aunt in about seven years. Still, maybe she was new.

After telling a man with a canary to take a seat in the waiting area, Kerry turned back to Poppy and picked up the phone. 'I'll check with him now.'

'Thank you,' Poppy mouthed as Kerry spoke into the phone. It would all be cleared up now she was talking to Gavin.

She looked down at Dougal, who was still lying exactly where she'd lowered him. The sooner the blood test results came back, and treatment could start, the better.

'Just as I thought. Thank you.' Kerry ended the call and looked up at Poppy. 'I'm afraid there isn't a discount or a tab. You'll need to settle your bill, please.'

'But...'

'Please. I need to see to our other patients.'

Twisting around, Poppy reddened. She hadn't realised a queue had formed.

'Daffodil? Do we have Daffodil the canary, please?'

Glancing around, she saw the vet had emerged from his treatment room. This was her chance. She looked down at Dougal before deciding he probably wouldn't be going anywhere and rushed towards the vet as he waited for his next patient.

'Excuse me. You've just seen Dougal.'

'Oh yes, hello again.' He smiled broadly.

'There seems to be some sort of misunderstanding. I'm helping out at Wagging Tails Dogs' Home and Dougal is a rescue dog. I'm being charged for today's appointment, but I was of the understanding that the charity only paid for medication and Dougal hasn't had any medication. Only the examination and blood test.'

The vet lifted his eyebrow and looked at her. 'I'm afraid I don't have any special deal with any charity. An animal is brought to me for treatment and the treatment needs to be paid for. I'm terribly sorry.'

'But...' Poppy glanced back at Dougal and then at the large sign in the waiting room. She pulled out the card she'd found on the counter back at the home. Yes, she was in the right place, the right surgery. She sighed. What if the card she'd found wasn't the surgery Wagging Tails used? Someone might have dropped it or left it accidentally or the surgery may even have popped it through the letter box scouting for business.

Alex had mentioned the vet's name was Gavin. Why hadn't she checked she was in the right place when she'd first arrived? She should have done. This was her fault. Her mistake. Sighing, she nodded.

'Ah, Daffodil and Mr Gregory, of course. Lovely to meet you

both. Come on through.' Holding the door open, the vet lifted his hand and smiled at Poppy again.

Joining the back of the short queue, Poppy pulled her credit card from her purse. She just had to hope there was sixty-five pounds still on there to use.

4

'Oh, lovely, sorry you had to pay. I'll pay you back. What did you say the surgery was called?'

Sitting at the table, Flora stroked Dougal, who had curled up on her lap, his front legs dangling over her knees. He looked as exhausted as he had earlier, even after a bite to eat.

'Thank you, but, no, it's my fault for taking him to the wrong one. Trestow Veterinary Surgery.'

'Trestow? That's the one we normally go to. I'll call them, get it sorted. There must have been a misunderstanding.' Leaning across the table, Flora rubbed Poppy's arm.

'Oh, really? I told the receptionist I was from Wagging Tails, and I spoke to the vet too, and although he was very apologetic, he just said he doesn't have deals, discounts or tabs with anyone.'

'That's odd. May have been a locum, though. I'm sure we'll get to the bottom of it. I'll transfer the money as soon as we've settled this one in his kennel.'

'There's no need. I should have explained myself better to them or something.' She picked at her nail varnish, the pale blue flaking to the floor. 'Besides, they'll probably give me a refund when you explain, anyway.'

'True, they will. Still, I'll transfer it as it sometimes takes a bit of time. Are you still having to pay half of the bills? Or has Ben taken that over now you've moved out?'

Poppy grimaced. 'After this month, I'll just be paying my half of the mortgage.'

It was a good thing really, being as two days ago had been her last day of supply teaching until after the school Christmas holidays.

Flora looked up at the kitchen door as someone walked through. 'Ah, here's Alex. Alex, this is my niece, Poppy.'

'Hey, Poppy. Great to put a face to the voice on the phone.' Alex strode in and grinned before looking down at Dougal. 'Oh, this must be our new addition. How much does he look like Bella and Tiger?'

Flora chuckled. 'That he does. Poppy, we had two little cockapoos in this summer. Real characters they were. Though the poor things were thrown over the fence. But they have a new forever home now.'

Kneeling down next to Flora, Alex began to fuss the small dog. 'Have you heard from their new family recently?'

'I have. They sent me an email just yesterday evening, actually. I've popped some photos they sent to us on the fridge.' Flora nodded towards the under-the-counter fridge, where two A4 photographs were clamped with little dog magnets to the door.

Turning around in her chair, Poppy looked at the photos. One showed two small cockapoos running through some woodland whilst the other depicted a nose, a huge, black shiny nose aimed straight at the camera. She laughed.

'That picture is great, isn't it? Bella and Tiger's new mum said she'd just got the camera out and Tiger must have thought it was a treat, the attention he gave it.' Flora chuckled.

'Aw, they do look happy, don't they?' Alex turned the tap on, filling a glass before leaning back against the counter and drinking it in one go.

'Yes, they seem to be getting on really well. It's always such a relief when we can rehome a pair who come in together.'

'Absolutely,' Alex said, kneeling down again in front of Flora and fussing Dougal behind the ears. 'What's happening with this little one, then?'

'We won't know what's wrong with him until tomorrow when the results of his blood test are back.' Poppy frowned.

'We've enticed him with a little chicken. He only ate a morsel though, and it was obvious that was difficult for him.' Flora sighed. 'We'll have a bit of a move around and pop him in the kennel closest to the reception and leave one empty next to him. Just in case. I know the others are all up to date with their vaccinations but until we know what's wrong with him, I'd rather take all the precautions we can, so washing hands after handling him and making sure we wash his bowls separately.'

'Good idea. We can never be too careful.' Giving Dougal a final fuss, Alex stood up and went to back the sink. 'I'm assuming it was another false alarm with Mr Thomas then? He wouldn't allow you and Ginny to take any of his dogs into our care?'

'Nope, not one.'

'Maybe next time?'

'We can only hope.' Flora shook her head sadly. 'Right, I'd better get a wriggle on, too. Can I give you this little one?' Flora nodded down at Dougal.

'Yes, of course.' Poppy pushed her chair back away from the table as Flora transferred him to her lap. 'Do you want me to do any admin whilst I'm sitting here with him? I made a start on writing up

Fluffles' details for her adoption advert. I can carry on with that if you like?'

'Oh yes, please. I'm terrible at writing those. I'll bring the notebook through.'

Poppy stroked Dougal's back. He hadn't seemed to notice being moved at all. His eyes were still as lacklustre as they had been earlier. She stroked his nose and swallowed. Poor little thing.

* * *

Poppy pushed the notebook away from her and pinched the bridge of her nose. She could feel one of her headaches coming on again. The funny thing was she'd never suffered from headaches, not until she and Ben had separated, so they were definitely stress related.

She took a sip of her water. What was it they said? Water cured most things, including headaches?

'How's it going in here?' Flora peered through the slightly open door before stepping inside and closing it quietly.

'Okay, thanks. Dougal's still sleeping.'

'Poor little poppet.' Flora placed her hands on the back of the chair opposite Poppy. 'I've spoken to the vet's and there wasn't a mix-up. Gavin has sold the surgery. I knew he was planning to. I just hadn't realised he'd found someone to buy him out, let alone that it would go through as quickly as it has.'

'So that couldn't have been Gavin I saw with Dougal earlier then?'

'No. Apparently, that was Mack, the new owner.' Flora leaned her elbows on the chair back and leaned forward.

'No wonder both he and the receptionist looked at me as though I'd grown another head when I said about the tab and the agreement. The receptionist must be new too?'

'I believe so, yes. Yvonne, who used to work there, was only a couple of years away from retirement. She'd been speaking about quitting and looking after her grandchildren to save her daughter some money on childcare. With Gavin selling up, she must have decided it was the right time.'

'Good for her. So you just need to set up another tab and speak to Mack about giving free treatments, then?'

'Unfortunately, no. According to him, everything needs to be paid for. Treatment, medication, everything...' Flora sighed.

'Really? He seemed such a nice guy. He was really interested in Dougal and doing his best for him.' Poppy frowned. She'd been certain he was a proper animal lover, not one of these vets who only worked for the money.

'I'm sure he is, and from what you've told me about the way he was with Dougal, I'm sure his intentions are good, but there was no budging on his decision. No movement whatsoever.'

'What are you going to do?' Poppy looked down at Dougal, who was still asleep on her lap. He needed treatment and because of how poorly he was, it was likely to be expensive.

'I don't know. I'd ask Freya but the veterinary surgery she works at is in the opposite direction, past Penworth Bay, well over an hour away, and we really need to have them registered at one closer. Some of the dogs we get coming through don't travel well in the car and, of course, in case of emergencies.' Flora straightened her back and tapped the back of the chair. 'Never mind. We'll figure something out.'

5

Poppy yawned and lowered herself down next to where Ginny sat in Dougal's kennel. Poppy had woken early to check on him but had found Ginny had got there first, with the small dog strewn across her lap.

'How do you not look tired? How long have you been here?'

'Ha ha, I've always been a bit of an early bird.' Ginny tilted her head. 'Well, and a bit of a night owl, too. I guess I can just function on next to no sleep some days.'

'I don't know how you do it. Don't get me wrong, when I do force myself to get up early, I love it, but I find it much easier to stay awake until the birds' dawn chorus and then go to bed rather than wake up in time to hear the birds sing their first song of the day.' She took a long gulp of coffee, swilling the drink around her mouth before swallowing in the hope that somehow she'd extract more of the caffeine.

Ginny grinned. 'You're up early today.'

'Yes, not as early as you, though. I think half past six is my limit.' She nodded towards Dougal. 'How's he been?'

'The same.' Ginny frowned. 'I managed to coax the tiniest piece

of chicken down him, but it was barely as big as my fingernail...'
She held up her little finger.

'I do hope Mack rings back today with some good news.'

'Yes, hopefully it's something easily treatable.'

Poppy crossed her fingers before moving her legs in the hope of
slowing the pins and needles which were already creeping up her
legs. 'I still can't believe he's not even prepared to give us a
discount.'

'Yeah, you would have thought he'd be willing to offer something at least, even if he wasn't going to give the treatment for free.'

'I wonder if Aunt Flora will end up going somewhere else?'

'Maybe. I don't think she wants to because of the distance, but
I'm sure Freya would help.'

Poppy stroked Dougal between his eyes. 'Oh, she mentioned
Freya. Is she a friend?'

'She used to volunteer at Elsie's bakery before deciding to stay
down here and taking over the surgery. You know Elsie, right?'

'Elsie? Yes, the lady with the bakery in Penworth Bay? The one
with the famous cheese and onion pasties?'

Ginny grinned. 'Yep, that's the one.'

'Oh, I have missed those. I don't think I've had one since I was
last here, five years ago.' Poppy could almost hear her stomach
rumbling at the mere thought of them. She hadn't been hungry
when she'd woken up – who can eat at half past six in the morning?
Definitely not a night owl like her. But now she was starving.

'We'll have to pop up there on our lunch break one day.'

'Yes, that's a good idea.'

It almost felt as though she'd known Ginny for months, not just
a day. She guessed it was because Aunt Flora had been speaking
about her so much, about all the staff, volunteers and dogs at the
home, in fact. Partly to take Poppy's mind off what had been going
on in her own life, but she was sure partly because her aunt had

known she'd relent and take up Flora's invitation of taking a break down here and had wanted her to feel at home. She smiled.

'Great. Maybe tomorrow?' Ginny said.

Poppy nodded as the small bell above the door into the reception area tinkled, signalling someone had just walked in. 'I wonder who that could be at this time?'

'Oh, that'll be Darryl, my partner. He promised to pop in on the way to work to collect the adoption advertisements. He dedicates a column in the local paper to Wagging Tails.'

'Aunt Flora mentioned that. She said it was having a real impact on adoption rates.'

'Yes, that's right. I'm just hoping it continues.' Ginny grimaced before gently transferring Dougal from her lap to Poppy's. 'I'll be back in a mo.'

Poppy listened as Ginny left the kennel and went to greet Darryl. She couldn't hear what they were saying, but by the tone of the chatter, they were both happy to see one another. She sighed. She couldn't remember the last time Ben had spoken to her with any interest, let alone as much joy in his voice as Darryl and Ginny had for each other.

Though, to be fair, Poppy had been the same, struggling to drum up any enthusiasm for the relationship by the end. It just fizzled out eventually. The love had faded over the years, and she'd begun to feel like a spare part, just a small irritating dot in the distance, somewhere on his horizon.

Leaning her head back against the concrete wall, she listened as the Christmas music was turned up a notch. She closed her eyes as laughter penetrated the chorus, followed by a loud thud and more laughter. It sounded as though something had been knocked over. They must be dancing along to the music.

She'd never have that again. Not the type of love where she'd be happy to mess around and make a fool of herself without fearing judgement. Had she felt as comfortable in her relationship with Ben as Ginny obviously was with Darryl? At the beginning, maybe. But she remembered being self-conscious and worrying that the daftest remark or a habit of hers would annoy him, drive him away.

Of course, she'd eventually got to a point where she'd felt comfortable with him. Possibly not ever 'in his league', but comfortable. Opening her eyes, she turned her mug in her hand and watched as the coffee swilled precariously close to the rim before settling back at the bottom of the mug again.

That wasn't fair. It had been her lack of confidence, her insecurities which had led to her feelings of inadequacy. It hadn't been his fault, but, if she was honest, it may have been partly due to how she'd felt, which had led to the demise of their relationship. If she'd felt more confident at the beginning of their journey together, they would have likely pursued more common hobbies. She'd have stepped out of her bubble, and they would have built shared interests, and everyone knows that shared interests help cement a relationship, don't they?

She listened as the landline rang and the music was turned down. A few moments later, the door to the kennels was opened once more.

Ginny came to stand outside Dougal's kennel, her hand holding the metal bars.

'Poppy, that was Mack, the vet, on the phone. He said he's had the test results back already and wants to see Dougal as soon as possible.'

'Already? I'd assumed they wouldn't be in until this afternoon at the earliest.'

'Yes, he sounded quite serious too.'

'Right.' Poppy looked down at the small pup, a lump forming in her throat.

6

Sitting on the plastic chair, Poppy looked out of the large window opposite and willed her legs to stop shaking. It was no good, of course. She couldn't stop them; it was a habit of hers whenever she was nervous and she wasn't sure if she'd ever been as nervous as she was today. Dougal was the first dog she'd seen to be so poorly, and that was in all the time she'd been visiting her aunt and helping at the rescue. Of course, she had no doubt that Aunt Flora would have shielded her from the most terrible of cases when she was growing up, but she'd still seen her fair share of mistreated dogs come through as an adult. Dogs who had been neglected, abused, abandoned.

'Dougal?' The door to the treatment room opened and Mack indicated Poppy to step through.

Lifting Dougal into her arms, she stood up and mumbled as she walked through the open door. She just wanted to get this over and done with, to be told the bad news and get Dougal started on treatment. 'Hi.'

'Morning. How's this one been overnight, then?' Closing the

door behind them, Mack indicated for her to place Dougal on the examining table.

'The same, really. Very lethargic. Just sleeping constantly.' Once she'd lifted him up, she fussed his ears. 'He ate some chicken, but not much, just the tiniest piece.'

'Right. Unfortunately, that's to be expected. We've received the blood results back and I'm afraid I'm going to have to be the bearer of bad news.' Mack placed his palms on the table and looked down at Dougal, his mouth turned down.

'Oh.' Poppy swallowed. She'd known there might be something really wrong with him. Her aunt had warned her as much last night. Anyone only had to glance at him to know he'd have a fight on his paws at best. She wiped away a tear.

'No, no. I'm not giving up on him. I'm sorry I didn't...'

Mack placed his hand on her forearm briefly before looking down and replacing his palm on the table. 'He has lungworm. And unfortunately, he's suffering from a serious infestation.'

'Lungworm?' Was that it? 'Isn't lungworm common? I mean, they can pick it up from snails and slugs. That's the one, isn't it?'

'It is. Dogs are usually protected from it as part of their worm and flea treatment, and in most cases where they do happen to miss a preventative treatment and pick it up, the next treatment cures the issue.'

'In most cases?'

'Yes.' Mack nodded slowly. 'In Dougal's case, though, I imagine he has not been receiving his preventative treatment. He came into your care yesterday, is that right?'

'That's right. With the note I showed you. Saying that he was poorly but his owner couldn't afford the treatment.'

'Right. Well, he must have caught the lungworm a good while ago and so they've had the chance to take a hold of his body.'

'The worms? So, he just needs worming treatment, and he'll

make a full recovery?' That was simple enough. 'I thought you said you had bad news?'

'No.'

'No?'

'The lethargy, the lack of appetite, the weight loss and...' Mack paused as Dougal began coughing. 'And the coughing. All of these symptoms point towards severe complications.'

'Really? And what does that mean? Can it be treated?'

She had a million questions spinning around in her mind. Taking a deep breath, she looked into Dougal's eyes, which were dreary with a tiredness that could not be relieved.

'There are treatments, yes. We'll start him on a course of lung-worm treatment right away, which he'll likely have to take for a good few months. Alongside that, I'll take him in and X-ray his chest. He has respiratory distress; we can see that due to his coughing and his laboured breathing. In severe cases, the lung-worm can cause pneumonia, so the X-ray will help us determine if he has that.'

'Pneumonia? You think he has pneumonia?'

'I'm certain he does, yes, but we'll give him an X-ray to confirm. We'll also put him on oxygen, help him breathe a little better, and get some fluids down him too. Hopefully, make him a little more comfortable.'

'But he'll make a full recovery?'

Poppy met Mack's eyes.

'It would be unethical of me to promise anything. All I will say is I will do my darn best by him.'

Poppy nodded slowly. 'Right. And what about the other dogs at Wagging Tails? Will they all catch it now?'

Mack shifted on his feet. 'Lungworm is not transmitted through direct contact but it can be passed on through snails and slugs. So, if a snail or slug happened to eat his faeces and then another dog ate or licked that snail or slug, then it can be spread that way. Your best line of defence is to make sure all the dogs are up to date with their preventative treatments and to clean the kennel Dougal has been staying in and any other areas he has toileted.'

'All the dogs have regular worming and flea treatment, so they should be fine.'

'Yes, they should be completely fine in that case.'

'Okay good, and Dougal will be too. I just know he will.' She shook her head. 'I just can't believe he's in such an awful way over something that can so easily be prevented.'

'Unfortunately not all worming preventative tablets guard against lungworm. And some that do need to be given every month, not the standard every three months. And if that hasn't been explained to an owner, then...' He shrugged. 'Dougal here should have seen a vet long before now. These things are easily treated if caught early, not to mention how miserable he must feel being as poorly as he is now.'

Poppy stroked Dougal's nose, his eyes flickering open and closed. This could have all been prevented with just one tiny pill.

'I know it's tough seeing him like this, but he will get the treatment he deserves now.'

Poppy nodded.

'Do you want to say your goodbyes before I take him out?'

'My goodbyes?'

He'd said he had a good chance of survival. Well, a chance anyway.

Mack cleared his throat. 'Sorry, your see-you-laters.'

'Right. Yes.' Leaning over the small cockapoo, Poppy whispered, 'You be strong, and I'll come and pick you up as soon as possible. You've got a lovely life waiting for you. Just be strong.'

She sniffed back the tears.

As soon as she'd stepped back, Mack scooped Dougal into his arms. 'I'll take good care of him.'

'Yes, I know. Thank you.'

And he would. She was sure of that.

With her hand on the door handle, she turned back to face him and cleared her throat. 'I know you were reluctant to offer a discount, but I have to ask again. Wagging Tails needs to support so many dogs. Is there any way you can give us some money off or come to some understanding similar to the one Gavin had with the charity?'

Mack looked down at the floor, his cheeks ashen, before glancing back up at her. 'I'm so sorry, I just can't.'

'Of course.' She nodded before leaving.

7

'And he just won't play. I've tried everything, wool, tinkly balls, a toy mouse...'

Poppy watched as the man in the queue ahead of her tapped the cat carrier he was balancing on the counter. It must have been at least ten minutes since she'd watched Mack carry Dougal away and all she wanted to do was to go and hide in Aunt Flora's car and cry. Instead, she was still standing here as the man tried to get Kerry the receptionist to agree to let him skip the queue in order for his cat to be seen fifteen minutes earlier than his allotted time.

'As I've already said, we have another patient waiting. I cannot just move your appointment up.' Kerry shook her head. 'Now, if you could take a seat, I can deal with our other customers.'

'But he normally loves his toy mouse,' the man muttered as the cat meowed loudly, either appalled at being asked to wait or simply disgusted at being trapped inside the small plastic box.

'Can I help you?' Kerry signalled to Poppy as the man reluctantly took a seat.

'Dougal. I've come to pay for Dougal's care.' She pulled the card her aunt had given her from her purse. But as she looked at it closely now, Poppy frowned. It wasn't the purple charity debit card; it was Aunt Flora's own credit card. She must have given her the wrong one by mistake.

'That will be three hundred and fifty pounds, please.' Kerry turned the card reader towards Poppy.

'Phew, that's not as bad as I thought.' She breathed a sigh of relief. She'd expected it to be a lot more. Maybe Mack had given them a discount after all.

'That's for the X-ray. Charges for treatment and board will need to be paid tomorrow on the collection of Dougal.'

Poppy closed her eyes momentarily. If the X-ray alone was three hundred and fifty pounds, how much would the treatment and him staying in for the night cost? She put the card in the reader as a teenage boy skateboarded into the surgery, causing her to step aside quickly. She watched as he flicked his skateboard into his hand and opened the door to the examining room.

'Oi! You can't allow that?' The man with the cat stood up. 'He's just skipped the queue. And he doesn't even have a pet!'

'The vet is still running on time.' Glancing at the man, Kerry pointed to the clock. 'Just enter your PIN when you're ready.'

Poppy raised her eyebrows, the man had a point. She shook her head before focusing on the card machine again as the door to the examining room slammed shut. For all she and the man with the cat knew, the boy might be popping in to see his poorly pet or be on work experience here or something. It was none of their business.

* * *

As Poppy scrubbed her hands in the sink, she watched the soap bubble on her skin for a moment before plunging her hands into the water. The last thing she wanted was to pass the lungworm on to any of the other dogs in their care. She'd never forgive herself. She slumped her shoulders. She was being daft; she knew she was. She knew the disease couldn't be passed on by her touching Dougal and then another dog, but just seeing him the way he had been, watching Mack carry him out of the examining room, his tired eyes looking back at her... She shuddered. She wouldn't forget that in a hurry.

'Poppy, lovely. How did it go at the vet's? Is Dougal in his kennel already?' Flora walked into the kitchen, closing the door behind her.

'He... umm... He has lungworm, a bad infection, and Mack is worried it may have caused pneumonia.'

Turning around, she dried her hands on the tea towel.

'Oh, my goodness, the poor little thing.' She dropped the notebook and pen she was carrying onto the table. 'Has he kept him in?'

'Yes, he's going to have an X-ray and oxygen. Mack is hopeful, but there's a risk he won't make it.' She looked down at her trainers.

'Poppy, he'll be fine. He may be weak and poorly now, but little Dougal has come this far. He'll make it. Come here.' Flora held her arms out.

Sinking into Aunt Flora's warm embrace, Poppy let the tears fall, leaving dark splodges on Aunt Flora's navy sweatshirt. 'He will, won't he?'

'I have every faith that he will, lovely. We need to think positively. That's all we can do now. There's no point in worrying about something that hopefully won't happen.'

Nodding, Poppy stepped back and wiped her eyes. 'Sorry.'

'Hey, don't apologise, but this isn't like you. Growing up, you were always the one to tell everyone else that you just knew even the poorliest of dogs would recover. What's going on?'

'I know, but... I don't know. It's everything at the moment, isn't it? Me and Ben splitting up, him going on that date, Dougal. Even work's been difficult these past few weeks. What if it's me? What if it's everything I touch?'

'You think you've cursed Dougal.' Holding Poppy by the elbows, Flora raised an eyebrow.

'No, yes. I don't know.' Poppy shrugged. It sounded daft. She knew it did but she had been the one to find Dougal and now he was fighting for his life.

'Dougal was lucky you found him. Imagine if you hadn't been here. No one would have been at the counter, keeping an eye on the CCTV when he was dropped off. Who knows what would have happened to him had he been left out in the cold in that cardboard box until me and Ginny had got back. You saved his life, Poppy.'

Aunt Flora was right. Well, maybe not about the saving his life bit, but about it not being her fault. 'I guess so.'

'Now, Dougal is in the best of hands so all we can do is to put our trust in Mack and focus on the other dogs.' Flora rubbed Poppy's arm.

'Yes, okay.' Poppy took a deep breath and nodded. That was all they could do. They had other dogs to feed, walk, care for. Worrying wasn't going to help any of them. 'Oh, you'd given me your credit card instead of the charity one. I'm sorry but I had to use it. I would have used my own, but with the mortgage payment coming out, I didn't have enough to cover it.'

'Silly me.' Flora chuckled and slapped her forehead. 'Never mind. How much was it?'

'The X-ray was three hundred and fifty, which is what I used your card for. We'll have to pay for the rest of the treatment when we pick him up.'

'Three...?' Flora frowned, deep lines forming across her forehead. She shook her head and seemed to force a smile. 'Never mind. Anyway, there's lots to be getting on with. I'm just about to write another letter to Mr Thomas trying to persuade him to relinquish some of his dogs to us. I could do with your help if you're not busy.'

'Yes, of course.'

8

Poppy jumped back as the hose took on a life of its own and spun around in her hand. Water sprayed into her face and across her top, the freezing cold liquid quickly penetrating her jumper. Wrestling it back under her control, she aimed it back onto the floor of Dougal's kennel and watched as the water burst the soap suds against the concrete flooring.

'Bubble in the hose?' A voice behind her rose above the sound of the splashing water.

Twisting around, she smiled. 'Alex. You made me jump!'

'Sorry.' Holding his hands up, palms forward, he laughed. 'Flora sent me to get you. It's time for the staff meeting.'

'Already? I thought I'd only been out here ten minutes.' Turning off the hose, Poppy checked her watch. She must have been more engrossed than she'd thought. She watched as the last of the soapy water circled down the drain in the floor. 'I've finished now, anyway.'

'I was going to say I don't think I've ever seen it as clean as it is now.'

Poppy grimaced as she wound the hose back up. 'I may have

gone a little overboard, but at least any lungworm eggs or anything won't be able to reinfect Dougal after we pick him up tomorrow.'

'True.' Alex nodded as he ushered her through the door into the reception area.

Poppy rubbed at the wet patches on her jumper before opening the door to the kitchen. Flora and Ginny were sitting at the table while Susan, her honorary aunt, who had been part of the Wagging Tails team for as long as Poppy could remember, bustled about making mugs of coffee, and Percy, the home's all-round caretaker, shook biscuits from a packet onto a plate. Sally, who had been busy scribbling into a folder, looked up as they walked in.

'I found her!' Alex grinned as he took a seat.

'Sorry, am I late?' Sitting down, Poppy took a mug from Susan. 'Thank you.'

'No, no, lovely.' Flora laughed. 'Alex is just a little enthusiastic about making a start.'

Poppy nodded and took a long sip of coffee, the bittersweet taste warming her throat.

'So, first on the agenda is fundraising.' Ginny shifted in her chair to face Poppy. 'We had our Christmas Fayre early this year in the hopes that we'd get more visitors. Last year, a few people had mentioned they'd have loved to have come but were too busy with other plans in December.'

'Yes, it worked, too. We had the best turnout ever, didn't we, Ginny, lovely? Thanks, in part, to the huge success of the Family Fun Day during the summer, people were excited to come to another one of our events.' Flora patted Ginny's hand.

Ginny shifted in her chair, her cheeks reddening. 'But there's always more money to be raised...'

Flora looked down into her mug, a shadow of worry briefly clouding her face.

'... So, as we do every year, we'll be joining West Par's village council and walking around the cove carol singing behind Santa's sleigh.'

Poppy frowned as Flora grinned again. Had she imagined Flora's worried look? She shook her head and looked across at Ginny. 'Santa's sleigh?'

'Yes, a tractor pulls Santa...' Ginny indicated Percy '... around the cove, house to house, and villagers join us singing carols and collecting money.'

Poppy nodded. That sounded sweet. She remembered tagging along with Ben's niece to something similar back home. Ben had worn a whole elf costume and moaned at her for being boring and only donning a red Santa hat. That was the difference between the two of them. He'd been the outgoing one, always striving to be the centre of attention, whereas she'd longed to fade into the background, unnoticed and quiet. Their personalities had been polar opposites, but it had worked. For a time, anyway. Maybe they'd just been too different in the end. Maybe separation had been the only possible outcome, the logical ending to a rocky relationship. And to think, Ben, the biggest Scrooge she'd met, had pranced around in an elf's costume. All to be the centre of attention, the best. He hated Christmas more than she did.

She took another sip of coffee.

'... and I've sent Mr Thomas another letter urging him to give up at least some of his dogs into our care, so I'll follow it up with a home visit in a couple of days' time. Give him the space to mull things over and come to a decision.' Flora crossed her fingers. 'And now, for the time Alex has so patiently been waiting for. Alex, would you like to take over?'

'I do. I do.' Alex picked up a red beanie hat from the work surface behind him and cleared his throat. 'It's that time of year again, folks. Secret Santa time!'

A small round of applause erupted around the table.

'Thank you, thank you.' He shook the woollen hat. 'Who would like to pull a name out of the hat first?'

'Oh, me. Me, please. I'll take my chances at pulling the first name.' Percy pushed his mug away.

'Of course.' After giving it a final shake, Alex held the hat across the table towards Percy.

Percy stroked his white beard before plunging his hand into the hat and swirling it around.

Poppy smiled. With his natural beard, she could well imagine him dressing up as Santa.

'In your own time, Percy.' Susan laughed.

'I have a good feeling about this one.' He pulled a small slip of folded paper from the hat, unfolded it, and hiding it with his other hand, he looked at the name.

'Who's next?' Alex shook the hat again.

'I'll have a go.' Flora nodded.

'Oh, hold on. Sorry, just a moment.' Percy waved his piece of paper in the air. 'Can I just have a quick swap? Got my own name.'

He took another slip of paper, which he checked, smiling, before dropping the first name back into the hat.

Taking her turn, Poppy plunged her hand inside the hat and hastily pulled out a name, glancing at it quickly before slipping it into her pocket. She'd be buying for Susan. She was happy with that.

Alex passed the hat around the rest of the room before pulling out the last slip of paper and throwing the beanie hat back onto the work surface. 'Right, we all know the rules, don't we? We buy a present for the person on our slip of paper. We usually spend about ten pounds. Buy anything you think the other person will like, something funny, personal, whatever, and we'll swap them on Christmas Day. Oh, and the most important rule...' Alex looked pointedly at Susan. 'Do not tell anyone whose name you have. Okay?'

'Yes, yes. Okay.' Susan grinned and held her slip of paper to her chest. 'In my defence, Alex, last year the gift I'd bought was just so good I couldn't keep the secret to myself any longer.'

Alex raised his eyebrows at her before shaking his head, a glint in his eye.

'Thank you for organising that, Alex. We do appreciate it.' Flora smiled before standing up. 'Right, I'd better get on. I'm going to brave the weather and take Ralph down to the cove. That's one advantage of the rain. The beach should be pretty quiet.'

Poppy nodded. Ralph was a complete softie with them, but was terrified of other dogs and reacted when scared, so it was best he was walked at times when the likelihood of running into another dog was low. Poppy looked down into her mug, the coffee now barely enough to cover the ceramic bottom. She'd been that thirsty after her morning of cleaning.

'I'd also better get on,' Percy said. 'I need to fix that tile on the roof of the cottage. If it cracks any more, you'll have rainwater flooding through your ceiling.' He nodded towards Flora before downing the dregs of his coffee.

'Oh, no you don't.' Flora tutted at him. 'Your responsibility is Wagging Tails, not my home.'

'If you and Poppy get poorly from living in damp conditions, then it affects Wagging Tails.' Percy held the door open for her. 'Besides, I've already got my ladder out ready, and you know what a muddle the storage shed is in. It took me half an hour to find it.'

'I can't expect you to fix the tile on my cottage.' Flora shook her head.

'You're not expecting me to, I'm offering.'

And with that, they both walked out, Percy shutting the door behind them with a click.

Susan chuckled. 'I'm assuming Percy is up to his old tricks again with the swapping of names?'

'Oh, yes. Indeed, he is.' Slumping back in his chair, Alex laughed.

'What do you mean?' Poppy looked from Susan to Alex and back again.

'You don't know?' Alex raised his eyebrows, trying and failing to stop laughing.

'Know what?' She looked across at Ginny, who ran her index finger and thumb across her lips pretending to zip her mouth shut.

'You can't not tell her now.' Grinning, Sally shook her head. 'I've only been here a few months, but I noticed it pretty quickly.'

'Tell me what? Yes, come on, don't keep me in suspense.' Leaning back in her chair, Poppy crossed her arms.

'Okay, okay, but don't shoot the messenger.' Alex held his hands up, palms forward.

'I won't, I promise.' Poppy laughed. 'Not unless it's really bad, that is.'

'We do Secret Santa every year and every year Percy takes out a name, looks at it and then makes up some excuse to pop it back in the hat to take another one out. This little tradition continues until he's found the name he wants.' Alex tapped the pads of his fingers against the edge of the table.

'I think last year was the worst, wasn't it?' Susan looked around the small group. 'He put the slips of paper back that many times he must have gone through all of the names until he found the right one.'

'Yes! Yes, I remember. He was getting that flustered, he just kept mumbling under his breath and putting his hand back in the hat.' Alex shook his head.

'Why?' Poppy asked.

'He wants Flora's name.' Alex slumped back in his chair dramatically.

'Really? Why?' Poppy frowned. There was something more to this, she could tell just by the way they were all acting. They'd been working together for years, longer than anyone else at Wagging Tails but judging by Alex's expression she had a feeling that wasn't the reason.

'Buying for her isn't the only thing he likes,' Susan loud-whispered across the table.

'What? Oh, he likes Aunt Flora? Like that?' Poppy's eyes widened. Percy had been caretaker for her whole life. Well, since shortly after her Uncle Arthur passed away, so *most* of her life. How had she never picked up on the fact he liked her aunt? 'Are you sure? I'm sure I would have noticed. How long has he liked her?'

'Forever?' Alex held his arms out and shrugged. 'Susan? You've been here the longest. How long have you been here? Has he always liked her?'

'Umm...' Susan counted on her fingers, ticking them off as she counted. 'I must have been volunteering for at least twenty years now. No, longer than that. I remember seeing you, Poppy, running around the paddock with some dog or other when you were only this high.' She held her hand up against the tabletop. 'Maybe twenty-five, twenty-seven years. Though I'm not sure how long he's had feelings for her. Definitely over fifteen years.'

'Wow. Seriously? Why has he never said anything?' Surely Aunt Flora would have noticed if everyone else had?

Susan shrugged. 'I remember him asking her out once, years ago, ten, maybe more, but she assumed he was joking so brushed him off. He's not built up the courage to ask again.'

'Why? Aunt Flora wouldn't hold it against him even if she said no.' Her aunt was one of the kindest people she knew, both to the dogs she rescued and cared for and the people she came in contact with. Unless they'd harmed a dog, that was. Then her fiery side came out, but she'd always been nothing but kind to everyone else, strangers, family and friends alike.

'I don't know. I think he just values their friendship too much to jeopardise it.' Ginny shrugged.

'Never mind. He'll show his true feelings when he's good and ready. In the meantime, we'll carry on letting him cheat at Secret Santa.' Susan pushed her chair back and picked up her mug.

'Oh, yes, we will. One day, hopefully, they'll both open their eyes and see what's right in front of them.' Alex pushed his chair back, too. 'They'd make such a cute couple.'

9

Poppy shifted her cotton bag higher up on her shoulders and looked down the street. She'd been wandering around the shops in Trestow for the past fifteen minutes and so far hadn't seen anywhere she fancied having a snoop in. She hated shopping. And shopping for Christmas presents was enough to make her feel sick. The only reason she was here was because Ginny had popped in to see Darryl at his offices and had offered her a lift.

Plus, after drawing Susan's name in Secret Santa yesterday and with Christmas only being three weeks away, she didn't have much choice but to join the crowds. Besides, they'd planned to pop into The Cornish Bay Bakery on the way back for one of Elsie's famous cheese and onion pasties.

Sidestepping around another young family, Poppy averted her eyes and looked in the window of a convenience store, pretending to be suddenly interested in the price of orange juice and noodles. Anything to avoid looking at yet another happy couple carrying armfuls of bags whilst pushing their perfectly content young child around in some stylish pushchair.

No. Between the glossy posters in the shop windows of happy

couples and families, and the real-life bubbles of couples swanning across the path or chatting over hot chocolates in the café windows, she realised it had been the wrong choice to come into town. How come other people managed to make Christmas shopping look so easy? Before Ben had left her to do the gift shopping on her own, it had always been a high-stress activity with more than the odd argument thrown in. Trestow town today was filled with couples strolling around the shops, stopping off at the coffee shop and seemingly enjoying the experience.

Because Ben had always got so grumpy when he'd joined her Christmas shopping, she'd stopped asking him for the last two years of their relationship. She'd gone on her own, rushing from shop to shop with a list of presents to buy as long as her arm thanks to his huge family. All he'd had to do was pretend he'd known about said presents when his family members opened them. Why had she done that? He'd never chosen or bought presents for any of her family.

'Not a fan of Christmas?'

Tearing her eyes from the juice and noodle advert, Poppy blinked as she realised the person was addressing her and she blinked even more when she recognised it was Mack speaking.

'Sorry?'

He held his hand up in a wave. 'Sorry, you probably don't remember me. I'm Mack, the vet treating Dougal. I just asked if you weren't a fan of Christmas?'

Glancing down, Poppy tucked her hair behind her ears. 'Oh, I know who you are. But, no, not lately anyway.'

Mack looked at her and frowned. 'I guess it can get a bit much, huh?'

Poppy shrugged. What was she supposed to say? That she didn't particularly feel like being happy at the moment? Or worse, that she didn't like seeing all the happy couples shopping for Christmas? A day they'd spend together, giving each other carefully chosen gifts whilst drinking eggnog or Baileys or champagne or whatever their choice of drink might be? On top of that she was worried about Dougal. Mack had rung earlier to tell her Dougal needed to stay in longer. 'I'm just not having much success finding the gifts I need.'

'In that case, I might just be able to help you. I'm on my way to the Christmas market in Trestow Community Hall.' He pointed down the road to the left. 'I can show you if you like? There's normally a decent range of stalls. It's the go-to for difficult gift-buying solutions.' He grinned.

'Really? Okay, yes, why not? That'll be great, please. Not that the person I'm buying for is difficult to buy for, it's more that...' She glanced back towards the shops.

'That you've not found the right gift yet?'

'Maybe.' She fell into step next to Mack as they began to walk away from the shops. 'How far is it? I've not got long until I need to meet Ginny back here.'

'Just around the corner. Not far. I've not got long either. I need to get back to the surgery for my afternoon appointments.' He looked across at her, softening his voice. 'I'm sorry Dougal couldn't be picked up this morning.'

'It's okay. I know it's the best thing for him. Though I must admit, I did fear the worst when you rang.'

'Ah, sorry, I didn't mean to give you such a fright.' He ran his hand over his face.

'Hey, stop apologising, you're doing your best for him and that's what he deserves.'

Shaking her head, Poppy laughed.

'What is it?' he asked.

'It's normally me that people tell to stop apologising, and it really irritates me. Sorry, I can't believe I just said that to you.'

'Ha ha, it's a tricky habit to get out of.' He indicated to his right. 'Here we are. Trestow Community Hall. Recently refurbished after a fire about a year ago.'

'Very nice.'

As they walked down the driveway and through the small car park, she looked up at the community hall. Small Christmas trees lined the entrance and festive tunes seeped out from the open doorway. Inside, stalls lined the perimeter of the hall, and another row was set up down the middle too. People bustled from one shiny gift to another, murmuring to their family, partners or friends. Small children skipped around wearing reindeer antlers and elf hats, their parents chatting and sipping hot chocolate bought from the kitchen at the far end.

'If you can't find something here, then I'm afraid you possibly won't ever.' Mack smiled, his eyes lighting up.

Mack was right; there was an array of everything you could think of on sale. From self-care treats like organic and handmade bath bombs, soaps and moisturisers to wooden handcrafted toys and trinkets, to hand-blown glass baubles and detailed hanging ornaments. The stall positioned near the entrance displayed beautifully knitted cardigans as well as scarfs, gloves and hat sets; the one next to it, incredibly lifelike animal portraits. Where did they start? What would Susan like? And Aunt Flora?

'So, what do *you* need to buy?' she asked him.

'I need to hunt out a stall selling personalised skateboards.' He looked around the hall. 'I also need to find something for Kerry.'

'The receptionist at the surgery?'

'Yes, that's right.' He grimaced. 'She's terrible to buy for. She was also at my old surgery and moved over with me when I invested in this place. I've always had trouble buying for her.'

'I'm sure you'll spot something here.'

'Hopefully. Or else I might piggyback off your choice for whoever you're buying and get the same.' He chuckled.

Shaking her head, Poppy laughed. 'I'm sure she's completely different to Susan.'

'Who's Susan?'

'Oh sorry. She's one of the volunteers at Wagging Tails. She's been there that long, since I was a child, that she's part of the family really.'

'You're probably right then.' Stepping towards the closest stall, he picked up a pack of three bath bombs. 'How about these?'

Leaning forward, she smelt them as he held them close. 'Yes, they smell nice. All flowery.'

Nodding, he looked back down at the stall and knitted his eyebrows together before quickly placing them back down and walking away. 'Seven pounds for bath bombs! Did you see that?'

'Seven pounds for three handmade bath bombs is pretty good.' Poppy frowned. 'You need to think of all the ingredients that the crafter would have had to buy, plus the packaging and you're paying for her time, too. When you look at it like that, seven pounds is really quite reasonable.'

Poppy wouldn't be buying them though as she'd have to buy something else to go with them and she just didn't have the money. However much she appreciated how much they cost to make, but Mack... He evidently had no such problem. He owned a veterinary surgery and charged extortionate prices for healing animals. He must have the money.

'Look over here. Now they look nice, don't they?' Mack made his way towards a stall.

Following him, Poppy weaved between the group of people surrounding the stall. What had he spotted? As a woman in front of her moved, the stall came into view. Make-up bags and boxes covered the table, from the plain to the exquisite. 'Wow, they're beautiful.'

'Aren't they just?'

Picking one up, Poppy turned it over in her hand. The svelte black make-up bag was smooth against her skin, the small stitched designer logo the only thing interrupting the glossy finishing. 'Do you think they're real?'

'I should hope so. For this price, anyway.' He held up a small price tag.

Whistling under her breath, Poppy quickly lowered the make-up bag back to the tabletop. Who would come to a Christmas market and spend that amount? She glanced around her. There certainly seemed enough interest so maybe they were discounted.

'Which do you think Kerry would prefer?' Mack picked up a slick purple make-up bag and a star-shaped gold one.

Opening and closing her mouth, Poppy shrugged. Was he really spending that amount on a Christmas present? He'd thought the handmade bath bombs had been expensive but apparently, he didn't think twice about spending a lot more on something designer. If he had that much to spend on a single make-up bag then there was even less reason for not giving a discount on the treatment for the rescue dogs. Heck, the bags were almost the price of Dougal's X-ray. 'I don't know.'

'Umm. It's a tricky one.' Mack looked from one overpriced make-up bag to the other before replacing them both and nodding towards the vendor. 'I'll have a think and pop back.'

Walking away from the stall, Poppy looked around. Of all the beautifully handmade gifts on display he was contemplating buying Kerry a designer make-up bag. She shook her head. It really was none of her business and she wouldn't be thinking twice about what he spent his money on if it wasn't for the fact he was so closed to the idea of helping a charity like Wagging Tails. What did that say about him? A vet who supposedly cared for animals and yet one who would rather waste money than offer a lifeline for the animals he cared for.

'You okay?'

Poppy took a deep breath and plunged her hands into her coat pockets. 'Absolutely.'

'Good. It's great here, isn't it? All the Christmas gifts anyone could ever want all under one roof.' Mack glanced back towards the stall they'd just left before looking around the hall. 'I think I'll carry on looking for a present for Kerry and fall back on the bag if I can't find anything else.' He nodded towards another stall. 'This one looks good. Look, one pound.'

A laugh escaped Poppy's mouth before she had the chance to look across at him and realise he was being serious. 'That's a raffle. It's one pound a ticket.'

'Sounds good. I might win a spa day or one of those head massage things.' He pointed to the prizes stacked on the table. 'Or, look, a retro radio. Now, that's cool.'

'For Kerry?'

'Yep. Why not?'

'Would she appreciate that?' Poppy frowned. Was he really going from being willing to spend an extortionate amount on one small bag to trying to win a prize for a pound to give her?

'Maybe not the radio, but yes, I'm sure she'd appreciate something else. Come on.' Cupping her elbow, he led her through the throngs of people milling around the stall until they got to the front. 'One ticket, please?'

'Certainly. Thank you.' The man took Mack's pound and held out a plastic bucket full of folded paper. 'Good luck. Would you like one, miss?'

'No thanks.' Poppy shook her head, she couldn't imagine either Aunt Flora or Susan would relish the idea of a spa day and although it had always been something Poppy herself had wanted to experience, it wouldn't end up being without cost – she'd have to invest in a new swimming costume and a floaty wrap or something.

'Yes!' Mack grinned as he held up his ticket. 'Number seventeen! The electric deep tissue massager. That's Kerry's gift sorted.'

Poppy waited as the man behind the stall congratulated Mack and passed him across his prize before turning to him and lowering her voice. 'Are you really going to give her something you've just won after spending a pound?'

'Of course. Why not?'

'It's just not very thoughtful, that's all, and you've only spent a pound on her, someone who I'm assuming left her old job to follow you to your new surgery and presumably works super long hours.'

'But it's a deep tissue massager. She'll love that. She's always had a problem with her shoulders.'

Poppy grimaced. It just didn't seem right. If he was struggling financially – not in the lucrative position he was in now – then, yes, she'd have been congratulating him on his luck, but it just didn't sit well with her. Just a few moments ago he'd been willing to spend loads on her and now... 'But I'm guessing she usually buys you a gift?'

'Yes.' Mack nodded slowly.

'And she, presumably, won't be giving you something she's just won in a raffle?'

'I don't know. Probably not.'

'Then don't you feel guilty? She's going to be spending more on you than you have on her, despite the fact I'm guessing you bring home a considerable amount more than she does.'

'So? That's her choice. I'm not expecting her to buy me a present. It's not in her terms of employment that she has to or anything.'

'No, but you're guessing she probably will do. And, say she

spends, I don't know, ten pounds or fifteen pounds on your gift and you give her this...' she waved her hand towards the box he was now carrying under his arm '... she's going to assume that you've spent loads on her, so next Christmas, or birthday if you exchange birthday gifts, she'll spend more to make up for the fact that she thought you spent more than she did.'

'I don't understand what you're trying to say. It's her choice as to what she spends on me and my choice what I spend on her. Besides, it's not about the money spent, it's about the gift. If I bought one of those make-up bags it would have cost a lot. Presumably a similar amount to what this would cost me if I'd bought it in a shop.' He patted the box.

'Right.' Poppy looked ahead. He clearly didn't understand what she was trying to say. Not that it was any of her business, anyway.

10

'Come on, it'll be fun.' Mack touched her arm and pointed ahead.

'What? No.' Poppy looked across to the Christmas display at the back of the hall next to the tables and chairs. A basket of elf hats and fabric reindeer antler headbands stood next to a large chalkboard saying, *Pop on a hat & take a Christmas pic to treasure!*

'Go on. Look.' Lowering the massager onto the table, he pulled on a bright green elf hat and jingled the gold bell on its tip.

'I don't know.' She glanced behind her hoping someone else was waiting to take a photo, any reason why she could excuse herself from the situation.

He rummaged through the basket, pulled out an antler headband and leaned forward, sliding it onto her head. 'Now this one would look good on you.'

'Urgh.' Rolling her eyes, Poppy placed the bag of hand-blown glass baubles she'd bought for Aunt Flora and the pawprint-covered tea towel and oven glove combo she'd bought for Susan on the table and repositioned the headband. 'Ouch.'

'Sorry, did I catch you?'

'No, you just pierced my skull, that's all.' She scrunched her nose up in an attempt to look moody. Not that she was. After their disagreement earlier it had been quite fun looking around the craft fayre. And she had to admit, he could pull off the elf hat quite well.

'That sounds serious. Shall I take a look, see if you need surgery to patch it up? Although the success rate will depend on how much of a gaping hole you have, you may need to just patch it up with some newspaper or some tape to keep the rain out or something.' Chuckling, he gently touched her head. 'Nope, looks as though you'll survive.'

'Now that's a relief.' She laughed, pulling her head away.

'Ha ha. Ready?' He nodded towards the Christmas scene, a backdrop of a winter woodland with huge stuffed polar bears and reindeer teddies positioned on the floor.

Rolling her eyes again – which she seemed to be doing a lot of today, in the presence of this man – she let Mack pull her forward, before grinning into the camera lens on his mobile. Why was she even letting him? She hated photos. And photos of her in a ridiculous reindeer headband would be even worse.

'Here, do you want me to take one with yours too? Give you an eternal reminder of the day you were dragged around a Christmas market by your dog's vet?'

He held out his hand for her phone.

'Why not?' Smiling, she fished her mobile from her coat pocket and passed it across to him. She didn't say anything about Dougal not being her personal dog – he knew. It was just a slip of the tongue.

'Look, Mummy, it's the vet.'

Poppy slipped off the antlers as a small boy pulled his mum towards them. The boy was wearing a bright red hand-knitted jumper with a sleigh adorned on it whilst his mum wore an almost identical jumper in festive green.

'Hey, buddy. How are Crumble and Custard doing?' Leaning

down, Mack high-fived the small boy, the bell on his elf hat jingling as he did so.

'Sorry, as soon as he spotted you, he wanted to come and say hello. I think you must have made quite the impression. He asks every day if it's time to bring the bunnies in for their next vaccination.' She waved towards her son. 'Come on, Harry, let them get on with their shopping.'

'Don't worry, it's fine.' Mack grinned.

'Are you an elf now? Are you being the animal doctor for Santa's reindeer?' The boy pointed to Mack's elf hat.

'Oh, this. Unfortunately not. Santa has his own special vet who lives up at the North Pole with the reindeer. It's a job I'd love to do one day, though. Do you want to wear it so your mum can take a photo of you?' Mack pulled off the hat and handed it to the boy.

'Yes, please. Mummy, can you take a photo of me as an elf?' Harry sat down on the floor amongst the stuffed animal teddies.

'Would you like me to take one of you both?' Mack held his hand out for the woman's phone.

'Oh, that would be lovely. Thank you,' she said as she passed her phone to him and grabbed another elf hat from the basket.

'There you go. I took a couple, just in case.' Mack waved at Harry. 'Say Merry Christmas to Crumble and Custard for me.'

Turning back to Poppy, Mack picked up the box with the massager in and passed her bag across to her.

'Do you need to get back to Ginny or have you got time to get a hot chocolate to quench our thirst after all that shopping?'

Poppy checked her watch. 'I've got a few minutes and I think we deserve one.'

'Great. Me too. Do you want to grab us a table and I'll get the drinks?'

After nodding, Poppy wandered across to the cluster of tables and chairs while Mack joined the queue for the drinks. People were laughing and chatting over mince pies and Christmas cake, their numerous bags spilling out from under the tables. She hoped there was a spare table. She looked around and was relieved to see there was one left, a small table for two squashed up against a large Christmas tree, the lights twinkling through the tinsel, an array of rainbow-coloured sparkles.

Slipping into one of the chairs, she pulled out her mobile.

Huh, Ben had rung. What did he want?

'I got us both a mince pie, too. I couldn't resist,' Mack said as he ambled back with the drinks. 'I hope you like them?'

Pushing the question of Ben from her mind, she helped Mack unload the tray.

'Thanks. They look delicious.'

'Oh, I'm sure they will be. Mrs Burton...' he waved back towards the kitchen '... used to have a cat called Honey who was a patient where I used to work. Whenever she had an appointment, she'd bring me a slice of cake or a chunk of flapjack.' He took a bite before wiping his mouth with a napkin. 'I wish she'd get another cat and bring it to the new surgery.'

Poppy took a bite of the mince pie he'd given her. She didn't usually care for mince pies or any of the usual traditional Christmas foods, but she had to admit this one was good. Picking up her mug of hot chocolate, she nudged a branch that was creeping into their space to the side before bringing the cup to her lips so she could lick off the cream.

'Can I ask you a question?' Mack placed the remaining half of his mince pie back on the plate and looked her in the eye.

'I guess so.'

'Hold on, you have a little...' He reached across the table and gently wiped the pad of his thumb across her lip. 'There. You had some cream.'

'Oh, thanks.' She wiped her lips with a napkin. 'What's your question?'

'What don't you like about Christmas?'

Scrunching up her nose, she shrugged. 'What is there to like?'

'Christmas trees, lights, all the gorgeous food and drink.' He signalled to the table. 'And above all, the kindness it brings out in people.'

'Really? That's such a cliché.' She laughed, dismissing him.

'Is it? Look around you. People are happy. They're helping each other out.' He indicated the surrounding crowds.

Sighing, she twisted around in her chair. He was right. Everyone here was either smiling, laughing, or generally looking as though they were having a good time. Mack touched her elbow and pointed across to the far side of the hall. Following his gaze, she watched as a group of people came to the rescue of a woman whose bag had split open, baubles, wooden ornaments and woollen hats spilling across the laminated floor. Shaking her head, Poppy turned back around and picked up her mug again.

'If a person needs a festive holiday like Christmas in order to be kind, what does that tell you about them? And of course, everyone here looks happy. They've chosen to come here. They're not being forced into anything. It's not like going to work or having a tooth pulled out. It's a Christmas market.'

'I think you're wrong. I think people are generally kind, the majority of them anyway. Christmas just adds that extra layer of magic; it brings people together.'

'Is that why you like it so much, Mr Christmas?' She smirked.

Leaning back in his chair, Mack looked around the room before meeting her eyes. 'I love this season because it offers hope. Whatever is happening in life, or however hard things are, Christmas is something to look forward to. Something to keep you moving forward.'

'That's pretty deep.' What did he know about hardship? He owned his own veterinary practice, he had enough money to splash out on designer gifts if he wanted to. He was happy. He clearly hadn't just been through a life-changing break-up.

'So I've told you mine. You need to tell me yours. You've still not said why you hate it so much.'

Poppy shifted in her chair. 'I never said I *hate* it. I'm just not so disillusioned to think that one day will have any positive effect on my life.'

'Have you never liked Christmas? What about when you were a child?'

Looking down at her nails, Poppy used her thumbnail to scrape off a little more of the blue polish. Had she liked Christmas as a child? Probably. As a young child, anyway. As a teenager, she'd always dreaded the day. The mornings had been lovely; walking across to her grandma's house with her mum whilst her dad had gone to the pub to meet her uncle. The afternoons though when they'd been back home, just the three of them? Not so much. In fact, she'd retreated to her bedroom as soon as Christmas dinner had been eaten and laid on her bed trying to block out the noise of her parents arguing whilst she began her new book.

'I used to get a new book for Christmas each year. It was a tradition I loved. Does that count?'

Mack took a slow breath in. 'Yes, I guess that does. What about as an adult?'

Poppy leaned back in her chair and sighed. She picked up her mobile, turning it onto its side, its front, its side, its back. She didn't really want to tell him about the Christmases at Ben's parents' house, experiencing the loving family atmosphere for the first time being made to feel as much as much part of the family as Ben himself. Up until a couple of years ago, when Ben's parents had started to go away to celebrate with his dad's brother in Spain and she and Ben had begun to spend their Christmas Days sitting pretty much in silence with old Christmas movies playing on a loop on the TV.

'Why all the questions?'

Mack took another sip from his mug. 'Just trying to get to know you, I guess.'

'Why? I'm just an owner of a patient of yours. Not even an owner.' She glanced at her phone screen, suddenly realising the time. 'I need to go. I have to meet Ginny.'

'Right. Of course. I should get back to the surgery too.'

Pushing her chair back, Poppy stood up. 'Thanks for the hot chocolate and mince pie.'

'No problem.'

She rushed outside, weaving between families and couples, gripping her phone in her hand. Why had Ben rung? What did he want to talk about?

11

'Hello?' Ben's voice sounded distracted, far away.

Poppy closed her eyes, remembering the years she'd been happy to hear his voice. Now, though? She shrugged. Part of her longed to hear him again, the other part, not so much. She needed to remind herself why their relationship had failed. She needed to remind herself that this was for the best.

'Ben? It's Poppy. Sorry I missed your call. Is everything okay?'

'Poppy? Oh, Poppy. Yes, sorry I didn't mean to call you.' He paused, the line going quiet. 'You got to your aunt's house okay?'

'Yep.' She swapped her phone to the other hand and leaned against the railings outside the community hall. She could still hear the cheerful Christmas music from here. 'We had a dog brought to us yesterday. A sweet little thing but—'

'I'm sorry, Poppy. I've...' He paused as a voice in the background interrupted him. 'I've got to go.'

'Right.' She pulled the mobile from her ear and looked at the now blank screen. She wasn't even sure how she felt after their brief conversation – relief that he wasn't sitting alone in their mutual home pining for her, or upset that she'd once been his all – his lover, best friend, confidante – and now he didn't even have the time to talk to her for a few seconds. No, upset was the wrong word. She wasn't upset – the separation had been mutual. She hadn't been any of those things to him within the last couple of years, anyway. But who had that been in the background? Where had he been? Work? She shook her head. Yes, it would have just been a work colleague. She looked across the street. What if it had been the colleague he'd had a date with? She pocketed her mobile. She was letting her imagination run away with her.

A large raindrop fell from the sky straight onto the tip of her nose, followed by another one and another. Great, rain. Turning away from the community hall, she began to walk back to the town centre, leaving the happy couples buying gifts and the young families taking their children to see Santa behind her. Stepping aside as a young family began to run towards the hall in an attempt to avoid getting wet, she paused and turned her face to the sky, letting the rain splash onto her skin and cascade across her face.

And that was why she had the churning sensation in the pit of her stomach. Not because she was missing Ben, but because her future, the future she'd been going to have with him, had *meant* to have with him, had disappeared. Marriage, children, their own happy little family.

'I'll take note. You don't like Christmas, but you do like the rain.'

Twisting her neck so hard she was shocked she hadn't given herself whiplash, Poppy turned around.

'Mack, what are you doing? Stalking me now?'

'Sorry, I didn't mean to startle you... Again.' He grimaced. 'You forgot your bag.'

She looked down at his hand as he held out her shopping bag and mumbled, 'Thanks.' Before turning on her heels.

She was still trying to figure out how she felt about that phone call. She didn't need Mack to begin his torrent of questions again.

Mack cleared his throat.

She turned around and this time, louder, said, 'Thank you.'

'Not that. It's just...' He rubbed the back of his neck with one hand and indicated the direction she was heading with the other. 'You're going the wrong way. The town centre is this way.'

'Oh, right? Of course.'

* * *

Back at the dogs' home, biting into her cheese and onion pasty from Elsie's bakery, Poppy closed her eyes. It really was the best she'd ever tasted.

The kitchen door opened, and Alex stood in the doorway, his hands on his hips. 'You got pasties from The Cornish Bay Bakery?'

'Yes.' Ginny nodded towards the paper bag in the middle of the table. 'Yours is in there.'

'Seriously? I blimming love you, Ginny!' He quickly strode across to the table and took his out of the bag, before leaning against the counter and taking a large mouthful.

'Has Tim been in touch?' Ginny asked, from where she sat next to Poppy. She lowered her pasty and looked at Alex. 'I know he's not been very well this week, so was off college. Have you heard if he'll be back on Monday?'

'Nope. Nothing. Flora might have heard from him, though.'

'Who's Tim?' Poppy took a sip of tea. Ginny had accidentally added sugar, and not having had sugar in her tea for so long, after giving up five years ago, she remembered why it had been such a struggle at first. She shrugged. She guessed there was no harm now. There was no reason not to any more. Just because Ben had tried to get her to go on a health kick, it didn't mean she had to continue it now.

'He's a college student studying animal care. He comes in to volunteer twice a week as part of his work experience. Sweet kid.' Ginny glanced at her. 'I was just going to sort the rota out for next week. But I'll assume he'll be in and if he isn't, we can work around it.'

'Good idea. With you, Poppy, here now, at least we're not going to be short-staffed.' Alex nodded towards her. 'In fact—'

The kitchen door burst open, and they all watched as Sally ran in, frantically looking under the table and behind the bins.

'Sally, is everything okay?' Alex raised his eyebrows.

'No, have you seen Fluffles? She's slipped her collar and now I can't find her.' But Sally didn't wait for a reply, running back out of the kitchen.

'Oh no, that'll be my fault. I gave her a bath this morning and must have put her collar on too loose.' Ginny pushed her chair back and stood up.

'Don't worry. We'll find the little tinker.' Placing his half-eaten pasty onto the work surface, Alex straightened his back. 'Operation Find Fluffles.'

Poppy followed the two of them out of the kitchen. 'She's the miniature poodle, isn't she?'

'Oh yes, although she may be miniature, she has the personality of a young boisterous Labrador.' Alex laughed at his own joke before turning down the corridor towards the kennels.

Stepping outside, Poppy pulled the sleeves of her jumper down and ran towards the left of the courtyard as Ginny ran towards the right. 'Fluffles. Come here, girl. Fluffles.'

Poppy ran towards the paddocks. Sally hadn't said where Fluffles had slipped the lead, but it was worth looking there. The gates and fences out of the home were secure, so Fluffles wasn't in any danger of getting out, but she still needed to be found.

As she made her way towards the bottom paddock, she glanced towards the cottage. After Poppy and Ginny had got back, Aunt

Flora had excused herself to go and take care of some admin at home, which was unusual. She'd never known her aunt to head back to the cottage unless she needed a change of clothes due to falling in the mud or some such thing. She shrugged. Maybe she just wasn't feeling great.

'Got her,' Sally called from the top paddock. From down here, Poppy could just about make her out, shutting the gate behind her, poodle in one arm.

'That's a relief. What a little pest you are.' Reaching her, Poppy fussed over the small thing. 'How's the training going?'

'Up until that little escapade, I thought it was going quite well.' Sally laughed and fussed Fluffles' ears. 'Now, I'm not so sure.'

'Aw, these things happen.' Poppy smiled.

'They certainly do, but she does seem to be a bit of an escape artist. That's one of the reasons her previous owner gave her up – because she kept escaping out of the garden.'

'Couldn't they have just made the garden more secure?' Poppy frowned. Fluffles could be a pain, but she was a gorgeous little soul who would happily sit curled up on your lap for hours at a time, too.

'I don't know. You'd have thought so, wouldn't you?'

After securing the gate to the bottom paddock, Poppy followed Sally back across the courtyard.

'How are you finding it here?' Poppy asked as they walked. 'You only started in the summer, didn't you?'

'That's right. I was thrown right in at the deep end, holding taster sessions at the Family Fun Day.' Sally smiled. 'Honestly? I'm loving every minute of it. It's my dream job, training dogs, and to be able to train the dogs here, as well as holding my own training sessions in the evenings. It's the best of both worlds and so rewarding.'

'That's brilliant.'

'Yes, and as you know, the team here at Wagging Tails is like a little close-knit family, and then there are all the volunteers. It has certainly gone some way in restoring my faith in human nature.' Sally shifted Fluffles to her other arm. 'How about you? Are you enjoying being back here with Flora?'

Poppy nodded. 'Yes, I am. It feels so good to be spending some time with my aunt. I've not seen her in a few years. And with the dogs, of course, I mean, they're all pretty amazing, aren't they?'

Sally grinned. 'Oh, they really are. Flora said Ralph had been here when you last visited, too. I bet it was good to see him again?'

Poppy opened the door to the reception and stood back, letting Sally and Fluffles through first. 'Yes, sad too, though, as I'd hoped he'd found his special home by now.'

'I know.' Sally frowned. 'But he has a wonderful life here, and he knows he's loved and always will be.'

'Yes, you're right.' Poppy smiled. Ralph had a special place in all their hearts.

12

———

'Are you off to pick up Dougal, lovely?' Flora paused in the reception area, Ralph's lead in one hand.

'Yep.' Poppy nodded as she buttoned up her coat. 'Mack has rung and said he's ready.'

'That's good news. Mack must think he's on the right road to recovery then.'

'I hope so. He's such a sweetheart.' Leaning down, Poppy fussed Ralph. 'And so are you, our wonderful one.'

'Ginny's in Trestow collecting some bedding donations. Shall I give her a call and ask her to swing by and pick him up, save you a trip?'

'No, don't worry.' Poppy shook her head. 'Thanks though. I'm happy to go and collect him.'

It was true. She couldn't wait to see Dougal again, but she also owed Mack an apology for the way she'd spoken to him after the Christmas market yesterday.

'Okay. Oh, here, take my card again. I'm not sure where the charity debit card is. I'll transfer it over later.' Flora pulled her purse out of her pocket and passed the card to her.

'Are you sure? I'd offer to pop it on mine, but I think I'm almost up to my credit limit and I've no idea how much Mack is going to charge us this time.'

'No, well, as long as little Dougal is okay, it doesn't matter, does it?' Flora patted Poppy's arm. 'Now, I'd best get this one up into the top paddock before Alex comes along with the puppies.'

'Okay. See you later.'

'Yes, lovely. Take care.'

Poppy watched as Flora went outside before turning towards the counter. She was sure she'd seen the charity debit card yesterday. She began to rummage through the drawer and yep, there it was. She tucked it into her purse next to Aunt Flora's card. She'd give both back to her when she returned to Wagging Tails with Dougal.

* * *

Poppy moved towards the window and looked out across the car park. Yesterday's rain hadn't returned. Instead, a thin layer of frost clung to the ground, the air freezing. A young girl walked with her father, carrying a small animal carrier in her arms. Poppy watched as the girl paused, breathing out through her mouth, so she could show her dad the white cloud evaporating into the air.

She smiled. She remembered doing just that. Aunt Flora had always called it dragon breath.

She sat down again on one of the hard plastic chairs of the waiting room, glancing quickly at the clock on the opposite wall. She'd been here twenty minutes already. Kerry had told her to expect a bit of a wait due to an emergency. She just hoped that the emergency wasn't little Dougal.

Placing her elbows on her knees and leaning forward, she

picked at her nail varnish, a bad habit she'd picked up recently. She really needed to repaint her nails.

The door to the surgery opened as the girl and her dad arrived, a cold burst of air filling the waiting room. The girl placed the carrier on the floor, kneeling in front of it and speaking quietly to the cat inside as her dad spoke to Kerry at the reception desk.

Twenty-five minutes had passed now. Poppy pulled her mobile from her pocket and scrolled through to her messages. Holding her breath, she typed out a quick text:

Hi, how's things going? Any news?

She deleted it. She shouldn't even be messaging Ben, but what had she meant by any news? Any news on the sale of the home? Or any news on the date he'd gone on last week?

She'd meant any news of the sale of their home, of course. Although she'd checked the estate agents' website this morning and their house, once her retreat from the world, was still up still for sale.

Yes, that was a legitimate question. She retyped the message.

'Poppy, do you want to come through?'

Glancing up, she quickly pressed send before following Mack into the examination room.

'That wasn't Dougal who you've been with all this time, was it? The emergency? It wasn't Dougal?'

'No, Dougal's doing just fine. He's a little fighter, that one.' Mack closed the door behind them, clicking it shut softly.

'Good, good. That's a relief.' Poppy nodded and swallowed. 'Look, I just wanted to apologise for the way I treated you yesterday. I must have sounded so ungrateful after you'd saved me from trailing around the shops and bought me hot chocolate and a mince pie, plus reuniting me with my bag. I'm sorry.'

'Hey, there's no need to apologise.' He held his hands up. 'In fact, it should be me saying sorry. I shouldn't have bombarded you with all those questions. It's a bad habit of mine.'

'Your questions were reasonable, given the fact we were at the Christmas market. It was me.'

'Shall we just agree to disagree on whose fault it was?' Mack crossed his arms and leaned back against the counter.

'Yes. Thank you.' Poppy looked around the room and pointed towards a skateboard leaning up against the wall in the corner. 'You found the skateboard stall in the end, then?'

'Yes, I did. What do you think?' Leaning down, he picked it up and held it across his arm.

'It's really cool.' She ran her finger across the stylish sketch of a skateboarder, swirls of flames coming out from the painted wheels.

'It is, isn't it? I got a good deal too. Managed to haggle the artist down ten per cent.' Grinning, he placed it back in the corner.

Here we go again. Did he try to save money on everything he bought? First using the raffle prize as a present and now this? Not that she thought the designer make-up bag had been worth the price – far from it. He really didn't like spending money, did he?

She shook her head and reminded herself it none of her business.

'Do you skate much?'

'Me?' Mack chuckled. 'Nah, I haven't skated in years. Not since I was a teenager. I'd likely fall off and break my legs if I tried nowadays. It's for my brother. When he's not in college, he's always down at the skate ramp practising some trick or another.'

'Oh, I didn't know you had a brother.' She rolled her eyes at herself. Why would she? She barely knew the guy. 'I'm sure he'll like that then.'

'Yes, I hope so. He's been following the artist who painted it for months now, so I'm hoping I've chosen a cool enough design.'

'I don't think anyone could say that wasn't cool enough.' She laughed. 'Although who knows what's on trend for teenagers at the moment?'

'True.' Mack nodded before picking up a clipboard from the side and replacing it before meeting her eyes. 'I enjoyed yesterday. Thank you for agreeing to come around the Christmas market with me.'

'You mean you enjoyed it until I snapped at you?' She grimaced before laughing. She really hadn't treated him very nicely. Her worries weren't his and she shouldn't have taken her bad experiences out on him. 'I enjoyed it too, thank you.'

He glanced down at the floor before looking back at her. 'Maybe we could do something else together? Without the stress of Christmas shopping, I mean?'

'Umm...' Was he asking her out? As in out on a date? Or just asking her to meet as friends? Either way she hadn't expected him to want to spend any more time with her after yesterday.

'You don't need to answer right away.' He shifted on his feet. 'Just let me know if you fancy it. You've got my number.'

'Have I?' She pulled her mobile from her pocket and looked at it. She didn't remember him giving her his number.

'On the surgery's business card, or on the website.'

'Right.' She nodded. 'Yes, of course it is.'

Mack pointed towards the door. 'I'll go and bring Dougal in for you now and we can discuss his treatment plan.'

As soon as the door clicked shut, Poppy placed her hand over her face. Could she have made more of a fool of herself if she'd tried? She plunged her hands into her coat pockets. Not that it mattered. She didn't care what he thought of her. Why would she? He was the home's vet, that was all. And a vet who didn't take into consideration that Wagging Tails was a charity trying to do their best for the dogs they rescued while he charged them full price for all treatment.

Of course she didn't care. He could think what he liked about her. It didn't matter. After today, she wouldn't need to see him again, anyway. She felt her phone vibrate against her fingers and she pulled it out quickly, her shoulders slumping as she read the message. It wasn't Ben. It was from Melissa asking her if she was settling in okay. She dismissed the text. She'd reply later. She could do with a good catch-up anyway. When she wasn't trying to figure out what Mack had meant by asking her out and when she wasn't wondering why she suddenly wanted Ben to reply to her texts.

'Here he is.'

Stuffing her mobile back into her pocket, she watched as Mack shouldered the door open, Dougal in his arms.

'Dougal!' she said, stepping forward. She grinned as she fussed his ears. 'It's so good to see you again.'

Mack lowered him to the table.

'He looks so much better already. His eyes are brighter and he's even wagging his tail. He didn't have the energy for that when I dropped him off.'

'That'll be the IV fluid he's had.' Mack reached behind him and placed a paper bag on the table. 'In here is the lungworm treatment. He'll need to take these regularly for several months to ensure the infection fully clears up. I've also had him on this medication…' He pulled a small box from the bag. 'To prevent seizures and these antibiotics.'

'Okay.' Poppy smiled as she looked into Dougal's eyes. They were glistening. He was almost like a different dog.

'I'd advise feeding him chicken for the next day or two as he regains his appetite and then high-calorie food to encourage weight gain would be beneficial.'

'Yes, okay. And he should make a full recovery now, then?'

'He's in a much better position than he was a couple of days ago, yes. He still has a way to go with treatment and building his strength back up, but, all being well, then yes, I'm confident he can overcome any more obstacles.'

'Great. Thank you so much.' Poppy swiped a tear away. Why was she even crying? Dougal was on the mend.

'Are you okay?' Reaching out his hand, Mack touched the sleeve of her coat.

'Yes, sorry. I don't even know why I'm being like this. Like you say, he's on the road to recovery now.' She looked down at Dougal. 'Aren't you, little one? You're on the mend.'

Mack smiled, the kindness reaching his eyes. 'If you book an appointment in for the end of the week, we can check him over and I can advise about the best foods for optimum weight gain.'

'Yes, will do.' Picking Dougal up, she shifted him in her arms before lowering him to the floor. 'I bet you'd like to walk now. You look as though you've got the energy, too.' She looked back at Mack. 'Thank you again.'

'My pleasure.' He bent down and fussed Dougal quickly before holding the door open for them.

Glancing back at him, she smiled before joining the short queue to the receptionist's desk. She couldn't believe the difference in Dougal in just the past two days. She watched as he sniffed at the floor before pulling on the lead to try to explore the waiting room.

'Hold on, Dougal.'

'Morning. Poppy and Dougal, isn't it? From The Wagging Tails Dogs' Home?' Kerry clicked at the keyboard.

'Yes, that's right.' Poppy pulled her purse from her pocket.

'Right, and you're to settle the bill today.'

It had been a statement, not a question. Poppy nodded.

Kerry twisted the computer screen towards her and clicked on the screen.

Gulping, Poppy forced her face to smile. How much? She pulled out the dogs' home's debit card. There was no point arguing or begging for a discount. She'd tried that. Sliding the card into the reader, she tapped in the pin code.

Kerry flicked her hair from her face and took the card out before pushing it back in. 'It's been declined. Please try again.'

'Oh, sorry.' Had she tapped in the wrong code? After pulling out her phone and checking the pin number in her notes, she entered it again.

'I'm afraid it still hasn't gone through. Do you have another card you could try?' Kerry held the card towards her.

'Umm...' She'd have to use Aunt Flora's one, after all. 'Yes, one moment.'

13

'Happy birthday, dear Susan, happy birthday to you.'

Poppy sang along with the rest of the staff and volunteers who had all crammed into the kitchen for Aunt Flora's weekly 'thank you' evening and to celebrate Susan's birthday.

Grinning, Susan stepped forward and blew out the candles before clasping her hands together.

Poppy grinned. She hadn't been to one of her aunt's 'thank you' dinners in years, but it was just as special as she remembered. There were new faces and names of the many volunteers to get to know, but Aunt Flora had still ordered pizza in as she had done all those years ago when she last stayed here, and Susan had still baked cupcakes to pass around. The buzz of excitement at all being together and the gratitude towards each other was still the same.

Susan clapped her hands together, and the room silenced, all attention on her. 'Thank you, everyone, for all the birthday wishes.' She indicated the cake. 'This was such a lovely surprise.'

'Three cheers for the birthday girl.' Percy held his mug up. 'Hip hip hooray!'

'Hip hip hooray!'

'Hip hip hooray!'

Blushing, Susan mouthed 'thank you' to Percy. 'Cake all round?'

Shouts of 'yes' and 'absolutely' filtered around the room as Flora passed Susan a knife and held out napkins.

Poppy took another bite from her slice of pizza and grinned. This was what Wagging Tails was all about, community, the coming together of like-minded people for the greater good. It sounded deep, but it was true. Each and every person here, staff members and volunteers alike, turned up each day or once or twice a week to give their time to the dogs. She'd missed this feeling of belonging.

The cheerful ringtone of the landline filtered in from the reception area and Poppy watched as Alex laid his slice of pizza back in the box and disappeared out of the room.

'Are you all right, lovely?' Flora said, passing her a piece of cake.

'Yes, I'm good, thanks.' Poppy took a bite of the cake, the moist sponge dispersing a burst of lemon across her tastebuds.

When Alex came back into the room, he clapped his hands and waited for silence. 'Sorry to break up the party, but that was Mr Thomas on the phone. He's letting us take four of his dogs if we can collect them tonight.'

'Really?' Pushing her chair away from the table, Ginny stood up.

'Quick, let's go before he changes his mind again.' Flora put the cake slices she was carrying down and glanced around the room. 'The rest of you stay, eat and enjoy. We're off to rescue some dogs!'

Standing up, Poppy followed her aunt through to the reception area. 'Can I come and help?'

'Yes, of course, lovely.' Flora shrugged into her coat before passing Poppy's to her.

* * *

Poppy placed the last of four feeding bowls on the floor and watched as the fourth and youngest dog wolfed down the meat. She looked around the kitchen; Aunt Flora was busy making coffee, Alex was slumped at the table with his head in his hands and Susan was sitting next to her partner, Malcolm, his arms around her and her head leaning on his shoulder, while Percy shook out biscuits onto a plate.

'Here we go, coffees for everyone. I think we deserve it.' Flora sunk into a chair. 'Come and take a seat, Poppy, lovely.'

Nodding, Poppy put the now empty feeding bowls in the sink before taking a seat next to her aunt.

'Here you go. Get that down you.' Flora passed Poppy a mug.

'Thanks.' Inhaling the hot bittersweet aroma of the coffee, Poppy watched as the four dogs made themselves comfortable on the duvets Susan had laid down for them.

'We'll let their food go down and then take them out for a quick walk in case they need to toilet before taking them to their kennel.' Flora looked around the room. 'Thank you all for coming with us to Mr Thomas's and helping get these four sweeties. And thank you, Malcolm, for staying behind after the dinner and tidying up.'

'No problem. Glad to have been able to help in my own small way.' Malcolm twisted his bow tie straight before rubbing Susan's back. 'What was Mr Thomas's house like? Was it as bad as it was last time you were allowed in or had he tidied up a bit?'

'Worse.' Alex raised his arms above his head and yawned. 'It didn't look as though he'd let the dogs, or the cats, out for days and he definitely hadn't been cleaning up properly after them.'

Malcom raised his eyebrows. 'Was it really that bad?'

Susan nodded, her head still resting on Malcom's shoulder. 'It was. But he's providing them with food, water and shelter so we can still only encourage him to give them up on his own terms.'

'Yes, poor Mr Thomas. The sooner he allows us to rehome them all, the better it will be for his health as well as his animals.' Flora glanced down into her coffee. 'You're all welcome to get off home. It's late.'

Poppy glanced at the clock. It was half past one in the morning. She hadn't realised how long they'd been at Mr Thomas's for. When they'd arrived, as expected, he'd changed his mind about letting them take the dogs, so Flora had spent a lot of time trying to reason with him. It had only been once he'd finally allowed them into the house that they'd realised the extent of the issue and thanks to Aunt Flora and her incredible negotiating skills, he'd eventually relented. After he'd managed to choose which dogs to relinquish, Flora had spotted a small whippet, Eden, whimpering in the corner. On closer inspection, they'd realised the dog must have been involved in a scrap with another dog and her leg had been seriously bitten. Another hour later and Mr Thomas had also agreed that they could take the whippet to the vet's in addition to the other dogs. And although Mr Thomas had insisted they return the whippet when the leg had healed, time would tell if Aunt Flora could talk him round to the idea of them being allowed to rehome the poor little thing.

'I'm staying until Ginny gets back from the vet's,' Alex said, holding his hand up.

'Yep, we will too. I need to know if that beautiful whippet is okay.' Susan rubbed Malcom's hand.

'Me too.' Poppy looked down into her coffee. She dreaded to think how much Mack would charge them for seeing Eden out of hours.

Flora nodded. 'Okay, if you're sure. I'm so pleased he allowed us to take her. Even if it did take some persuading.'

'I didn't think he was going to,' Alex said as he leaned his forehead against the tabletop.

'Oh, I was optimistic. Mr Thomas loves those dogs, which is

why he's finding it so difficult to realise that he can no longer care for them as he used to.' Flora bent down and fussed over one of the Labradors they had been allowed to take.

Pushing her chair back, Poppy stood up. 'I'm going to go and check on Dougal.'

'Okay, lovely.' Flora patted her arm before turning back to her coffee.

Closing the kitchen door behind her, Poppy looked out of the window towards the front of the reception area. The only light was from the sliver of moon, which hung low in the sky. There were streetlamps up in West Par, the village up the road, but here, all she could see was night.

Taking a lead from the hooks behind the counter, she went to Dougal's kennel.

'Hello, sweetheart. Do you fancy a night-time stroll?' She fussed over the small dog as he walked across to her, his tail wagging. She then clipped the lead to his collar before leading him back through the reception area.

After shrugging into her coat, she stepped outside and took a deep breath, the cold air filling her lungs and waking her up.

'You okay, Dougal? Look how beautiful it is at night.'

Leaning her head back, she looked up at the stars. She'd missed this – being able to see the stars so clearly.

She walked towards the edge of the courtyard and paused next to the gate that led to the bottom paddock.

'There you are, love.'

Turning around, Poppy smiled. 'Percy. I was just thinking about you and how you taught me to love the stars.'

'Ah, yes, I remember bringing you out here one night when Flora had run off to rescue some dog or other.'

Poppy nodded. 'Yes, and after that I used to beg Aunt Flora to let me stay up late so you could show me the stars again.'

Percy chuckled. 'She relented in the end, didn't she? And you were allowed to stay up once a week...'

'Twice in my last week down here in the summer holidays.'

'That's right. I'd forgotten. Flora would make us hot chocolate and we'd set up those two old camping chairs, and we'd sit in the dark drinking our hot chocolates and talking about the stars.'

'I still remember some of the constellations you taught me.' She turned her face back towards the sky again. 'Look, that one's Orion, isn't it?'

'That's right.' Percy pointed to another cluster of brilliantly bright stars. 'How about that one?' He held his finger up, following the pattern they made as if they were dots on a dot-to-dot picture.

'Cat... something? No, I know, it's Cetus. Is that right?' She looked across at him.

'Yes, that's correct!' Percy grinned. 'Extra points if you can tell me its other name.'

'The whale.'

'Perfect.'

Car headlights swept across the courtyard and they both watched as Ginny pulled into the small car park.

* * *

'That's a good boy. You try to get some rest now.'

After one last fuss behind the ears, Poppy pulled Dougal's kennel door closed. Then she made her way through to the reception and hung up the lead before shrugging out of her coat and opening the door into the kitchen. Everyone but Alex had woken up and was listening to Ginny.

'... Mack is going to take an X-ray tonight, but he's hopeful the bite hasn't gone through to the bone and has put her on IV antibiotics.' Ginny took a mug of coffee from Flora. 'Thanks.'

'Poor little soul.' Flora shook her head. 'She must have been in agony.'

'Yes, she must have. Hopefully, this might make Mr Thomas realise it will be best for his pets if they're rehomed.' Ginny took a long sip from her coffee.

'I hope you're right. I really do.' Flora sank back into her chair.

Poppy took a biscuit from the plate and leaned against the work surface. She felt more awake after going outside for a bit, but she couldn't trust herself not to fall asleep if she were to sit down.

'Oh, and Flora, I meant to say the charity debit card wouldn't go through for some reason, so I popped it on my card.' Ginny pulled the card from her pocket and passed it to Flora.

Taking it from her, Flora shifted in her seat. 'Oh, sorry, love. There's been some issue with it or something. I'll transfer you the money and give the bank a call in the morning.'

'No rush. Wait until it's sorted, if you like.'

'No, no, I'll transfer it tonight.' Flora stood up. 'Right, I suggest we all head home to bed now. Everyone come in a bit later tomorrow morning, too.'

'Good idea. I'm bushed.' Susan yawned before walking across to Alex and gently shaking him by the shoulder. 'Time to wake up, sleepyhead.'

14

'Help yourselves to buckets, people.' Alex held up two blue collection buckets with the Wagging Tails' logo on.

Poppy took one.

'Ready, Percy?' Flora held out a Santa's hat.

Percy took the plush red hat from her, pulled it on, flicking the white furry pom-pom to the back, and grinned. 'I am now.'

'Good, good. Up you go then.' Flora indicated the trailer which had a wooden cut-out of a sleigh attached.

Gripping hold of a metal pole, Percy clambered into position on his sleigh.

'Are we all ready?' Farmer Nichols, who had volunteered to pull the trailer with Percy's sleigh on with his tractor, looked behind him.

'Ready.' A chorus of agreement rose from the small crowd of Wagging Tails' volunteers.

'Your hat.' Ginny nudged Poppy with her elbow.

'Oops. Thanks.' She pulled the green elf hat over her head. At least it should keep her warm.

Music boomed from the row of speakers lined up on the trailer, and the fairy lights on the sleigh began to flash. Slowly, the tractor pulled away from the side of the road. They were off.

Poppy fell into step behind Alex and Susan and, holding the bucket in one hand, she tried to button up her coat. She should have done it earlier. Trying one-handed was no mean feat.

'Here, let me.' Flora caught up with her and took the bucket from Poppy's hand.

'Thanks. I should have been more organised.'

'It's supposed to get colder still by the time we're due to finish.' Flora looked towards the sky. 'I wouldn't be too surprised if we didn't have a bit of Christmas magic and it began to snow.'

'Really?' Poppy squinted into the evening sky. Flora was right, there was enough cloud, and it was certainly cold enough for snow.

'Maybe.'

Glancing behind, Poppy frowned. 'Why are so many people joining us?'

After hearing the music of the sleigh, people were rushing out of their houses, shrugging into their coats, and were beginning to form a crowd trailing behind them. Didn't people usually just watch and then retreat back into their homes? That's what had always happened when she'd been a child and Santa's sleigh had made the rounds for the local charities.

'It's a tradition in West Par. They're showing their support. We'll all congregate at the village tree soon for drinks and snacks.' Flora shrugged before putting her arm through Poppy's and pulling her close. 'When you were younger, you used to love Christmas? Do you remember?'

Poppy frowned. 'No, I didn't. The only part of Christmas Day I ever enjoyed was going over to Grandma's for the morning. I hated the rest.'

'Ah, yes, your dad's mum was a lovely lady. I only met her twice, mind. Once at your parents' wedding and once more after.' Flora shook her head. 'No, I mean before that. Before the arguments between your parents began.'

'Before?'

'Yes! Don't sound so shocked. Even your mum and dad loved each other once upon a time. Admittedly, only a short-lived time, but they did. They used to travel down here the weekend before Christmas Day, and you loved it. I remember you dancing to the Christmas music, handing out gifts for the dogs because you weren't going to see them on Christmas Day. We'd have the whole works, gifts under the tree, crackers at the table. Your mum would make the biggest roast you ever saw.'

Poppy paused. 'I don't think I remember.'

'I'll fish out the photos when we get back to the cottage.' Flora pulled her even closer, her mouth right next to her ear. 'And, more importantly, just because you didn't enjoy Christmas in the past, it doesn't mean you can't learn to enjoy it now. Look around you.' She waved her hand, encompassing the sleigh in front of them; West Par's Christmas lights strung from lamppost to lamppost illuminating a warm glow beneath them, trees decorated with warm yellow lights the perfect addition to the magic; Percy grinning and waving whilst the volunteer elves ran from door to door collecting coins; parents hurrying to the end of their front gardens, children in their arms or jumping up and down spellbound by the 'Santa' in front of them.

Poppy sighed. 'However beautiful it all is, it doesn't change the fact that my long-term relationship has just ended. I'm basically homeless and my life has been turned upside down.'

'Maybe your life needed turning upside down.' Flora tilted her head and shrugged.

'Great. Thanks.' She raised an eyebrow. No sympathy from her aunt then.

'I'm being serious. You were unhappy. Every time your mum

rang me, she'd tell me about some drama or other you were having with Ben and when you managed to ring me, you didn't sound happy either.'

'Sorry, I should have been in touch more. I hardly called you before all of this and now I've just turned up to stay.' Poppy turned to thank a young boy who had run up to place some money in her bucket before looking back at her aunt.

'Don't be daft. That's not what I meant. It's wonderful having you here. But it's true. You weren't happy. I know it's easy to look back with rose-tinted glasses, but you need to remember it was a mutual decision between the two of you to call it a day. That's not to mean you weren't – and aren't – entitled to feel upset, of course you are, but you do need to remember that you made that huge, scary leap for a reason and now you have a blank canvas to restart your life, the way you want it. The way you deserve. And you can start by learning to enjoy Christmas.'

'Flora...' Ginny called from where she was walking next to Darryl, who was holding part of the string of fairy lights, just behind the sleigh.

'Oops, looks as though the lights are trying to escape. Think about what I said.' Flora kissed Poppy on the cheek quickly before rushing off to join Ginny and Darryl, already wielding a roll of tape in her hand.

Poppy glanced around her. She had to admit the atmosphere was magical. All the people here collecting, even the tractor driver had given up his time to come together and raise money for Wagging Tails. And if that wasn't enough, it was obvious that their presence, Percy's presence, was bringing joy to the community.

Was Aunt Flora right? Could she really come out of all this upheaval happier? Poppy shook her head. It did seem impossible at the moment. She still had to communicate with Ben while they sorted the sale of their house, and until that was all finalised, could she really move on with her life? She was still paying some of the mortgage as he couldn't afford to pay all of it. Until the house was sold, she didn't really have much of a choice but to stay stuck. Stuck on some infinite treadmill, running but going nowhere. Stuck because she couldn't financially move on. Heck, once last month's wage from the supply agency had gone, that would be it. And it was whittling down fast, what with her mortgage payment and the train ticket and taxi fare to West Par.

'Merry Christmas! Can I come and collect with you, please?'

Shaking her thoughts away, Poppy looked down and smiled at the boy who was tugging on her coat sleeve. 'Umm, well, I don't know. Are you allowed to?'

'Yes, I am. My biggest brother said I could, and he's super old.' The young boy, who must have been barely six or seven, pulled his navy bobble hat lower over his ears. 'He's over there.'

Poppy squinted into the darkness and looked across to where the boy was pointing. In the darkness, she could just about make out the silhouette of someone waving. 'Okay then. Do you want to hold the bucket?'

'Yes please.' The boy gripped the bucket in one hand and slipped his other hand into hers, pulling her across onto the path through someone's front garden towards a couple who were waving towards the sleigh, an excitable spaniel at their heels. 'We're collecting for the little dogs. Can you give us some money, please?'

Poppy stifled a laugh before adding, 'We're raising money for Wagging Tails Dogs' Home.'

'Of course. One moment.' The woman disappeared inside the house before coming out with her purse and shaking the coins into the bucket. 'Here you are. You do an amazing job. We got our Tyler from the home this summer and couldn't be happier.'

'Oh really? Well, thank you. It looks as though he couldn't be happier either.' Kneeling down, Poppy fussed the little dog behind his ears and his yapping was quickly replaced with the beating of his tail against the wooden hall flooring. 'He's beautiful.'

'We think so.' The man grinned.

'We need to go and get more money now, don't we, Poppy?' The boy gripped hold of her hand again, pulling her away. 'Bye!'

'Thank you and Merry Christmas.' Poppy waved at the couple. When they were back in the procession, she turned to the boy. 'What's your name, by the way?'

'Spencer.'

'And how do you know my name, Spencer?'

But Spencer didn't answer as he was distracted again, pointing excitedly to the large tree in the middle of the village square. 'Look, look, we're almost at the Christmas tree! Quick, let's go and get more people to give us their money,' he said, before yanking Poppy towards another house.

15

'Hello, Spencer, lovely. I didn't know you were helping us tonight.' Flora wrapped her hands around a takeaway mug.

'Yes, my brother said I could… I've been helping Poppy.' He rattled the bucket.

'Well, thank you very much. That's very kind of you. And I think that calls for a mince pie, don't you?' She held her hand out for Spencer to take.

'Urgh, I don't like mince pies. I might when I'm old, though. My brother said I would when I grow up, but I don't think I will…' Spencer took hold of her hand, still gripping the bucket in his other one. 'There are fairy cakes on the stall. The lady Elsie from the bakery promised me she would bring some fairy cakes.'

'Fairy cakes it is, then?' Flora turned to Poppy. 'Go and get yourself a hot chocolate, lovely. You'll need it to help keep you warm before we carry on.'

'And she said she was going to put sparkles on them.' Spencer turned his face up towards Flora. 'Will they be sparkles I can eat or will I have to pick them off? I hope I don't have to pick them off. I'm hungry and I don't want to have to wait.'

'I'm positive they'll be edible.' Flora grinned at Poppy as she led the way to the cake and mince pie stall.

Poppy watched as Flora weaved her way through the crowd which had gathered beneath the village Christmas tree. Children queued to have their photograph taken on the sleigh with Santa, their parents wiping a tear or two from their eyes; people mingled with cups of hot chocolate, watching as a few brave people danced beneath the tree.

Poppy joined the queue to the drinks stall, taking a deep breath, breathing in the warm aroma of the hot chocolate.

'Evening.'

Looking up, she saw Mack before her, picking up a cup before ladling hot chocolate in. 'Mack? What are you doing here?'

'Just doing my bit for charity.' He grinned as he held up a can. 'Cream?'

'Yes, please,' she said, still quite surprised that he would be here. He was doing his bit, supporting the village. 'I didn't think you believed in charity?'

'Pardon?' The last drop of cream dropped from the can onto the surface of the chocolatey liquid.

'Sorry, nothing. Ignore me.' She shook her head. It wasn't her place to question his intentions. Or him. But it was odd, wasn't it? That he'd give his time up to serve drinks and yet wouldn't even contemplate upkeeping the previous vet's agreement to give the dogs from Wagging Tails a discount or even just to provide his time free to help the dogs.

'Thank you for letting my brother walk with you. He's been so excited to see Santa, so being able to walk with an elf and help collect money will have been the highlight of his week.'

'Spencer is your brother?' Poppy took the cup. 'Thanks.'

'Don't look so shocked! Though I'll admit there's a *bit* of an age difference.' Mack chuckled as Spencer bounded over, a cake in one hand, bucket still in the other. 'Hey, buddy. Have you come over for some hot choc?'

'Urgh, you know I don't like hot chocolate.' Spencer shook his head with such enthusiasm his bobble hat worked its way off, falling to the floor.

'Just teasing, I've brought you a flask of blackcurrant. Let's put your bobble hat back on, though. You don't want to catch a cold, not for Christmas, do you?'

'Nope, I don't want a cold, but...' Spencer pushed the hat away as Mack tried to put it on him.

'But what, buddy?' Mack leaned down and Spencer whispered something in his ear. Straightening his back again, he chuckled. 'I'm afraid you can't have Poppy's hat. Then *she'll* get cold.'

Poppy pulled the elf hat from her head and pulled it down over Spencer's head. 'There you go, Elf Spencer.'

'Wow! Really? Can I really be an elf?' He shook his head from side to side, the yellow pom-pom on the tip of the hat bouncing against his cheeks.

'I think you'll make the best elf.' Poppy grinned as she picked up her cup which she'd put down in order to help him.

'Yes, look at you, buddy.' Mack laid his hand on Spencer's shoulder and nodded towards her. 'Now, what do you say to Poppy?'

'Thank you, Poppy. Thank you.' Spencer wrapped his arms around her waist, the bucket knocking into her back and the cake coming very close to her side, a smear of icing trailing across her coat.

'You're very welcome.'

'Now you can give Poppy your hat to wear, Mack, and then she won't get cold.' Spencer nodded to Mack's red beanie hat before returning his attention to his cake. 'I'm going to go and show Nathan my hat.'

He pointed towards a group of children playing under the Christmas tree.

'Okay, stay where I can see you, though.'

Mack watched until Spencer had joined his friends before pulling his hat from his head.

'Oh no, don't really give it to me. I'll be fine.' Poppy held out her hand, palm forward.

'Ha ha, you really think Spencer won't notice? Besides, I'm warm enough and you've still got the other half of the village to cover.' Stepping forward, he gently pulled the hat over Poppy's head.

'Thanks.' Poppy smiled and tugged it down to cover her ears.

'Here, do you want to come and take a look at the Christmas tree? Spencer will no doubt quiz you as to whether you've seen the bauble he decorated.' Mack glanced around the crowd. 'I think everyone who wants one has a drink already.'

'Why not? Did he make it at school or something?' Poppy walked over towards the large Christmas tree where she ran her fingers across the pine needles. It never failed to surprise her how soft they actually were.

'Yes. A local pottery teacher and artist visited and worked with each class in turn to make and decorate them. You might know her actually, she volunteers at your place. Carrie?' Mack cupped his hand around a brilliant blue bauble hanging on a branch near them. 'Here's the one Spencer made.'

'Oh, it's lovely.' She smiled. It really was. All of the baubles were. 'No, I don't think I've met her yet. Although I may have done at Aunt Flora's get-together the other day.' She shook her head and laughed. 'I'm rubbish with names.'

'Beautiful, isn't it?' Mack looked up at the tree. 'It always amazes me just how stunning it looks with lights on. Not that it doesn't look beautiful without lights on, that is. And the baubles really add something, don't they? This is the first year with anything but fairy lights on it, I believe.'

'It is pretty.'

'What's your Christmas tree like at home?' He took a sip of his drink.

'We don't have one at Wagging Tails.' She frowned. They usually did. Aunt Flora must have decided against it this year for some reason. 'Or do you mean at my old home?' She scoffed. What was home? Did she even have one at the moment?

She shook her head. She knew how upset Aunt Flora would be if she were to voice that worry. She knew she'd always have a home with Aunt Flora. For as long as she needed, her aunt had already told her that. She might not have her own house at the moment, but she did have a home. 'I didn't have one back at the house. We didn't really bother much with Christmas.'

'You and your ex, I'm presuming?'

Shifting on her feet, Poppy nodded.

'Sorry, I shouldn't have asked.'

She cleared her throat. 'No, it's fine. The relationship has been over a while now. It's just only been official really for a few months, and I guess I'm still trying to wrap my head around how different my life is now going to be.'

Mack nodded. 'These things can certainly pull the rug from beneath your feet, can't they?'

'Oh yes.' She took another sip of her hot chocolate. 'How about you? I'm guessing you have a Christmas tree.'

'Oh yes.' Mack grinned, his eyes glistening with the reflection of the lights on the tree.

'I guess you have to keep the magic alive for when your brothers visit?'

'They live with me, but no, I don't have a tree just for them. I believe we can all use a little magic in our lives, don't you think?

Life is too serious, so why not make the most of a special time like Christmas?'

Poppy looked at him over the top of her cup. 'It's funny you say that now. My aunt was just telling me how much I used to love Christmas. Not that I really remember. Sorry, I'm being so negative, aren't I? It's just Christmases for me haven't been quite so magical recently, that's all.'

'That's fair enough. As an adult life can have its tough moments.' Mack smiled at her. 'Maybe spending this Christmas down here with your aunt and at West Par might just change your mind?'

She shrugged. 'Maybe.' And maybe it already was. She looked around them. Everyone was still chatting, dancing or sipping hot chocolate. People were happy. Maybe she was beginning to feel a little more Christmassy already. Just maybe.

Mack grinned and looked up at the sky. 'Look, it's snowing. Now if that isn't magical, I don't know what is!'

Tilting her head back, Poppy looked up at the sky as snowflakes began to fall, illuminated by the lights from the tree and the surrounding lampposts. 'It's beautiful.'

From the other side of the square, Flora clapped her hands together.

'Right, let's get back to it and finish off our route.' She grinned as everyone got into their positions again and the last photo of Percy with an excited toddler was taken.

'Come on, come on. It's time to go. We've got more money to get for the doggies.' Spencer ran up to them, reaching for both Poppy and Mack's hands. They joined the group as the sleigh set off, the bucket knocking against Mack's knee as Spencer gripped hold of it.

As the tractor engine roared into action, the speakers blasted out cheerful Christmas tunes again and an excited hubbub filled the air.

'Quick, this way!' Spencer pulled them both towards a small cottage, relinquishing their hands before running up the stone steps to the front door.

An elderly couple opened the door and stuffed a note inside the bucket before giving Spencer a Christmas cracker. Poppy smiled as she watched.

'Hah, I knew it!' Mack grinned at her from the other side of the open gate. 'You *do* see the joy that Christmas brings to people.'

'I don't know what you mean.' Poppy held the gate open as Spencer skipped back through, holding up his cracker for them to see. 'That's just plain kindness. It's nothing to do with Christmas.'

'Umm.' Shaking his head, Mack leaned down towards Spencer and pointed to the next cottage along. 'Try there.'

'Are you really saying that those people would have answered the door to a, what, six, seven-year-old and been mean to him if, say, it had been summer, or spring, or autumn?' Poppy was right, and he knew it.

'Not mean to him, no, of course not, but Christmas does bring an extra layer of magic.' Mack nudged her shoulder gently. 'And he's nine. I won't tell him you thought he was six if you admit you're beginning to feel a tiny little bit Christmassy.' Mack held his thumb and forefinger a millimetre apart.

'Ha ha, very funny. You won't tell him.' Poppy laughed.

'No, you're right. I won't.' Mack chuckled.

She looked across at him and grinned. He was a good man, funny, caring, and he obviously thought a lot for his brothers, a real family man.

She looked away, a warm blush flushing across her face. What was she even thinking?

16

'This way, Alfie. That's it, good boy. And you too, Oscar.'

Poppy swapped Alfie and Oscar's leads in her hands in an attempt to untangle them before she ended up flat on her face. She laughed as Alfie sat down on the path whilst Oscar circled him. The two of them had been rescued from Mr Thomas, the hoarder, and although they had stuck by each other's side since arriving and refused to step outside their kennel without the other, they were like chalk and cheese. Alfie, a Lhasa Apso, loved nothing more than to rest and curl up on his bed, while Oscar, possibly a Pomeranian cross, had enough energy for the both of them and was constantly on the move. She didn't think she'd seen him sit still for longer than five minutes in total.

Quickly looping Oscar's lead around her hand, she hurried them along before Oscar could tangle them up any further. The dog with the poorly leg who had also been rescued, Eden, was still at the vet's. They'd have to remember to keep her separated from Oscar until her leg healed, at least. Although, if Eden was anything like Alfie, then she'd just ignore his energy, anyway.

'Come on, let's go down to the beach and look at the sea. Have you seen the sea before?'

Oscar paused, tilting his head as he looked up at Poppy.

'What's up, Oscar? You're still! I might just be able to give you a fuss now, then.' As soon as she'd reached down, Oscar darted between her legs, wrapping his lead around her ankles. 'Oscar!'

Catching her balance, she bent down and tried to pull the lead looser. It wasn't working. Oscar was just getting more and more excitable, obviously thinking that she was playing with him. At this rate, she'd be stuck standing here, wrapped up like a mummy forever.

She blew her hair out of her eyes. 'Are you getting as fed up with this game as I am, Alfie?' She watched as Alfie looked at her out of the corner of his eye, making it clear to her that he was as embarrassed of Oscar's actions as she was.

'Do you need some help there, love?'

Jumping round, Poppy twisted to peer behind her. 'Mr Euston! Am I glad to see you! And, that's not Gray, is it?'

'It sure is. Poppy, isn't it? Flora's niece? Well, I haven't seen you in these parts for a long time. How are you?' He paused a few steps away.

'Oh, you know. A little tied up at the moment.' She grimaced. 'Literally!'

'Yes, yes, of course. I'll give you a hand. Are these little ones okay with other dogs?' He nodded to his own, who was sitting patiently next to him on a lead, a little French bulldog.

'Yes, they should be fine. They've been living over at Mr Thomas's place with about twenty other dogs, so they're quite used to company.'

Nodding, Mr Euston stepped forward and leaned down, holding out his hand for Alfie to sniff before fussing him. 'You're a lovely one, aren't you? Very calm.'

'I just wish the same could be said of this little monster.' Laughing, Poppy gestured to Oscar.

'Oh, you're just excitable, I bet.' He moved from Alfie to Oscar and then fussed him behind the ears too. 'Are you excited to be going to the beach?'

Poppy shook her head. 'That's the longest time I've known him to be as still as he is with you.'

'Aw, it must be my calming influence.' He chuckled before eyeing up the tangled lead. 'Now, let's see what we can do here, shall we?'

Poppy watched as Mr Euston encouraged Oscar this way and that until the lead was loose enough for her to step out of it. 'Thank you so much.'

'You're very welcome, love.' He passed Oscar's lead back to her.

'Wow, you've grown so much, Gray, sweetie.' Bending down, Poppy fussed Mr Euston's small dog, tickling his tummy as he rolled onto his back.

'He sure has. He must have been just a pup when you last saw him? He's still as daft as he was then.'

Standing up, she wrapped Alfie and Oscar's leads around her wrists, making sure to keep Oscar's short. 'That's right. I'm pretty sure I remember you having to carry him on the way back from walks. He'd just stop and sit down.'

Smiling, Mr Euston chuckled. 'Oh, that sounds about right. Luckily for me and my back, he loves his walks now. If anything, it's him pulling me on the way home. Talking of which, I'd better get going or he'll be telling me off as it's nearly the young master's dinner time.'

'Lovely to see you both again,' she said, letting Alfie and Oscar have one last fuss from Mr Euston before they headed off.

'You too, Poppy, love. Have a good rest of your holiday down here.' He held his hand up and waved.

Poppy glanced down at Alfie and Oscar before looking ahead towards the lane down to the cove. 'On your best behaviour now please, Oscar, as I don't think there'll be anyone else at the beach to rescue me if you tie me up again, not in this weather.' She shuddered against the wind, wishing for the twentieth time since stepping outside that she'd remembered her hat, scarf and gloves.

As they reached the beach, Oscar bounded ahead, oblivious of the fact that the cobbles had quickly turned to sand. Alfie, on the other hand, was a little more wary and, much to the annoyance of Oscar, held back, a little reluctant.

'It's okay, Alfie, sweetie. It's just sand. It's not going to hurt you.' Fussing him behind the ears, she encouraged him one step at a time until he was a little more confident with the change underpaw. 'That's it. Clever boy, Alfie.'

Once the dogs were happily running around the beach, Poppy looked out to the sea, watching as a small fishing boat was thrown from side to side. She swallowed. She didn't mind being on the ocean – she'd enjoyed the trips out to see the seals when she'd been younger – but she definitely wasn't brave enough to venture out there on a day like this.

The ping of a text message sounded through her pocket and, swapping both leads to one hand, she pulled out her phone.

Not sure if you've seen on social media but Ben is now in a relationship. Sorry to be the bearer of bad news but thought it best to let you know before he told you. Melissa xxx

Ben was in a relationship? An actual relationship? Since when? He'd told her he was going on a date but that had only been, what, two weeks ago? If that? Yes, it must have been. She'd finished her supply contract at the beginning of December, and it was still almost two weeks until Christmas.

Squinting at the screen, she reread the message. Did anyone actually declare being in a relationship after two measly weeks?

Sinking to the sand, she straightened out her legs and looked out to sea; the waves being washed upshore, further and further with the tide. She felt Alfie's head flop onto her knee at about the same time as Oscar's lead pulled taut, and he came trotting back to see what the delay was.

'Oscar, come here. Have a bit of a rest.' To her surprise, he sunk to the sand and laid his head on her other knee, almost a mirror image of Alfie's position. 'Thank you.'

Closing her eyes, she focused on the sound of the rushing waves as they crept further up the beach.

Two weeks ago, Ben had gone on that date. Someone from work, he'd said. She knew he wasn't a cheater. She knew he wouldn't have been seeing this woman behind her back and if he was dating her whilst Poppy had still been living there, living their separate lives under one roof, she knew he'd have been honest and told her upfront.

Yes, he would have told her, which led to one conclusion and one conclusion only – that he'd fallen head over heels for this woman. That Poppy had been easily replaceable, not irreplaceable as she'd hoped.

Taking a deep breath, she stood up, trying to shake the thought away. What had Flora said? This could be a fresh start, down here. It wasn't too late for her to turn things around. She just had to focus on herself and rebuilding her life and let Ben do the same. Yes, it was a shock he'd seemingly moved on so quickly but maybe this would be the complete, definite closure she needed.

'Ready to head back now? It'll be your dinner time soon.'

Clutching the leads, she retraced her steps back to Wagging Tails.

It was fine, she told herself. It really was fine. She wanted Ben to be happy. It was good he'd found someone else. Good that he'd moved on so easily.

She swiped the back of her hand across her eyes. Just fine. Absolutely.

17

'Sorry.' Poppy took Flora's handkerchief and wiped her eyes and her cheeks. 'I don't even know why I'm crying. It was a mutual decision. He's a free man. He's allowed to find someone else. I want him to find someone else. I'm glad he has.'

Flora pulled out the chair next to her and sat down, clasping her hands on the table. 'It's a big change. A shock to the system, even if you know it was for the best. And to find out he's got into another relationship so soon...'

'Exactly.' Poppy nodded before blowing her nose. 'It shows that he hasn't felt anything for me for ages, years probably. If he can just jump straight into something serious so quickly.'

'You don't know that's the case.'

'I'm pretty sure. The facts don't lie, do they? He hasn't loved me for years. Maybe he never did. Maybe I was just convenient. Right time, right place. Or wrong time, wrong place in this instance.'

'Oh, lovely. He did love you.'

Poppy shrugged. 'I know. I know he did, but it's just difficult finding out about this woman from work. I just don't know what to think.'

'That's understandable.'

'Is it? It wasn't as though our relationship was any good for either of us. For the last couple of years, we'd been living more as friends really. And then, over the last few months after we separated – strangers.'

'Poppy, lovely. You need to give yourself time to grieve. I remember when my Arthur went...' Flora shook her head. 'It took me an awfully long time to get used to the idea of him not being around, not always being there for me, not to have him to turn to.'

Poppy shook her head. 'No, Uncle Arthur passed away. You had a right to grieve. I don't.'

'Oh, you do. More than you realise. When Arthur went, it was so so difficult. I missed him, but as well as mourning for him, I mourned the future we had planned together. Running this place, starting a family.'

Poppy turned to her aunt. 'I didn't know you wanted children.'

Flora nodded sadly. 'I did, which was why I treasured those summers when you visited all the more.'

How had Poppy never known that? Her mum, Flora's sister, had never mentioned anything.

'But what I'm trying to explain is that it isn't just Ben you're missing.' Flora laid her hand over Poppy's. 'And I don't mean the Ben you know now, I mean the Ben from when you first started dating, when your relationship first began to get serious. It's not just him, it's everything life promised you as well.'

'I know.' Poppy sniffed and wiped her nose. 'I thought I'd have kids, too. I was so determined to create the happy home environment that I didn't have.'

'You're young still. You'll find someone else. You'll have your perfect little family.'

'I don't know if I want anyone else. I don't think I can go through all this again.' She shrugged. 'I probably don't deserve it, anyway.'

Flora shook her head. 'Of course you do, lovely. You deserve the world. And you'll fall in love again.'

'How can you be sure? You didn't, did you?' Poppy glanced at her aunt. She'd never asked her why she hadn't remarried before.

Sighing, Flora pulled another handkerchief from her sleeve and patted her eyes. 'No, I didn't. I threw all of my energy into this place, into doing my best for the dogs that have come and gone. I lived to see the dogs in my care find their forever family and live their best lives. I sometimes wish I'd found someone, though, had another relationship, another chance at the life I once thought I'd have. I know that's what Arthur would have wanted.' Flora smiled, a short quick smile and patted Poppy's hand. 'You, though, you're going to fall in love again. I can feel it in my bones.'

Slumping back in her chair, Poppy sighed. Even if she didn't, life would be better than if she'd stayed with Ben. She knew that. Even through the grief of the separation, she knew the decision had been for the best. Not that Ben wasn't a decent person, just that they hadn't been right for each other. Not right at all.

'Come here, lovely.' Twisting in her seat, Flora held her arms out, signalling for Poppy to lean into her embrace.

'Thank you.' She rested her head on Flora's shoulder and wrapped her arms around her.

'What for, lovely?'

'Everything. For always being there when I was growing up, for giving me an escape each summer, for taking me in now, even though I've not visited for years. Thank you.'

Flora leaned back lightly, holding her at arm's length and smiled. 'You don't ever need to thank me, Poppy. I'm your aunt, that's what I'm here for.'

'Hey... Oh sorry, I didn't mean to interrupt.' Alex began to back out of the door.

'Don't be daft, Alex. Come on in. I'm about to put the kettle on.'

'Huh, that was great timing then.' Alex picked up the biscuit tin from the work surface, opened it and offered it to Poppy and Flora.

'No thanks.' Poppy shook her head and slipped the handkerchief into her pocket.

Shrugging, Alex took a biscuit and leaned back against the work surface. 'Sally said Fluffles walked on the lead without holding it in her mouth for the first time today.'

'Ooh, I knew Fluffles had it in her,' Flora said as she clicked the kettle on.

'I don't know if Oscar does, though.' Poppy sniffed and tried to plaster a smile on her face. 'Poor Mr Euston had to untangle me before I fell over after Oscar wrapped his lead around my ankles.'

Alex snorted, biscuit crumbs flying from his nostrils. 'Sorry, sorry. I just had an image from a film or something then. Shame there wasn't someone recording you.'

'Ha ha, don't apologise. You definitely would have laughed if you'd been there.' Poppy smiled.

'Here you go, lovely.' Flora rubbed Poppy's shoulder as she leaned over and placed a mug of tea on the table in front of her.

'Thanks.' Poppy nodded. She'd needed that talk with her aunt. It had put things in perspective for her. Yes, it still hurt that he had seemingly replaced her but she'd needed reminding that things hadn't been all perfect with Ben and that there were many reasons why they were better off apart.

18

Poppy placed a mug of coffee in front of Ginny before leaning back against the work surface and taking a sip of her own.

'Thanks.' Ginny yawned.

'Did you come in early again?'

'Not that early. Only about six.' Ginny took a long gulp of her coffee.

'Umm, more like five, lovely.' Flora chuckled as she heaped a pile of towels onto the kitchen table. 'I saw your car headlights bouncing along the lane.'

'Here, I'll give you a hand,' Poppy said, putting down her mug.

'Thanks, lovely.'

Ginny grimaced. 'Aw, sorry. I didn't mean to wake you. I feel really bad now.'

'Don't be daft. I'm only teasing. I was awake already.' Flora shook out a yellow towel before folding it.

'Oh, you can't talk then. You're just as bad as me.' Leaning back in her chair, Ginny looked across at Flora and laughed.

Flora chuckled. 'I walked right into that one, didn't I?'

'You sure did.'

'There you go.' Poppy placed the last of the folded towels in the pile on the table and quickly drank the dregs of her coffee. 'I'm going to take Dougal out for a quick walk before that rain comes down.' She nodded in the direction of the window as huge charcoal grey clouds gathered above them.

'Good idea. Remember to wrap up warm.'

'Oh, I will. I made that mistake yesterday.' Poppy laughed as she walked into the reception area, but she stopped abruptly when she saw who was waiting at the counter. 'Mack? Hi. What are you doing here?'

'I've just come to check on little Dougal. See how he's doing.' Mack shifted from foot to foot.

'I'm just about to take him on a walk. I'll go and get him, and you can check him over before I go, if you like?' Poppy picked up a lead – a turquoise and white striped one – from the hooks behind the counter.

'I'm happy tagging along, if you don't mind. That way I can get an idea of how he's doing building his strength.'

'No, of course I don't mind. Great. One moment and I'll bring him out.'

* * *

'So what do you think? He's doing well, isn't he?' Poppy looked down at Dougal, who was happily padding across the cobbles at her heels.

'He sure is. He has a long road of recovery ahead of him, but I'm stunned by his progress.' Mack rubbed the back of his neck.

'He's definitely a little fighter.' Leaning down, Poppy fussed Dougal and smiled as he leaned in towards her. 'And absolutely gorgeous at the same time, hey, aren't you, Dougal?'

'He's enjoying that. Look how he's closing his eyes when you scratch behind his ear.' Mack nodded towards the dog.

'Aw, he's such a sweet little soul.'

She led the way to the lane down towards the cove where the cobbles faded away to sand.

'How's Eden doing?' she asked.

'Yes. Great. She's only got another couple of hours on the IV antibiotics and then the bite on her leg should be clear of infection.'

'That's great news.'

'Yes, it is. It's a good job you were able to rescue her from Mr Thomas's when you did. Had she been left like that any longer she might not have been so lucky.' Mack nodded.

Poppy looked across at him. 'You seem very quiet today. Is everything okay?'

There'd been no joking or teasing today and he seemed, well, deflated, as though there was something worrying him.

Mack kicked at the sand beneath his feet, unearthing a purple pebble. Picking it up, he smoothed it between his fingers. 'Oh, nothing.'

'Yes, there is. What's the matter?' She shook her head. 'Sorry, I keep forgetting that we've only known each other a short time, I feel as though I've known you longer. You don't have to tell me.'

Mack glanced at her before throwing the pebble in the air and deftly catching it with his other hand. 'I feel the same and it's fine. I don't mind you asking. I just feel bad boring you with the woes of my life, that's all.'

'Hey, look at you; woes of your life! I'm happy to listen but there's no pressure to tell me.' She frowned. There was clearly something wrong, he hadn't even raised an eyebrow at her yet let alone broken into one of his wide grins.

'Thanks.' Turning the pebble over and over in his hand, he took a deep breath. 'My dad got in contact today. He sent a

Christmas card. Well, three: one to me and one each to my brothers.'

Poppy looked over at him. His eyebrows were knitted together, seemingly concentrating on the task of rolling the pebble between his fingers. Only he wasn't. He wasn't concentrating on that; he was concentrating on keeping his voice light. She could tell because it was a trick of hers too, to pretend to focus on something small rather than allow her feelings to show on her face, in her posture.

'You don't hear from him very often? Your parents are divorced?'

Mack shook his head and looked out towards the ocean. 'My mum passed away when I was in my teens. My dad then went on to remarry, but to say they didn't have the best of relationships is the understatement of the century. From what I heard, anyway. I wasn't living at home at the time. I'd moved away. I only popped back every month or so to check in on my half-brothers.'

'You were at your old surgery?'

'No, this was when I was training.' He glanced at her before turning back to the water. 'Anyway, she eventually left and my dad couldn't cope with the boys, not by himself. That was when I transferred universities, moved back here, to West Par, to help take care of them and he upped and left without so much as a hint at what he was planning. I've not heard from him since. Not until today. Seven years of nothing from him and then he sends cards.'

'Oh, wow.' Poppy swallowed, trying to process all that he'd told her. 'You've been looking after your brothers since Spencer was two?'

'Yes, that's right.'

'What did the cards say?'

'I haven't given Spencer or Gus theirs yet. Gus is my other brother, by the way.' He shrugged.

'The teenager with the love of skateboarding?'

'That's him.' Mack smiled, a quick shift to pride, before

furrowing his brow again. 'I opened my card though. I almost didn't, but I made myself.'

'And...'

'And he wants to see them. He wants to start seeing Gus and Spencer. After all these years, after putting us through everything he did, just leaving them as he did.' Mack shook his head. 'It had been a normal weekend in the run-up to Christmas and he'd asked me to babysit so he could go and buy them presents.' He shrugged. 'And he just didn't come back. The next week a card landed on the doormat with just the word "sorry" in it.'

'And that was it? Just sorry, no explanation or anything?'

'Nothing.'

Poppy blinked. She couldn't imagine what effect that had had on little Spencer and Gus, or on Mack. He'd have had to have completely changed his life.

She looked at him. She'd known he was a good person, but to step up and care for his brothers like that... She shook her head.

'That's awful of him.'

Mack nodded slowly and shrugged. 'Anyway, that's why I'm a bit out of sorts today. I'm still trying to wrap my mind around it all.'

'I bet.' Without thinking, she reached across and hugged him, then pulled away immediately. 'Sorry.'

'Hey, don't apologise. Hugging is supposed to be the best healer, isn't it?' He chuckled sadly.

'Oh, Mack. I don't even know what to say. And there was me feeling all sorry for myself and you're going through this.' She rolled her eyes at herself.

'Tell me.'

'No, it's daft compared to...' She waved her hand towards him.

'It's not daft. Not if it's upset you. Besides, it would be nice to think about someone else's problems for a while.'

'Oh, thanks. Now it all comes out!' Poppy laughed. 'The real reason you're here – so you can make yourself feel better by listening to me talk about my sad old life.'

Mack raised his eyebrow. 'Well...'

'Oi!' Poppy looked at him in mock shock before smiling. 'Nah, it's not much really. I found out yesterday that my ex is in a new relationship. I mean, he'd told me he was going on a date two weeks ago but now apparently he's in a fully-fledged relationship with her. After two weeks!'

'I'm sorry. That sucks.' Mack sighed.

'Yes and no. I think it was more the shock of hearing it, to be honest. We decided our relationship was over months ago. If I'm honest, we'd both known it was inevitable long before that – a good couple of years at least – but because I didn't actually move out until the beginning of the month and he wasn't with anyone then...' She shrugged. 'It was just a bit of a surprise, that's all. I'm pleased for him. He's not a bad guy, we just weren't great together.'

'Still, I can understand why that came as a shock. Life's unpredictable, isn't it?'

'Yep. When I was growing up, I'd always thought I'd have my life sorted by now. And, if I'm honest, even up until a few years ago. You know, two point four kids, husband, house, probably a dog or two. That sort of stuff.' She grimaced.

'Ha ha, yes. I hear you. Same here.' Mack shook his head before chuckling. 'Isn't adulting supposed to be the easy part, where we get to make our own decisions and choose how our life pans out?'

As they reached the water's edge, Poppy paused and looked out across the cove towards the great expanse of ocean. 'I think we may have been lied to.'

'Yes. I think you may be right.' Mack chuckled. 'Still, I guess we're where we're supposed to be, and we just need to figure it out and get through it.'

Poppy nodded. 'Maybe. I quite like that actually – where we're supposed to be. Although whether that works for us two, you with your dad trying to walk back into your and your brothers' lives and me having run away to my aunt's house, with no house, no partner, not even a car.' She shrugged.

'The only way is up, hey?'

Poppy laughed. 'You are absolutely right. Well, here's to finding the right way up.'

Holding out her hand, she cheered an imaginary glass to the sky.

'Absolutely. To finding the right way up.' Holding his hand up, he copied her before checking his watch. 'Oops, I'd better get back. Lunchtime will be over soon.'

'Lunchtime? I thought you'd popped by for a home visit to check on Dougal?'

Mack shrugged. 'It was a home visit – just during my lunch break.'

'Oh no, I feel bad now, dragging you out on a walk. Now you've not had a proper rest or anything, let alone any actual lunch.' Turning, she began to walk back across the sand towards the lane.

'Don't feel bad on my account. This was exactly what I needed, sea air and a chat.' Falling into step with Poppy, he touched her arm, a brief, quick touch. 'Thank you for letting me offload to you. Just so you know, though, I hadn't planned on telling you all that. I don't want you to think the only reason I came was to burden you with my problems.'

She smiled. 'And thank you for listening to mine, too.'

'What are we both like?' He smiled, his eyes meeting hers.

'I don't know.' Feeling tension on the lead, Poppy looked down and nodded. 'I'm not sure about this one either. I think he's decided he doesn't want to walk any further.' Bending down, she fussed Dougal who had flopped onto the floor, his head on his paws. 'Are you all tired out? Do you want me to carry you back?'

'Here, let me.' Leaning down, Mack scooped Dougal up in his arms.

'Thanks.'

'My pleasure. There is an ulterior motive, I'm afraid. I'll be using him as my own personal hot water bottle as we walk back.'

Tucking the end of the lead into the crook of his arm, Poppy laughed. 'And there was me thinking you were being all gentlemanly and saving my back.'

'Oh no, I don't have a gentleman's bone in my body.' Mack chuckled.

'Umm, I'm starting to see that.'

'Oi!' Looking across at her, he grinned. 'Honestly, thank you for this.'

'Anytime.' She smiled.

They may have spent the walk talking about not-so-nice stuff, but she'd enjoyed spending the time with him and sharing their problems; she was sure it had done them both some good.

19

'So, we raised... Let me find it.' Ginny flicked through the notebook in front of her. 'Sorry, I've clean forgotten the amount.'

'While you look, let's see who can guess the closest.' Alex stood up, mug in hand, and looked around the table. 'Go on, Poppy, you can go first.'

Poppy looked around the kitchen and grinned. She enjoyed staff meetings here. After sitting through meeting after meeting at her old school, which usually focused on something that didn't affect her class one iota, she'd never in a million years dreamed that she'd be using the words 'enjoy' and 'staff meeting' in the same sentence.

'Umm, I feel this is unfair. This was my first time helping with the Christmas collection, but if I have to go first, I'm going to say... five hundred and fifty-eight pounds.'

'That's very specific for someone who doesn't have a clue.'

Poppy shrugged and grinned at Alex. 'That's all I have.'

'Fair enough. Sally?'

'This is my first one too, so I have no idea either.' Sally straightened her back. 'I'll go with six hundred.'

'Okay, next up is Susan.' Alex pointed to Susan, who was busy brushing toast crumbs from the table. She shook them onto her plate and closed her eyes momentarily. 'I'm going with six hundred and forty. I think that's what we made last year.'

Alex nodded. 'I like your style, basing your estimation on past events, although for us to collect the exact same amount as last year...? I don't know. I may stand corrected. Percy?'

Interlocking his fingers, Percy stretched his arms in front of him. 'I'm going to be optimistic and say one thousand pounds.'

'Ooh, very optimistic. We can tell who's in the cheerful Christmas mood. Flora?'

Shaking her head, Flora looked up from her hands clasped on the table and across at Alex. 'Sorry?'

'Where have you been?' Alex laughed. 'We're playing a guessing game. How much do you think we raised at the weekend on our Christmas collection run?'

Flora shook her head and wrapped her hands around her mug of coffee. 'Oh, I don't know... umm... Seven hundred?'

Poppy frowned and looked at her aunt. Something wasn't right. She'd never seen her as distracted as she'd been these past few days. She was obviously worried about something. But what? Mr Thomas and his dogs maybe? Although there was always something to worry about at Wagging Tails, whether it was the dogs in their care or cases of neglect or mistreatment they had heard about on the grapevine and were in the process of trying to rescue them, and Aunt Flora had always been an expert at boxing worries up and focusing on the here and now, what they could control. She picked up her mug. Maybe it was because they'd been speaking about Arthur and Flora having wanted children. She'd have to catch her later and check everything was okay.

'Okay. My turn. I'm going with eight hundred and ninety-three pounds and fifty-two pence.' Alex took a sip of his drink before looking at Ginny. 'How about you, Ginny, what's your best guesstimate?'

'Ah, I'd be cheating if I had a guess.' She held up her notebook. 'I've found it.'

'Well, don't keep us in suspense, then. Let us know if we're millionaires.' Alex sat back down.

'Ha ha, not exactly millionaires, I'm afraid, but we did well. Better than last year, anyway.' Ginny grinned.

'Ooh, Percy, your optimism may pay off yet.' Alex gestured to him with his mug.

'Not quite. We raised seven hundred and ninety pounds and thirty-seven pence.' Ginny smiled.

A round of applause broke out in the small kitchen.

'Well done, everyone.' Percy nodded around the table.

'What do you think, Flora? Seven hundred and ninety. We're up from last year.'

Flora pinched the bridge of her nose before looking up and shrugging. 'It will barely make a dent in this month's vet bills.' Pushing her mug away, she stood up and left the room.

Poppy watched as Flora walked past her. Was that what she was worried about? The money?

Alex waited until the door had closed behind her before looking around the table.

'That's not like Flora. She's always so happy when we raise money. She'd usually be made up if we raised eight pounds, let alone almost eight hundred. Do you think something's wrong?'

'I don't know.' Susan frowned. 'She has been pretty quiet these last few days.'

'I'll try and speak to her.' Percy pushed his chair away and left the room.

'She's been quiet back at the cottage, too.' Poppy sighed.

'And she normally loves the run-up to Christmas.' Ginny took a sip of coffee.

'All this with Mr Thomas might be having an effect. You know how she gets when there're dogs she wants to help but can't for whatever reason.' Susan picked up her plate and opened the door to the dishwasher. 'And the vet's bills on top. What with Dougal and now poor Eden needing treatment as well.'

'Yes, you're probably right. As she said the money we've raised won't even cover all of what we're going to owe for Eden's vet's bills.' Alex nodded. 'And if there are any more who need treatment...'

'I guess we've just got to hope that Mr Thomas lets us take them in soon enough and there are no more surprise vet costs for the time being.' Susan knocked on the tabletop. 'Touch wood that we can manage.'

'I think he'll let us take them soon enough and we didn't notice any others with anything obviously wrong.' Ginny shifted in her chair. 'You all saw what the house was like. He can't carry on like that. I don't think it will be long until he realises that us taking the dogs and the cat rescue taking his cats is the best thing for all involved.'

'That's it. If he could just keep one of the more elderly dogs, they'd have all of his attention. And maybe I could go and help him train them to use the garden for toileting.' Sally shrugged. 'They'd have a nice life, but the number of animals he has at the moment just isn't sustainable. Not for anyone, but even less so for him with his ill health.'

'It's sad, isn't it?' Alex slumped against the back of his chair. 'His heart's in the right place. He's taken in all these animals over the years and given them a home, but he's just not known when to stop.'

'It is sad.' Susan grimaced. 'I remember being caught scrumping apples back when he owned the farm. Me and my sister were petrified when we saw him speeding up to us on his tractor.'

'Speeding? On a tractor?' Alex raised his eyebrows.

'Okay, well, trundling then.' Susan laughed. 'It had felt as though he was speeding up to us at the time. Anyway, when he got to us, he gave us a wicker basket and told us to take as many as we could carry. We'd never been caught before, and I remember thinking we'd be thrown into jail for the rest of our lives.'

'And there was me thinking you were all sweet and innocent and law-abiding.' Alex laughed.

Susan tilted her head to one side and grinned. 'We all have our moments, but I think stealing apples from Mr Thomas's orchard was probably the height of my criminal career.'

'Good job too. We wouldn't want you teaching the dogs your bad ways.'

'Oi!' Laughing, Susan threw a tea towel across the table towards him. 'On that note, I'm going to take Fluffles out on a walk. See if I can find any apples to steal.'

'You'll be lucky in this weather.' Looking out of the window, Alex shivered. 'I think I might put myself on kennel cleaning out duty today.'

'I don't blame you; it's freezing out there today.' Ginny downed the dregs of her coffee before standing up. 'But I've promised Ralph a game of fetch in the top paddock, so I'll be braving it.'

'Yep, and I'm determined to try to eliminate the danger of Oscar wrapping anyone else up with the lead. Wish me luck.' Sally grimaced as she placed her empty mug in the dishwasher.

'Good luck.' Poppy smiled as she put her mug next to Sally's.

'Thanks. I have a feeling I'm going to need it. Catch you later.'

Poppy looked around the now-empty kitchen and smiled. These people had been strangers to her a couple of weeks ago, all bar

Susan and Percy, but they had happily welcomed her into their lives.

Walking towards the kitchen door, she peered out. Flora was standing hunched over the counter, scribbling something into her notebook. Was Ginny right? Was it the amounting vet bills and the whole situation with Mr Thomas and his dogs that was getting her down, or was there something else? She couldn't remember seeing Flora like this before.

Picking up the biscuit jar, she opened the kitchen door. 'Hey, thought you might like a biscuit.'

Straightening her back, Flora blinked. 'Thanks, lovely. Sorry I was short in there. I just didn't sleep very well, that's all.'

'No worries. Are you sure you're okay, though? You know you can talk to me.'

'I know. Thanks, Poppy, lovely.' Flora rubbed Poppy's forearm before taking a bite into her biscuit and turning back to the notebook on the counter.

20

Poppy looked down at her list and shifted her shopping bag further up her arm. She had found most of the ingredients she needed, but the small supermarket in the centre of Trestow had been out of courgettes, of all things. She would probably have had more luck at the large supermarket on the retail park on the outskirts of town, but she'd wanted to pop into the florist's to pick up a bunch of tulips, Flora's favourite.

She stepped off the path to make room for a double pushchair and jumped back up the kerb, looking back down at her list just as she collided with someone.

'I'm so sorry. I didn't see you.'

'That's what happens when you're too engrossed in what you're reading.' Mack chuckled.

Looking up, Poppy grinned. 'Mack! Am I glad it's you I've bowled into instead of knocking into some poor stranger.'

'I'll take that as a compliment, I think.'

'Ha ha, yes. Have you just finished work?'

'Yep. I just need to pick up a couple of bits from the bookshop. How about you? Working through your Christmas list?' He nodded towards the scrap of paper in her hand.

'Very funny. No, I'm making Flora her favourite meal in an attempt to cheer her up. Veggie moussaka.' She slipped the list into her pocket and shifted her bag into the other hand.

'Oh, is she okay?' Mack frowned.

'I'm not sure. She's not been herself the last few days. Although she says she's just tired. I thought making dinner is the least I can do after all she's done for me.'

'I'm sure she'll love it. And veggie moussaka...' Mack smacked his lips together. 'I've not had that in years.'

'Nor me. I just hope I can still cook it.' She shrugged. 'I can't find any courgettes though, so think I'll end up at the retail park.'

'Is that all you've got left to get?'

'Courgettes and tulips. Tulips are her favourite flowers, so I thought a bunch of those might be a nice touch.'

'Well, I know a little grocery shop down one of the side streets. I tell you what, I just need to pop in there—' Mack nodded towards a small bookshop on the corner of the street '—and then I can show you it if you like? Unless you're in a rush?'

'No, it's fine. Yes, that'll be great, thanks.'

She followed him into the bookshop, and pausing by the door, she looked around. Shelves and shelves of books lined the shop, tables piled high with displays perched around small Christmas trees, and character teddies filled the shop floor. She took a deep breath.

'You like it too?' Mack raised an eyebrow.

'Was it that obvious?' She laughed. 'But yes, nothing beats the musty, comforting smell of books. It reminds me of hiding out in the school library whilst it rained outside, choosing my next adventure to lose myself in.'

'Ha ha, I can relate, and no, it wasn't obvious. I only noticed because that's what I do every time I come in here.'

'What? Stand and sniff the air?' She grinned.

'Pretty much.' He chuckled.

'Mack, good to see you.' A man behind the counter waved at them. 'I have those books you ordered in. They arrived this morning.'

'Hi, great. Thanks so much for that.' Mack shook the man's hand before turning to Poppy. 'Poppy, this is Evan. Evan, Poppy.'

'Lovely to meet you.' Evan held out his hand.

Swapping her bag to her left hand, Poppy returned the handshake, which was stronger than she'd thought it would be. 'Great to meet you.'

Evan nodded before bending down and rummaging through a cupboard beneath the counter. 'Ah, yes, here we are.' He pulled out a paper bag marked 'Mack'.

'Fantastic. Thank you.' Mack took the bag and headed towards the door, his hand held up. 'See you.'

'Bye and Merry Christmas if I don't see you both again before then.'

'Merry Christmas.' Mack grinned as he turned back towards the door, patting the bag. 'He's the best. He always manages to track titles down for me.'

'Something special?'

'Just some books for Gus and Spencer. It's a bit of a tradition of ours. I always get them a couple each for Christmas. Not that Gus has read any of the ones I bought him last year, too busy skateboarding or playing online with his mates, but I'm forever hopeful that I'll somehow stumble across the one book which will reignite his love of reading.'

'Oh, I love the idea of that tradition. I always used to get a book for Christmas too.' Poppy smiled as she closed the door behind them.

'It was what my nanna used to do, as well. Send me books each year. It's how I found my love for animals. There was this one series about a vet that really planted the seed. She used to send me one from that series for my birthday and another one for Christmas.'

'Aw, that's really lovely.' Poppy smiled.

'Yes, it was. Right, shall we find those courgettes now?'

Poppy nodded as he led the way down a small side street.

'Have you decided what to do about the cards your dad sent?' she asked.

'I have. I've decided I'll speak to the boys about it when I get home today. Which is probably one of the reasons I'm postponing going to pick them up from my neighbour.'

'What do you think they'll say?'

'I think Gus, in true teenage fashion, will shake it off and say he's not bothered, and then will probably get into trouble at school tomorrow or something. Spencer, I'm not sure. Because he was only two, I don't think he remembers much about his dad anyway, so he'll either refuse to see him or be curious enough to want to. Either way, I know I'm going to have a few rocky days ahead as everyone adjusts to the idea of Dad walking back into our lives.' Looking ahead, he swallowed.

'Do you think he'll want custody?'

'No, I don't, and if he does, then he's in for a darn good fight, I can tell you.' Mack shook his head. 'But, no, even if he suggests it, when I get the solicitors involved, he'll back down pretty quickly.'

Poppy paused and looked over at him. 'Do you need a hug?'

Smiling, Mack looked back. 'I could do with a proper hug, not a quick one like yesterday on the beach.'

'Ha ha, yes, okay. That was pretty awkward, wasn't it? But in my defence, I didn't know if I was overstepping the mark by giving you a hug or not.' She grimaced.

Mack chuckled as he held his arms open. 'I don't think there's a written rule about vets hugging former patient's owners.'

'You know what I mean.' Stepping towards him, Poppy could smell his scent – oaky, with a touch of something softer, something sweet, cinnamon maybe. She wrapped her arms around him, her arm gently leaning against his back, and closed her eyes as she felt his embrace. She smiled. 'Now, that's what I call a real hug.'

'Same here.' His breath tickled against her ear.

She could stay here in his arms forever. She couldn't remember a better hug.

The loud tinkle of a bicycle bell interrupted them, and they both jumped apart as a small boy rode between them, a length of tinsel unwinding from a trailer attached to the back of the bicycle and dragging along behind him.

Poppy looked across at Mack as a man, presumably the boy's dad, rounded the corner pushing a buggy in pursuit of the boy.

'Sorry, sorry.' The man looked at them quickly before raising his voice. 'Slow down, Finley. I can't keep up – not with your baby brother. And your tinsel...'

The young boy squeezed on his brakes as he came to the road, the trailer tipping at the sudden change in speed.

They watched as a mound of Christmas decorations fell from the small trailer, baubles unwrapping themselves from the numerous lengths of tinsel and rolling across the path.

The man expertly weaved the pushchair this way and that avoiding the baubles until he slowed to a stop next to his son's bike.

Bending down, Poppy and Mack began picking up the strewn decorations as the young boy jumped from his bike and ran towards them, his small arms outstretched.

'Here you go, buddy.' Mack placed the decorations in his arms.

'What do you say, Finley?' the man called towards his son.

'Thank you.'

'You're very welcome.' Mack grinned as the boy ran back

towards his bike before retrieving the remaining decorations from Poppy.

'Thank you.' The man held his hand up in thanks before they set off on their way again. The tinsel, this time, tucked neatly into the trailer.

Mack chuckled and nodded towards the young boy. 'That's just what Spencer was like at that age. Always full of energy and in a rush.'

Stepping towards him again, Poppy tucked her hair behind her ear and laughed.

* * *

'They're so beautiful and I love the smell, too.' Holding the bunch of yellow and red tulips to her nose, Poppy breathed in the floral scent of the flowers. 'It always reminds me of honey.'

'Really?' Leaning over, Mack took a deep breath. 'Oh yes. I've never realised that before, but they do.'

Poppy grinned. Now she had all of the ingredients she was all set to make Flora's favourite dinner and, being as Flora was on the late shift today, she'd have more than enough time to get back to the cottage from Trestow and bake the moussaka.

'Whereabouts are you parked? I'll walk you to the car.'

'Oh, don't worry, thanks. I took the bus into town today.' Poppy nodded down the road. 'The stop's only just down there.'

'When's the next bus?'

'Umm...' Holding the bunch of tulips out, she shook her coat sleeve up and looked at her watch. 'Only twenty minutes or so.'

'Do you want a lift? I'm happy to drop you off?'

'No, don't worry. Thanks though.'

Mack nodded. 'Right, well, good to run into you again.'

'Yes, you too. We seem to make quite a habit of it, don't we?'

'That we do.' He smiled. 'See you later.'

And with that, he raised his hand before turning away.

Poppy watched him disappear around the corner before heading towards the bus stop. She enjoyed their run-ins, random or not. And that hug...

Poppy paused as the sky opened and large fat raindrops fell, which quickly turned to a torrential waterfall. Within a couple of minutes, the path had become covered in water and she had to run towards a shop doorway to take shelter.

She sighed. Was there much point? She was soaking already and there was quite a while before the bus came. She looked down at the tulips in her hand. With the rain pounding against the delicate petals, they wouldn't last long.

'Hey, under here.'

Twisting around, Poppy held her hand over her eyes, trying to see more than the few feet in front of her the rain would allow. As the person got closer, she realised it was Mack again, holding his coat over his head. As he reached her, he lifted his arm across her shoulders, so she was shielded from the rain, too.

'Are you sure you don't want that lift? Because I'm not sure how long I can keep my arm up like this.' He chuckled; his face close enough to hers she could feel his warm breath on her cheek.

'Can I change my mind?' Poppy grinned.

'Please do.'

'Then, yes, I'd love a lift, please?'

'Great. I'm parked just down there.' He nodded behind them before pivoting, his coat still protecting them from the onslaught of rain.

'I think you've rescued my tulips just in time.' She looked down at the bunch of flowers cradled in the crook of her arm.

'What can I say? I'm an everyday hero.' He twisted his elbow out in an attempt to rummage in his pocket for the car keys without pulling his coat away from over both their heads. 'Got them.'

As he rolled the keys through his fingers to reach the button to unlock the car, they fell to the ground, landing in a huge puddle at their feet.

Poppy ducked at the same time as Mack, bumping heads.

'Ouch.'

'Ow.' Standing up straight, Mack chuckled as he reached out to rub Poppy's head. 'Sorry.'

'No, I'm sorry.' Touching the side of his head, she looked into his eyes, their eyes locking. She leaned towards him as Mack did the same, their lips touching. Both frozen to the spot, the light touch soon turned to a proper kiss. Was this what she wanted? What he wanted? She reached her hand behind his neck as he did the same.

Stepping back, Mack pulled away. 'I'm sorry. I can't do this.'

'Sorry, I...'

He'd been the one to make the first move, hadn't he? She hadn't been imagining it? Shaking her head, she picked up her bags and Aunt Flora's tulips and turned away.

'Poppy...'

Looking back, she watched as he moved his gaze to the ground and rubbed his palm over his face. 'Let me give you a lift back.'

Swallowing, she backed away slightly. 'No, it's fine. Thanks.'

'But...'

Turning on her heels, she half-ran back down the road towards the bus stop. The rain plummeting around her, a welcome source of distraction as it cooled her burning face. What had actually just happened? Why would he have kissed her and then pulled away, telling her he couldn't?

Keeping her head down, she picked up her pace and ran the last few metres to the bus stop, not caring or noticing as she ran through the puddles, staining the bottom of her jeans a dark blue.

21

Yawning, Poppy used the measuring cup to scoop out a portion of dog biscuits into Eden's bowl. She'd hardly had any sleep last night. In fact, she wasn't so sure she'd had any at all. Flora couldn't have had much either, as every time Poppy had ventured downstairs to grab a hot chocolate or some painkillers for the lingering headache, Flora had been sitting in the kitchen or looking out of the living room window, looking drawn.

'Is that Eden's breakfast you're making up?' Ginny walked into the kitchen with a pile of water bowls which she proceeded to rinse and refill.

'Yes. Why?'

'Because it's Eden's biscuits, but you're putting them in Ralph's bowl.'

'Oh.' Dropping the scoop back in the bag of biscuits, Poppy tilted the bowl and looked at the name. How had she missed that? As a long-term resident at Wagging Tails, Ralph was the only dog whose bowl had a name on and she'd still managed to mess up. 'Sorry.'

'Are you and Flora okay? You both look absolutely shattered

Has there been some bad news in your family or something?' Ginny turned the tap off, the bowl in her hand half-filled with water, and looked at her. 'Don't feel you have to tell me. I know I'm probably sticking my nose in, but something's going on with you both and I'm worried. Like I said the other day, I haven't seen Flora like this before.'

'I'm not—'

'Morning, Ginny.' Flora placed her mug on the counter before coming up to them.

'Morning.' Ginny turned the tap back on.

'Poppy, lovely, why don't you go back to the cottage and get some rest?' Flora patted Poppy's forearm. 'You were up a lot last night. You can't have had much sleep at all.'

'I'll be okay.' Stifling a yawn with the back of her hand, she looked back at Flora. 'You didn't get much either.'

'No, I didn't. Maybe there was a full moon or something, hey?' Flora chuckled and clicked the kettle on. 'Do you both want a coffee?'

'Yes, please.' Ginny grabbed another bowl to fill.

'Poppy?'

'Umm...' Hearing the shrill ringtone of her mobile, Poppy fished in her pocket and pulled it out, her heart sinking as she read the name. 'No thanks. I'd better take this.'

She hurried out of the kitchen and stepped outside, immediately regretting not taking the time to put her coat on as the cold penetrated her thin jumper. She crossed her free arm around her middle in an attempt to keep some small part of her warm and held the phone up to her ear. 'Ben?'

'Hi, Poppy. Thanks for answering. I won't take up much of your time, but I've got some news.'

'Right.'

This was it. He was going to tell her about his new relationship.

Why did he think she would want to know? It had been bad enough that he'd told her he was going on a date with someone, but that had been face to face; he might have felt he should tell her for some reason. But with her down here in Cornwall, hundreds of miles away, why? She'd much rather not have this conversation.

'I think you'll be pleased.'

That's it, drag it out.

She took a deep breath. She'd burst his bubble; she'd tell him she already knew. 'You don't need to tell me. I know already. Melissa told me.'

The line went quiet.

Holding her phone away from her ear, she checked he hadn't hung up. He hadn't.

'How did Melissa know? I've only just had the call myself.' The confusion in his voice was audible.

'Oh, maybe we've got crossed wires. Sorry, what was it you'd rung to tell me?' She looked down at the ground and kicked a lump of dirt by her feet. It was frozen solid.

'Okay.'

She could almost hear him shaking his head at her, the way he'd done so often when they'd been together, and probably more so since they'd separated.

He cleared his throat before announcing, 'We've had an offer put in for the house.'

'An offer? Really?'

'Yes, really.'

She bit down on her bottom lip, willing herself not to say something. Not to ask him why he sounded so proud, insinuating through his tone that she should be forever grateful to him.

'How great is that?'

'Yes, yes, it's great news.' And it was. It was what she'd been waiting for, hoping for. Once she got her half of the equity, she'd be able to move on. Find a little place for herself. Probably near the centre of town, far enough away from the estates Ben would likely move to so she wouldn't be running into him every ten minutes, and close to the local schools so she'd be able to walk to work if she was lucky enough to get more supply work. Her life would be...

She kicked at the frozen lump of dirt again. It still wouldn't shift.

'The other thing... the thing you said Melissa had told you, I'm guessing that's something to do with me changing my relationship status on social media...'

Poppy frowned. He was doing a good job of sounding sincere.

'You don't have to tell me.' Please don't.

It had been enough of a sucker punch when Melissa told her, but to hear it from Ben himself... She didn't need that.

'You deserve to know.' The line crackled as he cleared his throat again, this time his voice void of the confidence he'd had before. 'I've been seeing Davina from work. It started after we'd separated. I want you to know that. I'd never, ever have cheated on you.'

Davina. She nodded. She knew her. She'd met her at one of Ben's summer work dos a couple of years ago. Davina had been friendly, lovely even. She remembered thinking that at the time.

'Davina's nice. I'm pleased for you.'

'Are you sure? You don't sound very pleased.'

She was just talking normally. What proof did he want? Maybe she should switch to video call and do a cartwheel across the court-yard. Then she could show him how pleased she was. She snorted at the thought.

'You're not crying, are you? I didn't want to upset you, I just wanted to be upfront and honest.'

Credit to Ben, he did actually sound concerned.

'Sorry, no, I'm not.' She shook her head. 'I am pleased for you. I remember meeting her and thinking she was nice.'

'You do? We only went on our first date that weekend you left for Cornwall, as I told you at the time, but it's been a bit of a roller coaster, if I'm honest. Everything's gone so quick, and I think I might actually l—'

'I'm sorry, Ben. Aunt Flora's calling me. I should go. Thanks for letting me know about the house. Please keep me posted.'

Pressing the end call button, Poppy walked across the courtyard towards the gate. Ben had been about to tell her that he loved Davina. Tell *her*, his ex.

She leaned her elbows on the gate, barely noticing the piercing cold metal, and looked out across the fields opposite. It was good news that an offer had been put in on the house. And she supposed it was good news that Ben had fallen in love with Davina. He deserved to be happy. Even if it hadn't taken him long to replace her. That was good. Good for him.

At least he was moving on.

Looking down at her phone, she scrolled through to Mack's name, the pad of her thumb lingering over the call button.

No, he'd made it clear yesterday's near-kiss had been a mistake. Of course, it had. Look at her. Homeless, jobless and quite almost penniless. She wasn't really a catch, was she? Mack had the house, the surgery, the stability.

She switched her phone off and slipped it back into her pocket. Who was she kidding? Thinking that Mack had actually wanted to kiss her? She laughed; her tone low, shallow. It had taken him less than a second to realise he'd made a mistake. Less than a second to weigh everything up in his mind and come to the conclusion that she wasn't good enough for him.

22

'We should celebrate the fact your house is now under offer.' Ginny grinned as they locked the kennels up for the night.

'Nah.' Poppy shook her head. Everyone else had already left. Besides, she wasn't really in the mood. 'It's too cold to go out.'

Ginny frowned and pocketed the keys before double-checking the door was locked. 'How about coming over to mine, then? We can grab a pizza and a film. It'll be nice to have a girly night.'

Poppy pulled her gloves on. 'I don't know. Maybe. As long as you don't think Darryl will mind?'

'Hey, I'm not one of those women who drops their mates and stops spending time with other people just because I have a partner.' Looking over at Poppy, she grinned. 'Come on, it'll be fun. Or at least warmer than standing out here chatting.'

'Okay, okay. It sounds like a good plan. I could do with doing something, even if it's only a takeaway and film.' She held her hands up.

'Great. And you're right, you should celebrate. This is a big moment, selling the house you bought with Ben. You deserve to mark the date.' Ginny pulled her car keys from her coat pocket.

'Yes.' Poppy nodded as she slipped into the passenger side. She hadn't meant that she could do with celebrating, she'd meant she could do with something to take her mind off things and that she stood a better chance of doing that if she wasn't wallowing at home.

* * *

'Yuck! Here's another one!' Ginny picked a sliced olive off her pizza and threw it back into the open pizza box on the coffee table. 'Is there really any need? Who likes olives anyway?'

'Umm, I do.' Poppy laughed and picked up Ginny's discarded olive slice before popping it in her mouth. 'I love them.'

'Eww.' Ginny squirmed as Poppy ate the olive. 'I'll just give you them if I find any more then.'

'Ha ha, please do. It'll save me from peeling them off the bottom of the pizza box.' Poppy picked up another slice of pizza, the stringy cheese dribbling from the dough. 'So Eden got a clean bill of health at her check-up this afternoon?'

'Yes, she did! She's just such a sweetie. The bite on her leg has completely healed now, and she's ready to be assessed and put up for adoption.' Ginny curled her legs beneath her on the sofa.

'She'll be snapped up, I should think.'

'I'm sure she will. In fact, I had a couple come over to me at the vet's as they recognised me. They adopted a dog last year – Tyler, a little spaniel.' Ginny laughed. 'I've never known a dog to love to play fetch as much as him. I mean, I know most dogs love it, but his obsession is on a completely different level.'

'I think I might have met him on the Christmas collection around the village.' Poppy was sure there'd been a spaniel in one of the homes she'd collected from and she was positive they'd said they'd adopted him from Wagging Tails.

'Probably. He lives in West Par. Anyway, they came over to talk to me in the waiting room as they recognised me and, of course, I had to say hello to Tyler and, guess what? They're looking for another dog. They love having Tyler and want to give another dog a home!'

'Oh, that's lovely.'

'Yes, yes, it is. They were asking about Eden and I've promised to ring them when she's ready to be rehomed so they can bring Tyler in to meet her properly.' Ginny placed the crust of her pizza in the box before picking up another slice. 'I'm keeping my fingers crossed because they were getting on so well at the vet's.'

'That's great. Let's just hope Mr Thomas lets us take the rest and we can find homes for them all.' Poppy took a sip of her drink.

'Definitely.' Ginny pulled a large fluffy throw from behind her and shook it out. 'Here, do you want some? It's cold even with the heating on.'

'Yes, please.' Poppy helped to lay the throw across their knees, grateful for the extra warmth. 'I keep expecting it to snow. I know we had a fluttering of it on the evening of the Christmas collection, but I mean like proper snow.'

'Same here. I really need to remember to buy some more logs for the wood burner. It'd have had this room heated in less than half an hour.' Tucking the throw around her, Ginny picked up her glass again. 'Mack was saying that he thought we'd have snow soon too when I saw him at the surgery today. He reckons we're going to have a lot this year.'

Poppy nodded, but kept her gaze on the TV, watching as Santa's sleigh was drawn into the sky, hoping that Ginny hadn't noticed her shift at the mention of Mack's name.

Ginny looked across at Poppy and frowned. 'He also asked me to pass on a message.'

Poppy jerked her head back to look at her. A message? She swallowed. 'Oh, yes?'

'Yes, it was really strange, actually. He just asked me to say that he was sorry and asked if you were okay.'

Poppy looked down at the throw laid across her lap and began winding the tassels around her fingers.

'Is everything okay between you? He was acting a bit weird when he asked me to pass that on.'

'In what way, weird?'

'Just quite serious, I guess. You know him, he's quite a positive person, but, I don't know, he was a bit... serious.' Ginny shrugged. 'Is there something going on between you?'

'No, there's not. There's absolutely nothing going on between us, as I found out yesterday.' Poppy began to wind the next tassel around her the next finger.

'What do you mean?' Ginny frowned. 'Sorry, I shouldn't have asked. If there's something going on between you, then that's your business. Not mine.'

'No, don't worry. There's literally nothing to tell, anyway. I was in town when that downpour started yesterday evening and... we had a moment.' Poppy shifted position again, drawing her legs up further onto the sofa. 'Or I thought we had a moment, anyway. He went to kiss me, I began kissing him back and then he pulled away, apologised, said it was a mistake and that was it. I've not heard from him since.'

'Oh.'

'I keep going over it in my head. It all happened that quick. I just keep wondering if I made the whole thing up, but I know I didn't and I know it was Mack who went to kiss me first.' She shrugged. 'I have no idea what I did wrong. I guess he just doesn't want to get involved with someone like me.'

'Hey, what do you mean by "someone like you"?'

'You know, someone with baggage. A house my ex still lives in No job to speak of. Yes, I can get work from the supply agency, but i can't always be relied upon. And besides, I don't even live here. I don't blame him. Anyone would run a mile.'

'All those things you've stated aren't a reason he wouldn't want a relationship with you. Everyone has baggage at our age. Literally everyone.'

Poppy shook her head. 'He's successful. He has his own surgery, for goodness' sake. He's...'

Lovely, that's what she wanted to say. Sweet, caring, strong, dependable, kind, the whole package.

'Someone like him would never look at someone like me. I don't blame him for realising it was a mistake.'

'He's only just taken over the surgery. And he has a history too. And I'm guessing that's the reason he pulled away, not because of you or your past but because of his.'

'Umm.' Poppy didn't know what to say. Ginny was just trying to make her feel better. And it was nice of her, but...

'I'm telling you the truth. I'm not just saying that.' Ginny turned on the sofa to face her. 'I've known Mack a few years now, and he's not had an easy time with relationships.'

'What do you mean?'

'He was in quite a serious relationship when I moved down here. I don't think they were living together, but they spent a lot of time together and his brothers got close to her, viewed her as part of the family, I guess. I mean, I moved down just over four years ago and so the little one, Spencer, would have been about five, right?'

'I think so. He's nine now.'

'Yes, that's right. And I know Mack and this woman had been together a couple of years by then, or at least I think they had, so he would have been really young when they got together.' Ginny took a sip of her drink.

'What's that got to do with me, though?' Still twisting the tassels around her fingers, Poppy looked across at Ginny.

'Because he's got to take the kids' feelings into account too. Mack and his ex splitting up would have had a huge impact on Spencer and Gus. Spencer would have likely only remembered life with her around.' Ginny reached out and touched Poppy's arm. 'So, you see, he's not just got himself to think about, he's got them to think about, too. And since they broke up, he's probably built his walls super high.'

'That makes sense.'

It did. It still hurt, but at least finding out why he'd reacted the way he had didn't make her feel quite so bad about herself. And she couldn't blame him for being protective of his brothers. She'd probably do exactly the same in his position.

'Give it time, though. If it's meant to be, then you'll get together.' Ginny smiled.

Poppy raised her eyebrow. 'I'm not sure if I believe in the whole destined to be together thing.'

'Ah, but if it's true, then you have nothing to worry about.' Ginny shrugged. 'Sorry, I don't mean to be flippant, I just mean that all you can do is to carry on getting to know him and see what develops between the two of you.'

'If anything does develop.' Poppy slumped back against the sofa cushions, shaking her fingers free of the tassels. 'It's probably for the best, anyway. I'll be back home soon enough, so there's no point in even trying to think about anything happening between us.'

'When do you head back?'

'I don't know. Aunt Flora suggested I get some supply work around here when the new term starts and stay with her until I get the equity through from selling the house. Then I could buy somewhere back home.' She shrugged. 'I can't afford to go back and rent even if I get five days' worth of supply each week, not until the sale is finalised and I no longer have to pay some towards the mortgage..'

'So, you're going to stay and move back once you can buy somewhere?'

'Yes, I think so.' Poppy nodded. Flora had only suggested the option to her earlier when she'd told her about Ben's phone call and the offer. Until now, she hadn't really had the time to process it, not between walking the dogs, clearing out the kennels and placing a food order, but it made sense. Perfect sense.

23

'Are you sure you're okay taking Fluffles for her booster?' With the door ajar and her coat in hand, Ginny looked back at Poppy, who was sitting behind the reception counter.

'Yep. That's fine. You two go.' Poppy waved Ginny and Flora off, watching them jump into the Wagging Tails' van.

It wasn't fine. Going to the vet's so soon after her and Mack's kiss was never going to be her idea of fine, but with Alex off for the day, Susan on a home visit and Sally down at West Par training Oscar to walk on the lead properly, she couldn't very well have refused. Not when Mr Thomas had agreed for Flora and Ginny to come and collect a few of his dogs.

No, she was a grown woman. She could face Mack. She *would* face Mack.

She tapped her fingers against the wooden top of the counter. Should she mention anything or just go in there and act as though the kiss had never happened?

Pretending nothing had happened was probably the easiest thing to do. Although should she let him know that she knew about his predicament? That she understood why he'd pushed her away.

It might be a good idea to clear the air. At least that way there might be a chance they could continue to be friends.

She shrugged. She'd figure it out when she got there. That was all she could do, really. See if he mentioned it or not. If he did, then she'd tell him she knew what had happened with his ex and that she got it. If he didn't, then she'd keep up the façade.

She pushed the notebook she'd been doodling in away from her and stood up. She'd better go and get Fluffles and leave, or else she'd be late for the appointment.

* * *

'You want to come and sit on my lap?' Poppy smiled as Fluffles pawed at her jeans. 'Come on, then.'

She only had to pat her lap once before the small dog jumped up.

'She's a sweet one, isn't she?' A woman perched on the seat next to her smiled, her arms wrapped around a cat carrier. 'I wish this kitty would be so affectionate. All I get is a hiss before she turns her back on me.'

'Aw.' Poppy peered into the carrier. 'She looks so sweet.'

'Hah, she's definitely a case of looks can be deceptive, I'm afraid. Still, I wouldn't have her any different. She's a true little character even if she rules the roost at home.'

Poppy laughed as the woman nudged her and nodded towards the front door.

'Look, isn't that the chap from the TV? The one from that countryside show?' She stage-whispered. 'I'd heard Mack, the new vet, had brought some of his old customers here. Lots of celebrities, apparently.'

Poppy looked as the man in question walked towards the reception desk, a frail old dog limping at his heels. She did recognise him, but she couldn't tell where from. She hadn't had much time to watch any TV recently. 'Maybe.'

'It is, I tell you. I watch that show every Sunday, I do. It's my favourite.' The woman glanced at Poppy. 'Do you think I can ask for his autograph? It might seem a little disrespectful being as he's here with his poorly dog, do you think?'

'I'm not sure.'

The woman shifted in her seat. 'I'll wait until he's been in. I can hang around the car park after our appointment.' She patted the carrier, a loud hiss erupting from the cat being disturbed. 'Yes, that's what I'll do.'

Poppy nodded. How was she supposed to answer?

'You're from Wagging Tails, aren't you? The dogs' home near West Par.' The woman nodded at Fluffles' harness. It had been Ginny's idea to get some made up with 'Adopt me' embroidered on, and so far they'd been helping get the word out.

'Yes, that's right. Fluffles will be ready to find her forever home soon.'

'That's lovely. I've always fancied getting a dog. Not that this one would ever share her home with anyone. Besides, she's enough to keep me on my toes.'

On Poppy's lap, Fluffles stood up and spun around before settling back down.

'At least you should get a good discount here because you're from the rescue centre. This one here managed to catch his claw and rip it. I'm expecting it'll cost me an arm and a leg.' The cat meowed loudly. 'Yes, I know. You're worth it.'

'Well...' Poppy shook her head. She couldn't very well tell a total stranger that Mack had refused to honour the old vet's deal with the home. Even though after hearing he had celebrity clients, she was even more sure he could spare the money. She heard a throat being cleared to the side of her, and she looked up, her heart skipping a beat when she saw Mack waiting for them.

'Fluffles?'

Swallowing, Poppy glanced at the woman. 'Lovely to have met you.'

'You too. And you, little one.' She patted Fluffles as they passed.

Poppy followed Mack into the small treatment room, where she picked Fluffles up and placed her on the table.

After closing the door behind them, Mack shoved his hands in his pockets. 'Sorry.'

Frowning, Poppy took a deep breath. She'd half hoped he wouldn't mention it. Half hoped they'd be able to get through the appointment as though nothing had happened between them.

'It's okay. I know why.'

'Right.' He came further into the room and fussed Fluffles before standing with his back against the counter on the far wall. He looked down at the floor before looking back up at her apologetically and taking a deep breath. 'After my dad left, things were really tough, money-wise. I almost quit training to be a vet.'

'Oh, really?'

What did that have to do with him not wanting a relationship?

'It was my old neighbour who persuaded me to stick at it. She told me I had to finish so I could turn our lives around and be in a better place to provide for Gus and Spencer.' He shifted his feet. 'Of course, I felt guilty at the time, and have ever since, but I knew deep down that she was right. She looked after them whilst I trained. She still looks after them now. She has them after school and whenever I need a few hours.'

'That's nice of her.' Poppy straightened Fluffles' harness. 'That must have been a really tough time.'

'It was. I was a state, broken. Looking back, I was probably still

in shock at being left with Spencer and Gus. She was – is – an abso-
lute lifesaver.'

'I'm so sorry to hear what you've been through.' Poppy looked
across at him. If they hadn't had that kiss and if he hadn't made it
crystal clear he didn't want anything from her, she would have
walked straight across the room and given him a hug. Instead, she
gripped hold of Fluffles' lead.

'I didn't tell you, so you'd pity me. I told you because I thought
you should know the reason behind my decision.'

Poppy nodded slowly, but then said, 'I'm sorry, I don't
understand.'

She laid her hands on the table, palms down.

What did that have to do with the kiss? Was he saying that he
wasn't ready for a relationship because he had to put the boys first?
He had to focus on his job? But he'd had that relationship in the
past – the one Ginny had told her about. She shook her head.
Maybe what had happened, how they'd broken up, had just
confirmed what he wanted, that he wanted to focus on his brothers
and his job. 'So you're not ready for a relationship then?'

'What?' Mack frowned, the lines between his eyebrows knitting
together.

'Just that. You're not in the right place for a relationship. You
want to focus on your brothers, on your business.' Poppy looked
down at her nails and begun picking off the already scuffed nail
varnish. He was in a better place than he had been back then. That
was obvious but he still didn't want her. 'I understand that you need
to look out for them, to put them first.'

'I...'

'Don't.' She blinked, willing with every bone in her body for the
tears not to fall. That she wouldn't show him how much he had
hurt her. She'd have rather just assumed his ex's actions had been
the reason he didn't view her in that way, not that he thought she

wasn't good enough. That he was too focused earning money. 'Can we get this over and done with, please?'

'Poppy, I don't understand.' Stepping forward, he held his hand out towards her before letting it drop to his side.

She shook her head and focused on Fluffles, who was now pawing at the table, trying to make herself comfortable on the cold, hard surface.

'Have we got crossed wires? I was trying to explain why I don't offer discounts or give my treatment away for free. I don't want to ever put my brothers back in that situation.' He gestured to the door. 'The woman you were sitting next to mentioned discounts...'

Closing her eyes, she took a breath before opening them again.

'I thought you were talking about why you were pushing me away, why you declared that kiss between us was a mistake.'

'What has that got to do with money?'

'That I'm not good enough for you because you've made something of yourself while I'm starting right back at the beginning again.'

'What? No. Jeez, who do you take me for? I couldn't care less whether you had a million pounds in your back pocket or ten pence.' Looking down, he shook his head. 'I don't mean that literally. Of course I'd care, but for you, not for me. How much you have or don't have or what position you are in with your life has no bearing at all on why I can't get into a relationship.'

'Oh, right.' She looked away.

'Poppy, I thought we were talking about the discounts. If I'd known you were talking about the kiss...'

'Well, not the kiss exactly. But... your past. I know about your ex getting close to your brothers and then leaving.' She shrugged.

'Oh. How did you...?' He rubbed the back of his neck.

'I'm not her though.' Poppy clenched her jaw shut. Why had she said that? She hadn't meant to.

'I know, I know you're not.'

Pushing all thoughts away, she stepped closer to the table. She didn't want to think about any of it, not here. Not with him standing a mere few feet away from her. She couldn't do it.

'Let's get Fluffles her vaccination.'

Mack cleared his throat. 'Yes, of course.' Turning around, he looked down at the counter before mumbling, 'I'll just go and get it,' and left the room.

24

'Merry Christmas. Have a good one.' The delivery driver stuck his hand up in the air as he stepped out into the cold.

'You too,' Poppy said automatically before turning to the package in front of her on the counter. She glanced around the reception area. She could hear Alex and Susan chatting and laughing in the kitchen behind her. Looking at the address label, she frowned. It was addressed to her, and she was certain it was Ben's handwriting; the Ps had that backward swoop of the tail he always used when writing her name.

She picked it up and shook it gently, holding it to her ear. Had he sent her a Christmas present? They'd never really bothered with presents. Of course, they'd bought for family and close friends, or she had bought them, to be precise, but early on in their relationship they'd agreed that there wasn't any point buying each other extravagant gifts when neither one of them was really bothered with Christmas. Over the years, even buying each other a little token gift or two had fizzled out.

Why would he have bought her something this year? And gone to the trouble of sending it to her down here, no less?

She looked down as Dougal nudged her with his nose. Dougal had looked so sad when she'd walked by his kennel this morning that she'd let him join her in the reception area. Most of the other dogs were either exercising or training, with the exception of Eden, whom Flora had taken to meet the Smiths, who were interested in adopting her.

'What do you think he's got me, hey, Dougal? It's too big to be perfume and he would have never known which one to buy anyway. Too hard to be clothes...'

She was being daft. Why would he start buying her presents now? When they had separated? If it wasn't for the fact he'd basically told her he had fallen in love with Davina, there might have been a small part of her that believed he had sent this to try to win her back. And there might have been a tiny, even tinier than tiny, part of her that may have welcomed it.

She shook her head and tore the brown parcel paper open, frowning as she was met with another layer of slightly darker parcel paper. After tearing that open, too and throwing it down on the counter, she sat back on the stool, snorting at herself.

'What an idiot I am, hey, Dougal? Thinking for even a second that Ben had sent me a present.' She picked up the parcel again and opened the lid of the box inside. Yep, just as she'd thought, the awful ornament she'd chosen and paid for to give to Ben's mum for Christmas from the both of them. After having it delivered, Ben had just wrapped it back up and sent it on to her without looking inside or wondering for one moment what it had been.

Closing the lid again, she shoved the whole box in the bin before scrunching up the parcel paper and chucking that in too. She sank to the floor and held her arms out as Dougal bounded towards her.

Wrapping him into a hug, she sank her nose into the top of his head and breathed in his warm, comforting dog smell.

'What would I have actually done if he had sent me a present? I know we're not good for each other and one measly present wouldn't have changed that fact.'

Closing her eyes, she leaned against the wall as Dougal laid his head on her lap. She knew why she was feeling the way she was, and it had nothing to do with Ben and the parcel.

It was to do with Mack. Yesterday's conversation had not only confused her further, but cemented how she felt about him. She couldn't help herself. She'd tried so hard to squash any feelings, but she couldn't. The reason for why he wouldn't give away any medication, or his expertise, for free didn't annoy or anger her; it made her like him. Value him even more. He was a good guy, and he had a good reason to be wary of his finances – he didn't want to put his brothers back in the situation they'd been in before. He'd worked so hard to build a life, a home for Gus and Spencer, that now he wasn't going to do a thing to jeopardise it.

She shifted her leg and fussed Dougal to settle him. Yes, he could more than likely afford to give his time for free, to see the dogs in their care without charging, but he'd been so close to losing everything that it made sense that he'd be scared to go back there. Petrified. Especially with his dad trying to muscle his way into their lives once again.

And as much as she wanted to hate him for the choices he'd made, for making life harder for Wagging Tails, she couldn't.

The loud *brring-brring* of the landline phone filled the office and Dougal immediately jumped up, searching for the location of the offending sound.

'Come on, we'd best find that.' Poppy pulled herself to standing and rummaged beneath the papers before pulling the phone out. Hi, Wagging Tails Dogs' Home. How can I help you today?'

'Poppy, lovely, it's me, Flora. I'm in a spot of bother and hoping you can help.'

* * *

'There they are.' Spotting the Wagging Tails' van at the side of the road, Poppy indicated and pulled onto the grass verge. She clicked on the hazard lights and glanced behind her at Dougal, reaching back to check he was still secured to the seat belt. 'You be a good boy and wait here a moment.'

Stepping outside, Poppy quickly buttoned up her coat before running towards Flora.

'Thank you so much, lovely. Did you bring the jump leads?'

'Yes, they were already in the boot, I checked.'

'Good, good. I thought they might be.' Flora unlocked the bonnet on the van before pulling it open.

Poppy peered at the engine. 'What happened? Did it just stop?'

'Pretty much. I slowed to let a car out at the corner, stalled the thing, and now it won't start.' Flora walked around to the boot of her car and took out the jump leads.

'How do you know it's the battery? It could be anything. Should we ring the breakdown service, so we're put on the waiting list at least? If the jump leads work, we can always ring and tell them we don't need their help.'

Poppy watched as Flora attached the leads to the battery in the van.

'I'm pretty sure it's the battery. It's been on the blink for the last couple of weeks now.' Flora nodded towards her car. 'Can you just pop the bonnet please?'

Slipping back into the driver's seat, Poppy reached down and pulled the lever, making the bonnet click open. She turned to face Dougal. 'You okay, little one?'

Dougal kept his eyes transfixed on the passing traffic, his head turning quickly from side to side with each car that passed them by

'Good. I'll be back in a moment then.' She closed the car door behind her and joined Flora again. 'Do you need any help?'

'I'm think I'm pretty much done here.' She clipped the remaining lead to the battery of the car. 'Just start the car engine and we'll give it a few minutes before I start the van.'

Poppy jumped back into the car and turned the ignition, the engine purring to life.

Opening the passenger door, Flora said, 'Thanks, lovely.' She sat down and looked behind her. 'Oh, hello, Dougal. Have you come out for a little adventure?'

'He's been so good in the car. He's literally just been sitting there watching the cars pass by.'

'He's a good little one, isn't he?'

As Flora fussed him, Dougal leaned his head on the little cubby between the two front seats.

'He really is, isn't he?' Looking down at him, Poppy smiled. 'I'm so glad he's on the road to recovery.'

'Absolutely,' Flora agreed and then, abruptly, slapped her knees. 'Okay, here's the moment of truth, then. I'll see if I can start the van. Keep your fingers crossed.'

'I will.'

Leaving the car, Poppy followed Flora towards the van and stood next to the open driver's door.

'Hold your breath.'

Taking a deep inhale, Flora turned the key.

Nothing.

'Ah, that doesn't sound good.' Poppy grimaced.

'Don't worry. We may just need to try again in a few moments.' Flora leaned back against the chair. 'I have some good news, though. It looks as though the Smiths are adopting Eden. Both she and Tyler got on beautifully. We met in the woods today, so they were both on neutral ground. We'll do that another day and then, all being well, I'll take her over for a play date at their house.'

'Oh, that's wonderful news.'

'It is, isn't it? Tyler is as energetic as Eden is calm, but it seemed to work. Eden seemed to benefit and grow a little more confident as the day wore on, and Tyler seemed to calm down a tad.' Flora laughed. 'Only a little, mind, but even a little is enough to make a significant difference.'

'That's great then. Eden was so nervous when she first came to Wagging Tails.'

'Yes, it didn't help that she'd had that injury either, bless her.' Flora shook her head. 'But we're getting there with Mr Thomas. Slowly but surely, he's coming round to the idea of handing his dogs over. His cats too.'

'That's good.'

'Yes, yes, it is. I'll just be glad when we have them all over at Wagging Tails.' Flora took a deep breath. 'Right, ready to try again?'

Poppy held up her hands, crossing her fingers tightly.

Closing her eyes, Flora held her breath and turned the ignition, and the engine spluttered to life. 'Yes!'

25

After hanging Ralph's lead up on the hooks behind the counter, Poppy rubbed her hands together.

Flora placed the landline phone in its cradle and looked at her. 'Cold, lovely?'

'Absolutely frozen.' Poppy cupped her hands together and blew into them, her warm breath hitting her skin.

'Ah, look. That's why.' Flora nodded towards the window.

'What?' Turning around, Poppy grinned. It was snowing! Huge flakes of snow drifting down from the sky, dancing in the wind before settling onto the slabs in the courtyard. 'Do you think it will settle?'

'Possibly, it's certainly cold enough for it to.' Flora looked at the kitchen door as Alex stepped through.

'Wow, it's snowing!' Alex ran to the door, without stopping to collect his coat, and stepped outside, staring up at the sky, his hands held out palms up to catch the flakes.

'What's going on?' Ginny let the kitchen door close behind her as she wiped her mouth with a tissue. 'Oh.' She grinned as she spotted Alex outside before walking towards the door and calling him. 'Are you not cold out there?'

Alex ran inside, stamping the snow off his trainers onto the doormat. 'Freezing! But it had to be done, it's snowing! Let's hope it starts to settle.'

'Umm, I hope not. I hate driving in the snow.' Ginny grimaced. 'Don't get me wrong, I love it, just not when I have to drive.'

'Ah, it'll be okay. Think of all the people who live in Alaska and the cold countries. They manage just fine.' Alex wiped his hands down the front of his hoodie.

'Don't they have winter tyres or different cars or something?' Poppy asked.

'No, not all of them. Most people's cars are just the same. It's more to do with the fact driving in the snow is second nature to them during the winter months. They have more practice. Plus, because it snows a lot, they're driving on compacted snow. We usually have a day or two of snow before it starts to melt, which then freezes overnight, so we end up either trying to drive on ice or new snow with ice underneath.' Flora shook her head. 'Not a good combination.'

'You should go and move to Alaska then, Ginny. You'll be fine driving.' Alex grinned.

'Oi! Thanks very much! Are you trying to get rid of me?' She held her hands up against her cheeks in mock-shock.

'Always.' Grinning, Alex ducked as Ginny threw her tissue at him. 'Yuck! What's on that?'

'Mayonnaise. I've just had noodles for lunch.'

Narrowing his eyes, he picked up the offending tissue between the tips of his thumb and forefinger and shook it at her. 'You're disgusting. How can you eat mayonnaise with noodles? Mayonnaise is bad enough when it's eaten with things it's meant to be eaten with like chips or in sandwiches.'

'Come on, you two, behave. We've got a visitor coming.' Trying not to laugh, Flora nodded towards the window.

Looking up from where she was ticking Ralph's name off on the Walk List, Poppy froze. It was Mack. What was he doing at Wagging Tails? And more importantly, how could she get out of here and quick without making it look as though she was avoiding him? Too late. The bell above the door tinkled as he stepped inside.

'Afternoon, everyone.'

Keeping her eyes fixed on the list in front of her, Poppy tried to focus on the names. Who hadn't been walked yet?

'Afternoon, Mack. What can we do for you today?' came Flora's warm voice.

'I've just come to drop off some medication for Eden.' He placed a paper bag on the counter. 'It's the rest of the prescription for her painkillers. Sorry we didn't have them all in when you last came, Ginny.'

'No problem. And thank you for bringing them.' Ginny took the bag.

'Great.' Mack shifted on his feet and suddenly she could feel his eyes on her. 'Hi, Poppy.'

Looking up from the list, she met his gaze before decidedly glancing back down. 'Afternoon.'

'How are the roads around here?' Ginny asked, shutting the bag of medication in the cupboard. 'Has much snow settled yet?'

'No, not really. It's—'

'Excuse me, please.' Poppy needed to get outside, to get some air.

Hanging up the clipboard with the Walk List next to the hanging leads, she squeezed around the counter and headed for the door.

'Sorry.' Mack stepped aside as she brushed past him.

Reaching the front door, Poppy pulled it open just as Mack

began to speak again, describing the effect the snow was having on the roads. She slipped through, shutting the door behind her, and thankfully, drowning out the sound of his voice. Pausing as the door closed with a click behind her, she pulled her gloves out of her pocket and put them on. She looked across the courtyard. Even in the short time since it had begun to snow, the large flakes were settling on the ground. What she was supposed to do now, she had no idea. Why hadn't she escaped into the kennels? She'd have been warm there and could have just hidden, pretending to be busy checking on the dogs or refilling water bowls or something. Now she was stuck outside trying to think of something to do so she didn't look as though she was just blanking Mack.

With her gloves on, she pushed her hands into her pockets. She'd walk across to the cottage. That was all she could do. That way, she wouldn't be here when Mack left the reception and returned to his car. And she wouldn't turn into an icicle whilst she waited for him to leave. It was the perfect cover.

As she began to walk across the courtyard, she heard the bell above the door tinkle again and the gentle click of the door being shut. Great, she'd messed around too long putting on her gloves and trying to work out what to do.

Taking a deep breath, she kept her eyes focused in front of her. She just needed to pretend she hadn't heard him behind her, avoid the temptation to turn around and instead keep heading towards the cottage.

'Poppy, hold up. Please?'

She held her breath, her eyes still focused ahead, putting one foot in front of the other. If she carried on he'd think she hadn't heard him.

'Poppy!'

His voice was louder now. He was closer.

Leave me alone, Mack, please.

He must have realised what she was doing. Why wasn't he letting her escape the awkwardness of the situation? She needed some time. Just a few days.

Poppy, hear me out. Give me a couple of minutes, please.'

She felt his hand on her shoulder, his touch gentle through her coat.

She had no choice but to face him now. Stopping still and plastering a smile on her face, she turned around. 'Sorry, I didn't realise you were behind me.'

Mack nodded, and then looked at the ground, avoiding eye contact.

'What did you want?' Why had he chased after her if all he wanted to do was to stare at the ground and not speak?

'I... I just wanted to apologise.' He looked at her, their eyes meeting. 'I'm sorry things have turned out the way they have between us.'

She let her smile slip. 'You don't need to apologise. I told you I understand. You've got a lot on your plate. You're in a complicated stage of your life. I'm in a complicated patch of my life. I have nothing to offer you.'

'No, it's not that. You have so much to offer. More than you'll ever know.' He took her hands in his. 'You're an amazing person, Poppy. Kind, thoughtful, funny, I could go on. Don't ever think you've got nothing to offer anyone. You have everything to offer.'

Blowing a snowflake away from her mouth, Poppy looked down at their hands. Their fingers were entwined. His grasp was gentle but firm. She took a deep breath.

'Maybe it's just bad timing,' she said.

Mack nodded slowly before frowning. 'Maybe it doesn't have to be.'

'What do you mean?' She could feel the warmth of his hands through the fabric of her gloves.

'Maybe we're the only ones really getting in the way.'

'I still don't understand what you're trying to say.' She looked him in the eye.

'I guess I'm trying to say: what if the only reason I'm pushing you away is because it's what I think is the right thing to do. What if I don't have to?'

'You're making no sense.'

'I know. I know what I want to say but...' Glancing away, Mack sighed before taking his hands from hers and stepping closer. Cupping her chin with the hook of his forefinger, he mumbled, 'May I?'

Nodding, Poppy stood still. If he was about to kiss her, she was going to wait for him to make the first move. She didn't want to be rebuffed or doubt who had kissed who again. As he leaned in, she could feel Mack's breath on her lips and then the warmth of his skin as he kissed her.

Closing her eyes, she placed her hand on his neck and drew him towards her, kissing him back.

When the kiss was finished – and what a kiss it was! – Mack took her hands again and grinned. 'Can we just throw caution to the wind and see where it takes us? Will you forgive me for getting cold feet?'

Laughing, Poppy nodded. 'Yes, and yes. I don't blame you. We can keep it between us if you like? We can tell Spencer and Gus we're just friends until we think they're ready?'

Mack smiled, relief sweeping over his face. 'I'd like that. Thank you. What with the uncertainty of my dad coming back into our lives, I'd rather wait to see where this goes before telling them. Are you sure you're happy with that?'

'Of course.'

And she was. Those two boys didn't need any more upheaval in their lives. This way she and Mack could see where things led without any outside pressure.

'Although, I'm not so sure we can keep it a secret from everyone else.'

'No?'

'No.' He raised his eyebrows and nodded towards Wagging Tails.

Following his gaze, she opened her mouth. Flora, Ginny and Alex were standing in the window watching them. As soon as he realised Poppy and Mack had seen them, Alex began clapping, with Flora and Ginny soon copying beside him.

Laughing, Poppy buried her face in Mack's chest, holding on to his coat to hide herself.

'Are they still clapping?'

'Oh, yes. Do you think we should take a bow?' He chuckled.

'Maybe.'

And with a little flourish, Poppy took Mack's hand, and they turned towards the window and bowed.

26

'Oh, I really don't know if I can do this. I don't think I've ever been skating.'

Poppy looked across the large ice rink. Skaters were weaving in and out of each other, some criss-crossing and making patterns on the ice. A huge Christmas tree sat in the middle of the rink, its coloured lights illuminating the ice below, the branches dancing as skaters passed close by. Fairy lights were strung up around the outside of the ice rink too, hot chocolate and mince pie stalls encircling the rink.

'You've never been skating?' Poppy asked.

'Not that I can remember, anyway.' Mack shook his head.

'But you love Christmas and it's a super Christmassy thing to do. Look at everyone.' She pointed at skaters swooshing past, wearing jumpers emblazoned with bright woollen baubles or reindeer.

'The question that begs an answer more is why in the world do you love ice skating? You haven't hidden what you think of Christmas.' Mack shook his head and chuckled.

Poppy shrugged. 'I remember Aunt Flora taking me one year. This is going back when I was a lot younger, five, six, maybe, when we still used to come down here and visit over Christmas.' Umm, maybe she did remember more about those early Christmases than she'd first admitted to Aunt Flora. She smiled. 'And I just fell in love with it. When I was a teenager and got my first weekend job, I began going again.'

'And you've been skating ever since?'

'I've had a break for a few years.' She hadn't been since she'd started dating Ben. He'd hated it. 'But apart from that, yes. I guess when I was a teenager, I was trying to recreate that happiness I'd felt when Aunt Flora had taken me and, if I'm completely honest, it makes me feel as though I have something in my life I can control. And besides, it's the best feeling in the world. Freeing.'

'So, there are parts of the traditions of Christmas you like?' Mack raised an eyebrow.

'Well...' Poppy laughed and bent to lace up her skate. 'I used to avoid the rink at Christmas. Too busy. It's a *winter* sport, not a Christmas sport.'

'Fair enough.' Mack took a deep breath. 'How about we get a mince pie and a hot chocolate and watch everyone else skate instead?'

Poppy looked up from where she was tying her lace and laughed. 'Nice try.'

'Or you can skate, and I can munch on Christmas cake while I wave at you?'

Straightening her back, she glanced towards the ice. 'Yes, okay.'

'Really?'

'Of course.' She grinned.

Yes, she'd have loved to introduce him to the joys of ice skating, but above all she wanted to spend time with him. She didn't really mind what they did.

'You do know we don't have to go ice skating, don't you? We can walk straight back out of here and go to the cinema instead, if you like? Or just go for a walk? I don't mind as long as we get to spend some time together.'

Holding the edge of the bench, Mack looked back across the ice rink.

'Nope. Let's have a go, but I apologise in advance if I fall on you and break your leg.'

'Ha ha, that won't happen. Besides, if it does, you'll be the one cleaning out kennels for six weeks.' Laughing, she stood up, balancing on the thin blades of her skates, and held out her hands for him. 'Are you sure you want to try?'

'Yes, I'm sure.' He grinned. 'Besides, the idea of having to spend six weeks scooping dog poop from the kennels is motive enough for me to be careful, so I think we'll be okay.'

'Oi! That shouldn't be the reason you don't want me to end up breaking a leg.'

Grinning, Mack began taking small steps towards the edge of the rink, towards her.

Poppy looked down at the ice to the side of them. 'Ready?'

'One question, how am I even supposed to balance on these things?' He lifted his leg, indicating the blades. 'Let alone balance enough to move.'

'You will. I'll show you how to.' Taking his hands again, she nodded at the rink behind her. 'Shall we? Are you ready?'

'As ready as I'll ever be.'

'Mack, are you sure you want to do this?'

Meeting her eyes, he nodded. 'One hundred per cent.'

'Okay, great. Then, do you trust me?'

'Again, one hundred per cent.'

'Aw, really?' She widened her eyes.

'Yes.' Mack chuckled. 'Of course I do.'

'Great. Just step onto the ice first.' Poppy watched as he did as she'd instructed. 'Did you ever roller-skate when you were younger?'

'Oh yes, I was a whizz at the roller disco.'

She laughed. 'In that case, this will be a breeze. Just pretend you're roller-skating.'

'On ice?' He grimaced. 'Rock solid hard ice.'

'You roller-skated on wooden floors, I'm guessing, so you'll be fine.' She grinned. 'Glide your feet out, one at a time. Just like you would if you were roller-skating.'

She watched as he pushed his feet out, one at a time, and began to glide forwards. Meeting his eyes, she skated backwards a little, her hands still in his.

'I'm doing it!' But when he looked down at his feet, he wobbled.

'Don't look down. Look at me. Look me in the eye.' Skating backwards a little faster now, Poppy smiled. 'Want to try on your own now?'

'On my own?' Mack's eyes widened.

'I mean, I'll hold your hand and skate next to you?' she suggested.

'Right.' Relief flooded his face. 'Yes, I like that idea better than you skating off and leaving me to fend for myself.'

Poppy shook her head and got into position next to him. 'As if I'd do that.'

'It depends how much you want to get out of cleaning the kennels. You might have been planning to skate off and break your leg somehow.' Mack raised his eyebrows and chuckled.

'Well, it's tempting, but I don't actually mind cleaning the kennels out that much. Most of the dogs keep theirs clean and when they don't...' she lowered her voice and leaned closer '... I find it strangely satisfying, making it clean again.'

'Ha ha, I have no words.'

* * *

'Yum, this is good hot chocolate, isn't it?' Poppy took another sip of the rich chocolatey liquid and savoured the taste in her mouth.

'It really is.' Mack lowered his cup and looked at her. 'Thank you for teaching me how to skate tonight.'

'It's fine. You were really easy to teach, probably because you used to roller-skate. You knew instinctively how to do it.'

'Well, thank you.' Mack looked behind her.

'What is it?' She turned around.

'There's a Christmas present lucky dip. Shall we have a go?'

'A Christmas present lucky dip?' She'd never even heard of such a thing. 'Is that even a thing?'

'Yes. Apparently so.' Taking her hand, he led the way towards the small stall nestled beneath yet another Christmas tree. 'What could be a better combination? Christmas and a lucky dip, all rolled into one?'

Poppy laughed as they joined the short queue. 'What do you think we'll get? A bag of chocolate coins or a wind-up Santa?'

'Ha ha, we'll have to wait and see. I'll choose one for you and you can choose one for me.'

'Good idea.'

The family in front of them moved aside, presents in hand.

'Two lucky dips?' The man behind the stall held up two fingers.

'Yes, please.' Mack passed across the coins before stepping back and indicating the red and green striped lucky dip box to Poppy.

'Okay, here goes nothing.' She rummaged through the shredded paper and tinsel mixture until she wrapped her fingers around a small parcel. Pulling it out, she held it up to show Mack and stepped back, letting him take a turn.

'Ooh, are there any left in here?' he said as he reached inside.

'There're some down the bottom.' Poppy laughed as he

pretended to get his hand stuck as he tried to free his gift from the box.

Mack nodded towards the man behind the stall. 'Thank you.' He held up his present. 'And Merry Christmas.'

'Merry Christmas to you both, too.' The man flicked the white pom-pom from the Santa hat he was wearing and turned to the next person in line.

Poppy followed Mack towards the railings that partitioned the ice rink and the small cluster of stalls.

'Here, you open yours first.' Mack passed her the gift he'd chosen.

'Thank you.' Taking the present from him, she lifted it to her ear and shook it, before squeezing the red wrapping paper. 'I wonder what it could be.' After slowly peeling off the paper, she lifted out a small plastic snow globe, with a tiny plastic reindeer sitting inside.

Mack smiled at her and held out his hand, asking to see the globe. He gently tipped it upside down before setting it straight again.

Poppy watched as the tiny balls of 'snow' fell from the top of the small plastic dome and floated to the bottom, covering the grass with a fine layer of white, the bemused expression on the reindeer's face unchanged.

'Merry Christmas.' Mack looked at her, their eyes meeting as he passed it back to her.

'Thank you.' She smiled and pointed to his present. 'Your turn.'

Grinning, Mack tore the wrapping paper off revealing a small stuffed reindeer toy.

'Aw, that's cute. And look, they both have the same beady eyes and wide smiles.' She held the snow globe up next to the teddy.

'They sure do.'

Poppy looked up at the Christmas tree. Baubles of every size and colour decorated its branches, as well as miniature stars, sleighs and reindeer, each one hanging from a short golden thread. Then she glanced back across to the ice rink. People were still skating, some travelling so fast across the ice that their scarves flew behind them whilst some wore Santa or elf hats, others were just content to make their way slowly around the rink, revelling in the sights of the fairy lights and Christmas trees.

'It's beautiful, isn't it?' Mack stood behind her, wrapping his arms around her waist, and kissed her on top of her head, his breath tickling her scalp.

'Yes, it is.' As she leaned back against his chest, Poppy smiled. She could almost feel a little of that Christmas joy he kept talking about. Not that she'd admit it. Not just yet.

27

'So, how was your date last night?' Ginny prised the tennis ball from Oscar's mouth and threw it across the paddock, watching as his small frame ran after it.

'Go on, you can chase it too.' Poppy nodded towards Alfie, who was sitting at her feet.

He glanced up at her before turning and running after the ball, although Oscar had already grabbed it in his mouth and was bounding back to them. Halfway back down the paddock, Oscar skidded in the snow, the balling rolling from his mouth, and Alfie quickly took the opportunity to take it whilst he could.

'Honestly? It was amazing. We went ice skating and then hung around the ice rink for a while. There were stalls and Christmas trees.' She smiled. 'It was really lovely. Definitely the best proper first date I've been on.'

'That does sound lovely.' After throwing the ball again, Ginny gave her a warm smile. 'I'm so pleased it's finally working out for you two.'

'Me too.' It was chilly out and Poppy stamped her feet, wriggling her toes to try to keep them warm. The ground was still covered in a blanket of white even though it hadn't snowed since the early hours.

'Oh, I know what I was going to ask you.' Ginny picked up a frisbee from the ground and threw it, watching it spin in the air, Oscar close behind, his fluffy ears bouncing as he ran. 'I went to order a new battery for the van this morning, but the payment wouldn't go through.'

'Was that on the charity debit card?'

'Yes, but I know Flora mentioned there was some problem or other with it. Do you know if she's managed to sort it out or if the bank is sending her a new one or anything?'

'I'm not sure. Sorry.' Poppy shook her head. Flora had said she'd ring them, but whether she'd got round to it or not, she had no idea.

'No worries. I'll ask her when I see her next.' Ginny took the frisbee from Oscar and the ball from Alfie and threw them both together. The two small dogs glanced at each other as if confused what to do.

'They're not sure which one to follow.' Poppy laughed.

Ginny shook her head and grinned as they both bounded after the ball, Oscar weaving in front of Alfie to take it at the last moment. Stunned, Alfie sniffed around and picked up the frisbee.

'Good jobs, you two.'

'Ginny! Poppy!'

Turning around, Poppy saw Alex running through the bottom paddock towards them. As soon as he reached the gate, he doubled over, taking in deep breaths.

'I don't think in all my time here I've ever seen you run quite so fast.' Ginny laughed. 'Not even after a dog.'

'No, no.' Catching his breath, Alex straightened his back, panic etched over his face. 'It's Flora.'

'What? What's happened?' Poppy ran towards him.

'She fell, tripped. Susan thinks she may have broken her leg. I've been searching for you both. An ambulance is on its way.'

'Oh no.' Poppy clasped her hands over her mouth, the lead she was holding clipping against her cheek. 'Where? Where is she?'

'Down in the courtyard.' Alex pulled open the gate and held his hand out. 'You both go. Give me the leads and I'll take these two in.'

'Right, yes.' Ginny gave him Oscar's lead before prising Alfie's from Poppy's hand and handing that over too. 'Come on, Poppy.'

Blinking, she looked from Ginny to Alex and back again. 'Yes, yes.'

As they ran through the bottom paddock, Poppy saw the familiar blue lights as an ambulance turned in through the gates of the courtyard. It must be bad if it had arrived this quickly. Wouldn't they prioritise the worst-off patients? Susan must be worried.

Storming through the gate to the courtyard, Poppy ran across the snow-covered slabs and knelt down next to her aunt.

'Aunt Flora, are you okay? Oh, I know you're not okay. That was a stupid thing to say.'

Wincing, Flora tugged the collar of the coat Susan had draped over her away from her mouth. 'I'll be fine, lovely. Just fine.' Flora looked from Poppy to Ginny and back again.

Having let the ambulance in, Susan ran back to them, the ambulance slowing to a stop behind her.

'Hello, Flora. You could have just picked up the phone if you'd wanted to see me. You didn't have to go to these lengths.' The paramedic smiled as she knelt down in the snow and held the pads of her fingers against Flora's wrist.

'Paige, lovely.' Flora looked from Paige to the other paramedic, who was now kneeling next to her too. 'And Pat. This is my niece, Poppy. You remember her, Pat?'

'I do.' Pat looked over and smiled broadly, igniting the laughter lines around his eyes. 'I remember when you were knee high.'

Poppy nodded.

'Can you tell us what happened?' Flora winced in pain. Placing her hand on Flora's arm, Paige spoke softly. 'We'll get you some meds for that pain, shall we?'

'Please.' Flora nodded before taking a deep breath. 'I just tripped over this lead. Daft, really. I was just trying to jump-start the van.'

Poppy looked down at the jump leads sprawled across the snow. Both the van's bonnet and that of Aunt Flora's car were propped open.

'You've got trouble with the battery, have you?' Pat placed a cannula into the back of her hand. 'Here, this should help.'

'Trouble with the battery.' Flora nodded before closing her eyes.

'Aunt Flora?' Poppy looked at Paige. 'Is she okay? What's happening?'

'It's just the medication. It's pretty strong stuff.' Paige looked across at Poppy and smiled softly. 'Why don't you jump in the car with Ginny, and you can follow us to the hospital?'

Poppy nodded as Ginny wrapped her arm around her shoulder and led her towards her car.

* * *

Poppy was pacing the small family room at the end of the ward Flora had been taken to.

'She'll be fine. She's the toughest person I know,' Ginny said, sitting by the window.

'I know. I know she is. But how long are they going to take? It's been ages.' Poppy looked out of the window. The car park was below, small dots of people walking from their car to the payment machine and then into the hospital or vice versa.

'She's in the best of hands.' Percy's voice cracked despite his calm demeanour. After waiting for Alex to secure the dogs, Percy had rushed across to the hospital with Alex, Susan and Sally to await news about Flora. 'And it won't be long now. She'll be out of theatre soon.'

Poppy nodded. Yes, Flora would be fine. Just fine.

She sunk down onto the other blue plastic chair by the window, the hard edges sticking into the backs of her knees. Clasping her hands together in front of her, she closed her eyes. She just needed a moment, a moment to think. Since Alex had told them about Flora's fall, everything had just been a whirlwind – the ambulance, the hospital, the waiting. And now Flora was in the operating theatre. How had she fractured her leg so badly by just tripping?

On hearing the door to the waiting room open and close, she kept her eyes squeezed tightly shut. It couldn't be the surgeon. Not yet. They'd been told the operation would be at least an hour, maybe two, and even though it felt as though it had been ten hours, she knew it had really only been twenty minutes. She'd checked.

She felt Mack's hand on her shoulder, gentle and firm, before she heard his voice. Opening her eyes, she stood up, leaning into his embrace and burying her head in the crook of his shoulder.

'I came as quickly as I could. Sorry, I had to get a locum in to cover. How is she doing?' His breath tickled her ear as he spoke.

Pulling away, she swallowed, trying not to let the tears fall. 'She's in surgery. They couldn't set the leg or something, so they had to operate.'

Mack nodded. 'Right.'

'I just don't understand. She only tripped. She just tripped over the jump leads. How can she be in surgery after tripping?'

'Hadn't she just replaced the battery after breaking down a couple of days ago?' Mack took her hands in his.

'Yes, no. I don't know. No, she didn't.' She looked down at their hands, their fingers entwined. 'I thought she was going to.'

'I'm going to get some coffee. Susan, do you want to come with me, and we'll grab everyone one?' Alex pushed himself out of his chair.

'Yes, I'll come and help.' Susan rubbed Poppy's shoulder as she passed.

Poppy couldn't do this. Every time she heard someone approaching, she'd jerk her head towards the door and take a juddering breath, before realising it was just a nurse or doctor walking past. She couldn't just wait, worrying every time someone came near.

She shook her head. 'Don't worry about me. I'm going to pop back to the cottage and get some things for Flora. I can't hang around waiting.'

'I'll come with you,' Mack spoke, his voice soft.

'No, don't worry.' She just needed some time alone, some time to process it all. 'Can you stay? Let me know if you hear anything? Please?'

Frowning, Mack nodded. 'I can give you a lift back. You'll ring if there's any news, won't you, Percy?'

'Of course I will.' Percy glanced up before looking back down at his hands, tightly clasped in his lap.

'No, it's fine. Honestly. I just need a bit of time.' Poppy shook her head. She didn't want to upset Mack by turning his offer down, but she needed the space to process what had happened.

'I'll give you a lift.' Ginny stood up and pulled her car keys from her pocket. 'I can feed the dogs whilst you're getting the bits Flora will need.'

'Thanks.' Poppy nodded, grateful of Ginny's offer before turning back to Mack. 'Thank you for offering though.'

28

Poppy sank to the bottom stair of the cottage and pulled out a crumpled receipt. She smoothed it in her hand, trying to read the list that she and Ginny had scribbled down on the way over. Things Flora would need for her stay in hospital.

She placed her elbows on her knees and laid her head in her hands, pushing the pads of her forefingers against her temples in an attempt to soothe the tension headache pounding against her skull. Everything had happened so quickly. One moment she and Ginny had been chatting in the top paddock, the next they'd been chasing the ambulance through the streets to Trestow General Hospital. How did a perfectly normal day change so quickly? She couldn't make sense of it.

Her phone rang in her coat pocket, a shrill tring in the silent cottage.

Pulling it out, she answered quickly, not wasting time looking to see who it was. 'Hello?'

'Poppy, it's Ben. Everything okay? You sound kind of...'

'Ben?' Ben. Why was he ringing? She needed him off the line.

She needed to keep her phone free in case Mack rang with news from the hospital. 'Ben, I can't talk at the moment.'

'That's okay. It's only a quick one. I'm off out in a minute, anyway.'

Poppy clenched her jaw. She could hear laughter in the background. Davina.

'I really can't...'

'I'll cut to the chase, then. I've pulled the house from the market. We're... I'm staying put. I'll buy you out.'

'What?' He'd pulled the house from the market?

'Yep. Great news, isn't it? We can wrap things up pretty quickly this way. Of course, with my job I won't be able to pay the asking price, but I'll message you over my offer.'

'Offer?' He was going to give her an offer? She couldn't do this. Not now. 'I need to go.'

Pulling her mobile from her ear, she ended the call, and stared at the now-blank screen. He was moving in with Davina. Not only that. He was moving Davina into their home. Her home. That's what he'd been going to say, wasn't it? *We're staying put.* He must have meant Davina and him.

She shook her head. This wasn't the time to be thinking about Ben and Davina. This wasn't the time to be thinking about the house. She was here for a reason, and she didn't have long. Both she and Ginny needed to get back to the hospital before Flora came out of surgery.

Pushing herself to standing, she heard her phone again. She paused and looked at it. Sure enough, true to his word, Ben had messaged with an offer. She squinted at the screen. How much was he wanting to pay her to buy the house out? That wasn't even close to the market value.

She stuffed her phone back into her pocket. She didn't have the brain space to think about that. Not now. She needed to focus on

Flora and getting Flora's things together so she could get back to her.

* * *

'Poppy, are you almost ready? The dogs are all fed and watered.'

Poppy looked up from the holdall she was stuffing Flora's washbag into. She'd packed underwear, a cardigan, clothes for on the way home. What else did she need? Pyjamas.

'One moment.'

'Okay. Do you need a hand?'

'No. I just need to grab some pyjamas. Won't be a second.' She yanked open the chest of drawers. There they were. She pulled out a floral green pyjama top and looked through the drawer searching for the bottoms to match. Huh, where were they?

As she pushed the clothes across to one side of the drawer, she noticed something poking out. Something that shouldn't be in the clothes drawer.

She frowned. What was that?

Beneath the clothes was a pile of letters. She wondered why Flora would be keeping post in her pyjama drawer, but then Poppy shook her head. It was none of her business.

And there were the floral green pyjama bottoms.

She pulled them out with a sigh, just as a letter fluttered to the floor.

Poppy picked up the letter and shoved it back into the drawer. But as she did so, she couldn't help the red printed words from catching her eye: 'Payment Contract'. What was that about? Picking it back up, she frowned. The letter was from one of the same-day loan companies she'd seen on TV.

What was Flora doing with letters from a loan company? Everyone knew the interest rates on these loans were more than extortionate. And anyway, Flora wouldn't need a loan. She didn't buy herself anything. Even looking at the pyjamas Poppy had just packed, the fraying around the ankles showed how old they were. Flora never bought anything for herself. She always said she had everything she needed.

Sliding the rest of the clothes in the drawer to the side, Poppy picked up another letter. A final reminder from a same-day loan company this time. A different one now. One from a different loan company. She pulled another one out. And another. How many same-day loans had Flora taken out?

She glanced at the date at the top of the letter. They were recent. Very recent. All in the last few weeks. It didn't make any sense. Flora must have borrowed thousands of pounds and over such a short period of time, too.

She laid the letters on the bed, covering the pale green stemmed yellow flowered pattern of the duvet cover. Returning back to the drawer, she looked again. That was the last of the letters. Now only a little notebook remained, tucked into the back corner of the drawer.

Poppy picked it up and flicked through the pages. Flora's handwriting, rushed and small. Pinching the bridge of her nose, she looked at the pages staring back at her. Names of dogs, dates, and amounts, all scribbled down.

Dougal – X-ray – £350

Dougal – treatment and stay – £750

Eden – bite – £250

The list continued. Each and every treatment the dogs had

received was itemised, the price next to it. Everything. It was all there.

Poppy perched on the edge of the bed.

Flora had been borrowing money to cover the vet bills. The funds in the charity account must have depleted. There hadn't been an issue with the charity debit card; there hadn't been any money left in the account.

That must have been why Flora hadn't replaced the van's battery. She just hadn't had the money. If she'd been able to afford to, she wouldn't be lying in the operating theatre now.

'Poppy? Are you sure you don't need any help?' Ginny's voice wafted up the stairs.

'No, no. I'm coming down now.' Standing back up, Poppy quickly gathered the letters together with the notebook and placed them back in the drawer. As she moved the clothes back across Flora's hidden letters, she felt something else beneath the softness of the fabrics.

She picked up the papers. It wasn't a letter this time, but pages printed out. She read the title: 'How to Remortgage your Home'.

Poppy could hear Ginny walking up the stairs now, the familiar creak-creak of the old floorboards. She couldn't let Ginny see these.

Replacing the papers, Poppy took a deep breath and composed her face into a neutral expression. Then she pushed the drawer closed, turned and picked up the holdall.

'Ready.'

29

Lifting the holdall further up onto her shoulder, Poppy pushed open the door to the waiting room then held it open for Ginny.

She kept her eyes focused on the floor, the strap of the holdall in her hand, keeping it in place on her shoulder.

'Have you heard anything yet?' Ginny asked the assembled group – Percy, Susan, Alex, Sally and Mack.

'Nothing. We should do soon, though.' Percy nodded.

'I'll go and grab you two a coffee now.' Alex jumped up from his chair before leaving.

'Hey, you okay?' Mack stood up and walked across to Poppy. 'Shall I take that?'

Ignoring him, she walked towards the window and shrugged the holdall from her shoulder before sinking onto the plastic chair. As she twisted the handle around her finger, all she could focus on was a stain on the floor. What was that? Blood? Coffee? It must have been coffee.

What had Aunt Flora been thinking? All of those loans. Same-day loans at that with the super high interest rates. And the information about remortgaging the cottage?

'Here you go, coffee.' Alex held out a plastic cup, the bittersweet aroma filling the room.

Poppy shook her head. She didn't want coffee. She couldn't drink at the moment. She needed to think.

'Are you sure?'

She nodded, too many thoughts in her head to even answer out loud. Remortgaging? That was a big deal, wasn't it? It would mean Flora's home being on the line. She'd lose it if she couldn't repay the money. What would that mean for the dogs' home? Possibly everything. Possibly nothing. The home would be separate from the cottage, wouldn't it? But where would Aunt Flora live?

'Don't worry. She'll be out of surgery soon.' Mack's voice was quiet, kind.

She frowned, keeping her eyes focused on the stain. She couldn't look at him. Not now. Not at this moment. Yes, she understood why Mack couldn't give discounts for the treatment he gave the dogs from Wagging Tails, but now she knew Flora had been struggling financially, knew what had led her to be in surgery, she just couldn't trust herself not to say something to him. Not to blame him, even though she didn't. Not really. She did understand but... No, it was best if she just tried to concentrate on waiting for Flora to get out of the operating theatre. However much she understood though, the facts were clear, if he had honoured Gavin's wish, continued giving veterinary treatment for free. Continued to only charge for medication. If he'd done that, Flora wouldn't have needed to jump-start the van again, she would have replaced the battery. If he'd honoured Gavin's wishes, Aunt Flora wouldn't be in so much debt, she wouldn't be looking to remortgage her home. And she couldn't lay that on him. She couldn't blame him. It wasn't fair.

'Poppy?' Mack touched her hand.

Pulling her hand away, she sat still. 'You should probably go. I don't want to keep you here.'

'Don't worry. I'm happy to stay. I want to support you.' He lowered himself into the chair next to her.

She swallowed. She couldn't have him here. She needed time to think. Space to think. 'It's fine. I've got Percy, Ginny, Alex, Susan and Sally here. I don't want to keep you.'

'You're not keeping me.' Mack shook his head. 'I can wait.'

Poppy chewed her bottom lip. He needed to go. She couldn't sit next to him. Not as though nothing had happened. Not as though she hadn't just found out he ultimately was the reason her aunt was here. 'Please, Mack. I'm fine. Just go.'

The confusion was clear in Mack's eyes, his brow furrowed as he ran his fingers through his hair. Still, he kept sitting.

Please just go. She squeezed the strap of the holdall tighter in her grasp. It wasn't his fault. He didn't know this would have happened. It wasn't his fault. 'Aunt Flora doesn't need us all here. She'll probably be embarrassed about what's happened.'

'Why would she be embarrassed?' Mack turned to face her and tried to take her hand in his again. 'There's no reason for her to be embarrassed. It was just an accident. It could have happened to any one of us.'

Poppy snatched her hand away again. She could taste the blood from her lip now. The strong metallic taste filling her mouth. 'It wouldn't have...' She caught herself just in time. She couldn't tell him that it wouldn't have happened to him, not with the money he was making off her aunt. She couldn't tell him that every time he spoke an irrational anger rose from the pit of her stomach. She knew it was just the shock, she knew he could never have foreseen what had happened, that he was just trying to look out for his family. But she knew if he stayed here, in this small room, sitting next to her for a moment longer then she'd say something she'd forever regret. 'She doesn't need to come around and have *strangers* around her bed.' She winced at her own voice. She hadn't meant for the word strangers to escape, hadn't meant to sound so impersonal. 'Just leave. Please.'

Standing up, Mack shifted on his feet, unsure of what to do.

'Please.' She looked up at him, blinking back the tears behind her eyes. She knew she'd hurt him but she couldn't cope with this. Not now. Not yet.

'I don't understand.' Mack's voice cracked as he shoved his hands in his pockets. 'I—'

Poppy took a deep breath. There was only one way to get him to go. She'd have to tell him all of this was his fault. 'You—'

Susan laid her hand on Poppy's arm and nodded towards the door as another family filtered through, pausing and looking at them, seemingly trying to decide if it was safe to enter.

'This isn't the time or the place.'

Poppy glanced at the family, who were gingerly taking their seats, and then back at Mack before shaking her head and slumping back against the chair. She clasped her hands again, squeezing her fingers together, her knuckles turning white. She could hear hushed voices whispering around her, the door clicking shut behind Mack. She felt Susan's hand on hers.

* * *

She swiped at the tears running down her cheeks as she looked out of the car window. Ginny was driving but she was just as focused on the road ahead as Poppy was on the thoughts running through her head.

How could this have happened? How could Aunt Flora have kept quiet about the piling debts for so long? Why hadn't she spoken to her? To anyone? She shook her head. Of course she wouldn't have spoken to her, Aunt Flora knew Poppy was having money troubles of her own. She wouldn't have been able to help and her aunt wouldn't have wanted to burden her, to worry her. But it wasn't right she'd kept quiet about it. No wonder she'd been so distant recently, so distracted. She'd been dealing with all this worry on her own.

She ran her finger along the door, right beneath the window seal. And Mack. What was she supposed to do about him? To think about him? Yes, he was careful with his money for a reason, but he could have given up his time for the dogs in his care. How would that have affected him?

She snorted. Of course, it would have meant he would have lost out on money. If he didn't charge for his appointments with the Wagging Tails dogs, then he would be missing out on appointments with paying customers.

'You okay?' Ginny glanced at her quickly before turning her attention back to the road. 'Sorry, I don't know why I asked that. It was a stupid question. Of course you're not okay after what has just happened.'

'I know what you meant. I'm fine. You?'

Ginny sighed. 'Yep.'

Nodding, Poppy turned to look out of the passenger window again. Not that she could see anything in the dark. She clasped her hands tightly in her lap. She'd really thought there could have been something between her and Mack. She'd felt it. Despite their differences of opinion about him charging the home vet's fees, she'd felt something. Something big. Something real. A connection. But now? There couldn't be anything between them. She'd always blame him, rightly or wrongly, for Aunt Flora's accident. It would always be there, hanging between them. The accusation, the anger, the sadness.

'Here we are. Home.'

Poppy watched the car headlights illuminate the cottage as Ginny swung onto the driveway. How much longer would it be either hers or Flora's home? 'Thank you.' She jumped out of the car before Ginny could give her a hug. She knew she wouldn't be capable of keeping it together if she did.

At the door, she turned and waved as Ginny's car disappeared back down the lane. Closing it behind her, she leaned against the wood of the door as large fat tears rolled down her face. How had they got to this? Aunt Flora had lived in the cottage, ran the dogs' home for thirty-five years, how could all of her hard work be unravelled in a few short weeks?

She sank to the doormat, ignoring the cold as the snow from her shoes quickly soaked into her jeans. And Mack? Why was everything going wrong?

Tucking her head in her arms, she let herself weep – for Aunt Flora, for the dogs. For Mack and what could have been. Her shoulders shook, her shoulder blades hitting the door as they did. But she didn't care. She couldn't.

* * *

Poppy threw a scrunched-up tissue onto the coffee table. She couldn't cry any more. She didn't think she had any tears left to cry. Not after spending over two hours crying on the doormat. No, she needed to figure out a way to fix this. And she needed to do it now. Before the sun came up. She needed to find a solution before she visited Aunt Flora, before she spoke to everyone back at the home.

She glanced at her phone as it flashed and ran the pad of her index finger over the notification. It was from Mack. He'd sent another message. He was worried about her. She knew that, but she just couldn't bring herself to message him back. She just couldn't make sense of any of it. Mack was so kind, caring. He showed that in the way he'd stepped in and brought up his brothers as well as the way he was with the animals he cared for, but... if it wasn't for him refusing to continue Gavin's discount scheme with Wagging Tails then Aunt Flora wouldn't be lying in a hospital bed right now. And she didn't know if she could get past that. She couldn't. She knew he had money. The car he drove, the fact he was willing to spend hundreds on a Christmas present for Kerry. He had the money.

Her phone pinged again. Another message. Pushing it across the coffee table, she turned back to the letters she'd found in Flora's drawer. Picking up the next one, she searched for the amount Flora owed and added it to the tally she'd made. It was more than she'd thought. The number just kept getting bigger and bigger.

She took a gulp of the coffee she'd made hours ago, the bitter-sweet taste somehow sharper now it was cold, and looked around the living room. It was strange being in the cottage without Aunt Flora. Her slippers were still by the fireplace, her favourite mug still on the little nest of tables, her reading glasses perched on the arm of her favourite armchair, the neck cord hanging down.

Looking back at the figures, Poppy pinched the bridge of her nose. No wonder Flora had turned to looking for advice on remortgaging. What other solution was there?

Unless... Unless... Poppy picked up her mobile again and scrolled through her contacts.

She just had to hope he'd be awake at this time of the morning. 'Ben?'

* * *

Pulling the door into Wagging Tails' reception open, Poppy shifted the papers in her arms. She could hear voices – Susan, Ginny, Percy

Alex, Sally. Were they talking about her? She wouldn't blame them. Not after her outburst in the waiting room yesterday.

'I hope she's okay.' The worry was audible in Susan's voice. In all their voices. 'I'll pop over to the cottage, check up on her.'

Poppy kicked the reception door closed behind her as she walked in, a waft of cold air filling the room, and the voices from the kitchen suddenly fell silent. Straightening her back, she entered. She could feel everyone's eyes on her. At least they were all here. She'd hoped they would be.

Walking to the head of the table, she let go of the papers in her hands, the letters she'd found, the figures she'd scribbled down, the information about the remortgaging all fluttering to the surface of the table.

'Poppy, love. You've not changed. Have you been up all night?' Susan jumped up from her chair. 'Let me get you a coffee.'

Ginny leaned across the table and picked up one of the letters. 'What's this?'

'Yes, what are all these letters?' Alex's voice was full of curiosity.

'What's going on?' Percy stroked his beard as he balanced his reading glasses on the bridge of his nose and picked up a letter.

'Bills? They're all bills.' Sally frowned.

Poppy cleared her throat. 'This is why Flora is in hospital. This is what she's been protecting us all from.'

'What do you mean?' Alex frowned.

'She's been getting into debt to pay the vet bills.' Ginny flicked through Aunt Flora's little notebook before looking across at Poppy. 'I'm right, aren't I?'

'And she's remortgaging her cottage?' Susan looked at the sheet of paper detailing the remortgaging process and clasped her hand over her mouth.

'That's why you were so off with Mack, isn't it?' Alex waved the letters in front of him. 'You blame him.'

'Oh.' Percy rubbed his hand over his face.

'It's hardly Mack's fault that Flora tripped, though. Despite all of this.' Sitting down, Susan leaned towards Ginny and indicated the notebook. 'Mack didn't *make* her fall.'

'The battery has been dodgy for a while.' Ginny lowered the notebook and looked at her. 'If Flora had had the money, she would have replaced it. That's what you're thinking, isn't it, Poppy?'

Poppy shifted on her feet. It didn't feel right to share them. She knew her aunt would be mortified if, or more likely when, she found out Poppy had shown the others her bills, disclosed how much in debt she was in, but it was for the best. She knew in her heart it was. It shouldn't just be Aunt Flora's problem. They all cared for the dogs and if they couldn't solve this, if Wagging Tails had to close... She shuddered. It would break her aunt's heart. If they could share the problem, the worries, maybe, just maybe, they could stop this ever happening again. She nodded. 'You're all right. Flora has been taking out same-day loans to pay for the vet treatment and if Mack had honoured Gavin's wishes and continued with the same arrangement, she wouldn't have taken out those loans, she wouldn't be thinking of remortgaging her cottage and she wouldn't have tripped over the jump leads and broken her leg, because she'd have had enough money in the charity account to replace the van's battery.'

Her voice was flat. She'd done all the crying she had in her last night. After the way she'd spoken to Mack, she'd been on autopilot until she'd got back to the cottage. A few hours of more tears and questioning everything and she'd been ready to face the problem, ready to try to find a solution.

She looked around the small kitchen. Everybody was silent. Still taking it all in, still looking at the debt letters on the table.

Percy coughed. 'We'll figure something out. I can remortgage my house. Or downsize. Never much liked it anyway.'

'I have some savings. And I can ask Malcolm if he has any.' Susan flapped the letter in her hand.

'And I have my credit card. I can even open a couple of zero interest ones.' Ginny nodded.

'Me too. I'll apply now.' Alex pulled his mobile from his back pocket.

'No, no. I've not brought all this here so you feel you have to pay it off. I just wanted you to all be aware of what's been happening. Of the position Wagging Tails is in. So we can make sure nothing like this ever happens again.'

'That's why Flora's been so quiet recently.' Sally shook her head sadly. 'Why didn't she tell us? We could have helped.'

'You know Flora. She's always been the last person to ask for help.' Percy sighed before looking across at Poppy. 'Let us help, love. Between us, we can get this cleared.'

Poppy shook her head. 'It's fine. I've come up with a solution, but going forward, we need to work something out. We need to raise some money. When Mr Thomas relinquishes those dogs, we're likely to have more vet bills.'

'I feel so useless. I knew something was wrong. She's been so preoccupied recently and then all that bother with the charity debit card. I should have put two and two together.' Ginny pinched the bridge of her nose. 'Poor Flora having to deal with all of this...' She indicated the letters and bills strewn across the table. 'I should have figured it out. I could have helped. We could have helped.'

'Don't blame yourself. If anyone is to blame, it's me.' Susan looked down at the letter she was holding. 'Flora confided in me that she was worried about the vet bills but when I tried to push her for details, she just told me not to worry, that it was all in hand. I should have questioned her, I should have...'

'I didn't work it out either, not until I found these last night. And I've been living with her. She's so good at hiding her worries.' Poppy reached out and rubbed Ginny's forearm. 'But now we need to focus on how we stop this ever happening again. How we make sure we'll be able to pay for any future bills.'

'I suppose you're right.' Ginny began to bundle up the letters. 'I'll speak to Freya. I know her surgery is over an hour away and Flora didn't want to take the dogs that far, but we can see if she'd be happy to treat the dogs she can – who are okay travelling and for non-emergencies.'

'Good idea. I'll draw up some Christmas cards to sell,' Alex suggested with a weak smile. 'I know we've only got another few days until Christmas, but every little helps, right? We might get some sales... I bet this is why we've not got a Christmas tree here this year. I did wonder.' He sighed dramatically.

Poppy gripped the edge of the table as more ideas came flooding out – Sally raising money through training sessions, Susan arranging a sponsored dog walk. She closed her eyes. Aunt Flora had all of these people surrounding her, people who cared both for her and the dogs they rescued. Why hadn't she spoken to them earlier? Why had Aunt Flora buried the problem? Always worrying about others and never herself.

Poppy slumped back in her chair, a wave of sadness sweeping over her.

'Poppy, love, you said you had a plan to pay off the debts?' Percy asked. 'I am more than happy to raise the cash.' He patted her hand.

Poppy looked down at her nails, picking off the fresh nail varnish she'd applied days before and straightened her back. She wasn't sure how the others would react to what she was going to tell them. But whatever they said she'd made up her mind and nothing they said would change that. 'I... umm... Don't be mad at me, but Ben is buying me out of the house and I'm going to use that money to pay off the debts. You know how much Wagging Tails means to me, and how much Flora has helped and supported me my whole life so I'm happy to do this and I've made up my mind so please don't try to talk me out of it because it won't work.' There, she'd said it. She slumped back against her chair again.

'I thought it was on the market? Is he buying you out now?' Ginny looked across at her.

'Yes.' Poppy nodded. 'He's moving his girlfriend in.'

Ginny blinked, her eyes widening. 'Seriously? That's quick.'

Poppy shrugged. 'I think he is anyway.'

She'd ring and speak with her friend Melissa. She'd know if he was but it didn't matter. Ben was the least of her worries now.

'I don't know what Flora will say about your plan, love, but I admire you for offering.' Percy leaned back in his chair and stroked his beard.

Poppy nodded. She knew she'd have a fight on her hands to get Aunt Flora to accept, but it was a fight she wasn't willing to lose.

* * *

'Great. Thank you, I'll make sure someone gets back to you as soon as possible.' Poppy put the phone down in its cradle and turned to Ginny who was checking off the Walk List. 'That was Patricia, a woman living over in Trestow, ringing up enquiring about Fluffles. She saw Darryl's write-up in the newspaper and wants to come and meet her.'

'Wow, that's brilliant. Did she sound nice?' Ginny put the clipboard back on its hook.

'Yes, she did. We could do with a little good news after all that's happened.' Poppy picked up a pen and scribbled Patricia's details down in the notebook. 'I said someone would get back to her. Is that okay? I haven't dealt with an adoption in so long I wasn't really sure what to say.'

'Yes, of course. I'll give her a call back and go through our requirements. And then hopefully we can arrange a meet-up and a home check.' Ginny grinned.

'Thank you.' Poppy passed the notebook across the counter to Ginny just as the bell above the door tinkled. Looking up, she froze. It was Mack. She wasn't ready for this. Ready to tell him what she thought of him. Not yet.

'Hi.' Shutting the door behind him, Mack paused.

'Right, I'll go and give Patricia a call now.' Ginny raised her hand to Mack before grabbing the notebook and phone and disappearing into the kitchen.

'Thanks.' Poppy picked up the closest thing to her – a clipboard – and walked towards the door, stepping around Mack as though he wasn't there.

'Poppy, have you got a moment?' Turning, Mack followed her out into the courtyard.

'I don't, sorry. I have to...' She looked down at the clipboard in her hands. It was the stock list. 'I have to check the stock.' She changed direction and walked towards the storage shed.

'Just a moment. That's all I'm asking.'

Looking ahead, she paused. She could hear the confusion in his voice.

'Please. I don't understand what's happened between us. One moment everything was going really well. Or so I thought. And the next... at the hospital...'

She shook her head and carried on walking, picking up her pace. 'You really don't get it, do you? You really don't understand what you've done.'

'What I've done? No, tell me.' He jogged to catch her up, stopping just in front of her.

Pausing again, she looked at him. He didn't look as though he'd had much sleep either. She glanced down at the ground before looking him in the eye. 'I just can't do this right now.'

'Hey, I know you're worried about Flora. Let me support you. Let me be there for you.' He reached out and touched her forearm.

Jerking her arm away, she stepped back. 'Please. I just need some space. I need time to think.'

'Space? From me?' He shifted on his feet. 'I thought things were going well between us?'

'They were.'

'Then what's changed?'

'Everything.' Holding the clipboard to her chest, she turned around.

'Poppy? Speak to me. Explain what's going on.'

Closing her eyes momentarily, she tried to suppress the anger rising in the pit of her stomach. She knew it was irrational. She knew he didn't realise what was going on, but there was nothing she could do. She just couldn't hold it in any longer. Twisting around, she glared at him. 'This. All of this... the debt, Aunt Flora being in hospital... it's your fault. You're to blame.'

She could hear his gasp as he stopped in his tracks. His face falling.

'I'm sorry. I shouldn't have said anything. Forget it.' She waved her words away. She'd hurt him.

'I... My fault. How is it my fault Flora is in hospital? What debts?'

Looking down at the ground, she kicked at a piece of frozen snow too stubborn to melt, and mumbled, 'She'd taken out a load of same-day loans. She's up to her eyes in debt. She was going to remortgage the cottage to pay them off.'

'Same-day loans?' Mack rubbed his hand over his face.

Poppy nodded. 'That's why she hadn't replaced the battery in he van. Why she tripped over the jump leads.'

'But how can you blame me?'

She took a deep breath. 'She's in debt because you wouldn't

keep up Gavin's agreement to discount the vet bills. She wouldn't have fallen over the jump leads if it wasn't for you.' There, she'd said it. She couldn't have spelled it out any clearer. She turned and began walking away again.

'Because I hadn't given the home a discount?' He swallowed, his Adam's apple bulging in his throat. 'I couldn't. I can't. You know why I couldn't.'

Spinning around on her heels, she faced him once more. 'Do I though? You have the money. More than enough money. You no longer have to worry about providing for your brothers. You know you can. All you needed to do was to give your time up for free and we wouldn't have gotten into this mess.' Seeing he was about to speak, she held her hands up in front of her, palms forward, the clipboard knocking her chin as she did so. 'Please don't come up with any excuses. You drive around in an expensive car, you were willing to spend hundreds on a stupid little bag for Kerry – hundreds on a make-up bag – and your clients include celebrities. I know you have the money so don't try to tell me otherwise.'

'I won't. You're right, I do. But you also know why I try to be careful with it. You know my past.' He spoke quietly.

'Don't. Just don't.' She'd heard enough. She did know his past but she also knew he had the ability to choose where and how to spend his money and if he could be willing to spend hundreds on a little bag without thinking twice then it was his priorities he had wrong. Nothing else. 'You have the money. It's your priorities you've got wrong.'

'Poppy, please?'

She turned away and walked the last few metres towards the storage shed. She could hear the pain in his voice. Perhaps the realisation that she was right? Perhaps just a lack of understanding? She wasn't sure but she couldn't turn to face him again. She couldn't see the hurt etched across his face. The hurt she was causing him.

30

Poppy looked in the mirror and dabbed another layer of concealer over the dark circles beneath her eyes. She didn't want Aunt Flora worrying about her. She'd already asked why she looked so tired yesterday when Poppy had picked her up from the hospital. Her aunt didn't need to know that Poppy hadn't slept again last night.

Putting the concealer back down, she loaded her make-up brush with powder before dropping it halfway to her face. Sighing, she looked down. A fine dust of powder had covered the items on the dressing table, the rest of her make-up, her hairbrush, her mobile... the snow globe Mack had given her.

She picked it up and perched on the bed. She pulled the sleeve of her cardigan over her hand and wiped it, the face powder transferring from plastic to fabric. Gently tipping the globe upside down, she righted it again and watched the tiny balls of 'snow' float back down, covering the reindeer with his beady eyes and smiling mouth and the grass around him. Some Christmas this was turning out to be. So much for Mack telling her that it was the season for kindness.

Throwing herself back, sinking into the thick duvet, she pulled Aunt Flora's crocheted blanket over her head. She missed him.

She held the snow globe above her head, making a little tent under the blanket. She'd felt something for him that day. She'd believed that what they had together could be something special. Why had she let herself feel that way? So quickly? And so soon after Ben? She'd come down to Cornwall to get away from a failed relationship and all the issues that surrounded it, and she'd walked straight into another one. From one failed relationship to another.

She scoffed at herself. What was she even thinking? She could hardly describe what she'd had with Mack as a relationship. They'd hardly known each other. It had been more like a fling. Not even that.

The quiet beep of her phone signalled a message. Wiping her eyes dry, she sat up and picked up her phone, the snow globe still in her other hand.

She rolled her eyes. It was as though he knew she was thinking about him. It was Mack. She dismissed it without reading it. She didn't want to hear from him. She didn't want to remember the expression on his face when she'd confronted him. To feel the guilt she did for blaming him. Yes, it was his fault, but it hadn't been intentional. He hadn't known what had been going on, just as she hadn't. None of them had. Standing up, she shoved the snow globe in a drawer and went downstairs.

* * *

'Are you following me, hey?' Poppy shoved the last of the dog bedding into the washing machine and looked down at Dougal who was sitting by her feet.

'You've got a real soft spot for little Dougal, haven't you?' Ginny said.

'I have.' Poppy picked him up and cuddled him. 'He's just such a gorgeous little soul.'

'He is.' Smiling, Ginny nodded to the kettle. 'Do you want one? I've just come in from walking Ralph and it's absolutely freezing out there.'

'Oh yes, please. I need to go and walk Alfie and Oscar, and after that, go over and get Flora some lunch.'

'I popped by earlier. She seemed okay. Frustrated at not being able to do much but happy to be home from the hospital.'

'Yes, she is. She's been talking about hobbling over here to help, but I keep telling her to give herself a bit of a break. I don't want her to do too much and end up back in hospital needing her leg reset or something.' She looked over at Ginny. 'You didn't mention anything, did you?'

'About the debts? Of course not.'

'Thanks. I will talk to her about it all, I just haven't found the right moment yet.'

'I understand. I won't say anything.' Ginny poured the water from the kettle, the coffee granules quickly dissolving and emitting their bitter aroma.

'I have a plan to keep her occupied and to rest up at the same time though, and it involves this little one.' Poppy fussed Dougal's ears. 'I'm going to pop him over at lunchtime. He hates being in his kennel and Flora hates being over there without the dogs, so I thought they could go to her. Or Dougal to begin with, anyway.'

'That's a good idea.' Ginny grinned.

'I figure it will help them both.'

'Have you heard from Mack again?' Ginny asked as she passed Poppy a mug.

'It depends what you mean by "heard from".' Poppy sighed. 'He's been messaging and ringing but I've not read any texts he's sent or listened to any voicemails.'

Sitting down, Ginny indicated the chair opposite for Poppy. 'It's difficult, isn't it? I mean, I understand why you feel as though Flora's fall was his fault, but he didn't plan for any of this to happen.'

Poppy sat down, placing Dougal on her lap. 'I know, but he knew that Wagging Tails is a charity. He could have offered us something, even a discount, anything. I just don't understand how he can be so self-centred. Did I tell you that he's planning on giving Kerry, the receptionist at the surgery, a prize he won in a raffle for Christmas? A one-pound prize.' She rolled her eyes. 'Although before he won that, he'd been happy to spend hundreds on a little scrap of a make-up bag for her.'

'I didn't know that.' Ginny shifted in her chair. 'I guess he's got his brothers to provide for, though.'

'Yes, but all it would have cost him to help Wagging Tails was to give up his time. He could have carried on Gavin's agreement and charged for medication and all that still.'

Ginny nodded. 'Are you going to speak to him? He might have an explanation.'

Poppy shrugged. 'I did. I spoke to him yesterday when he came over and I told him what I thought of him.' She shifted in her chair. 'And to be honest, all I feel is guilt now. Me. For telling him I blamed him.'

'Oh. I guess...'

'Hello?' A voice wafted in through the open door from the reception area.

'Paige, is that you? Coming.' Ginny called out before standing up and leaving the kitchen.

Poppy followed her.

'Hi, Ginny. Hi, Poppy. How's Flora doing?'

Poppy smiled. 'She's okay, thanks. Frustrated with not being able to get out and about as normal, but glad to be out of hospital.'

'I bet.'

'Thank you so much again for everything you did the other day.'

'My pleasure. Just glad to hear she's on the mend. And lovely to properly meet you.' Paige hugged her.

'And you. Did you want a coffee?' She indicated the kitchen door.

'No, I'd better not. Thank you though. I've just popped by to give Flora this. I went to the cottage, but there was no answer.' Paige held up a gold gate link charm bracelet. 'Me and Pat found it in the ambulance. I'm sure it's Flora's?'

'Yes, it is. Thank you.' Poppy took the bracelet and ran the pad of her forefinger over it. 'Uncle Arthur gave it to her on their wedding day.'

'Oh wow, glad to be able to reunite her with it then.'

Poppy looked down at the bracelet and smiled. Flora would be relieved to have it back.

'How's your day been then?' Ginny leaned her elbows on the counter just as the bell above the door tinkled again and a blast of cold air entered the room.

'Hi.'

She recognised that voice. She kept her head bowed, pretending to be transfixed by the bracelet in her hand.

'Mack, hi.' Ginny nodded at him.

'Hi, Paige. Hi, Ginny. Poppy.' Mack's voice was quiet, unsure.

'Oh, Paige, come on through and I'll get you that coffee now.' Ginny's voice was forcibly bright as she ushered Paige through to the kitchen.

'Right, of course. Thanks, I'm parched.'

Poppy knew what they were doing. She knew Ginny hadn't suddenly forgotten that Paige had declined the offer of a coffee. She closed her eyes for a moment. There was no way out of this situation, was there?

Then she looked across at him, her heart sinking as she watched him shift on his feet. They'd been so good together.

'Poppy, please, just let me explain.' He cleared his throat. 'How's Flora today?'

'As fine as she can be after having surgery on a broken leg.'

Mack winced. 'I feel so guilty. I understand why you blame me, but I never, ever intended anything like this to happen. I never once thought...'

'Whether you intended anything or not, you as good as pulled that jump lead from beneath her.' Poppy's voice was low. She watched as his face fell. She was right. She was. So why did she feel guilty telling him so? She'd been too harsh. He'd never intended any of this. No one could have foreseen what had happened, but she could still feel the anger inside her bubbling up. Rightly or wrongly.

'I...' Mack reached behind him and rubbed his neck. 'I didn't know about the debt. I didn't realise what was going on. I'm sorry. I didn't think my decisions would have such an effect on Wagging Tails. On Flora.'

'Didn't you? What did you expect then? You know Wagging Tails is a charity.'

'I know. I know. You were right yesterday. I've made a lot of wrong choices regarding the money I've spent. Maybe I should have done more to help but I've always had to be so careful with money and even now I struggle to...'

'Be kind? To make the right choices. You're happy to spend your cash on ridiculously expensive cars and presents but you can't bring yourself to give a couple of hours of your time up to a charity?'

'No, no.' His jaw flinched, his voice cracking as he spoke. 'Is that what you think of me?'

'I don't even know what to think any more, if I'm honest.' She didn't. She just didn't understand him, his motives, anything. How could he act like the kindest man in the world, only to be so callous and selfish when it came to money? She shook her head. That wasn't fair. He wasn't selfish or callous, just... 'I have to go and get Flora her lunch.'

And with that, she scooped Dougal up and walked outside.

31

'Oh, Poppy. What a lovely idea. Thank you so much for bringing Dougal over.' Flora pushed her empty lunch plate across the coffee table and patted her lap for him to jump up.

'I thought you might like some company. Do you want to keep him over here for the afternoon? He gets so upset in his kennel.'

'I'd love him over here.' She turned to Dougal. 'Are you going to keep me company, yes?'

'Aw, he looks so happy to be back in a proper home.' Poppy fussed Dougal before standing up from the sofa.

'I've had a fair bit of company today. Percy, Susan, Ginny, Alex. Elsie from the bakery popped over too and brought me that bunch of flowers over there.' Flora pointed to a vase brimming with amaryllis standing on the window ledge.

'They're lovely.'

'Yes, they are, aren't they? She said they're her favourite winter flower and whenever she sees them, they make her smile. They go nicely with the tulips you brought me last week, don't they?' She nodded towards the vase in the middle of the coffee table. 'You bought them that day you ran into Mack in Trestow, didn't you?'

Poppy shrugged. 'I don't remember.'

She did.

'That's one person who hasn't popped by. Mack. Do you know why, by any chance?'

Poppy looked across at Flora. Had one of the others said something? They must have. They would have.

'That's a good thing, then.' The last thing Poppy wanted was for Mack to somehow let something slip about the debt. Not before she'd had the chance to speak to her aunt herself.

Flora frowned. 'Percy mentioned you'd had a bit of a set to at the hospital. I hope you haven't really fallen out over me? You were getting on so well.'

Poppy looked down at her nails. She should have painted them again. At least then she'd have something to focus on. She picked at her cuticles.

'Poppy, lovely, what's going on?'

She swallowed, still focusing on her hands. 'I found the debt letters,' she mumbled before glancing up at Flora. She still felt awful for finding them, even if it was by accident and even if it was the best thing she could have done. 'I wasn't snooping or anything. I'd never do that, but I saw them when I picked out the pyjamas I took to you at the hospital.'

Flora nodded.

Poppy leaned back against the sofa cushions and looked at her aunt. 'I'm sorry.'

'No, lovely. I'm sorry. I'm sorry you had to find them. I'm sorry to have got myself in such a pickle.' She patted Poppy's leg and sighed.

'Don't be. I just wish you'd have told me, us. Maybe we could have done something.'

'I'm normally so careful when it comes to our finances. I keep he money for Wagging Tails separate from Arthur's pension. This ime, though, I just didn't know what else to do.' She glanced across at Poppy and gave her a quick smile. 'Things will be all right, though. I'll sort it out.'

'Please don't remortgage this place. This is your home.'

'Ack, it's a building. My home is over there with all those dogs. It always has been. If they won't remortgage this place, I'll sell it and get myself a cosy little static caravan. I'll be happy over in the court-yard. Closer.'

'Aunt Flora, you don't need to remortgage and you don't need to sell.'

'I need to do something, lovely, but it's my worry, not yours. I don't want you to go worrying about it.'

'You don't need to worry about it, either. Ben's buying me out. I'm going to use the money to pay off the debts.'

'What? No, no, you won't. You'll need that for when you go back home, you'll need a deposit to put down for your own place.' Flora shook her head 'And what do you mean Ben's buying you out? I thought the house was on the market?'

'It was, but he's decided to stay, to move Davina in. I think at least.' She still hadn't rung Melissa to find out the truth, but it all felt somehow irrelevant now. She was past caring.

Flora's eyes widened. 'So, all this time when he's been telling you he couldn't afford to pay your half of the mortgage, she's been living there?'

Poppy shrugged. She hadn't thought about it like that, but Aunt Flora was probably right. He may have already moved her in.

'Maybe, but it's done now. Anyway, I've been thinking I might hang around here a while, anyway. Start doing some supply work in Trestow maybe, or in one of the villages. I can stay here while I save up for a deposit. If you'll have me, that is?'

'If I'll have you?' Flora grinned. 'Of course I'll have you. It's been wonderful having you to stay. The only part of that plan I'll be putting my foot down to is the part you say you'll pay off my debts.'

'They're not just your debts, though. You're in debt for the dogs. Please, just take it. It makes so much sense.' Poppy squeezed Aunt Flora's hand.

'I can't do that, lovely. It's a beautiful gesture, but it would be wrong of me.'

'No, it wouldn't. Besides, if you end up selling this place, then where am I going to live?'

Flora chuckled. 'I'm sure I can find room for you in my caravan.'

'No. This is your home. You deserve a home. You've dedicated your whole life to Wagging Tails, to the dogs.'

Flora shook her head slowly. 'Let's just see if we can come up with another solution? Yes?'

'Okay. But if not, you'll take it. Won't you?' Poppy looked at her. She had to. What other solution was there?

'Sit on it a while and we'll talk about it again.'

'Do you promise?' She couldn't let her aunt bury her head in the sand again. That was why they were in the mess they were.

'Like I said. Give me a bit of time to think things through.' Flora turned her attention back to Dougal, the conversation about the money over. 'There is something I want to talk about now though.'

'What?' Poppy perched on the arm of the sofa.

Leaning forward, Flora took an abandoned crust of bread from her plate and gave it to Dougal. Then, turning back to Poppy, Flora raised her eyebrow. 'You still haven't told me why you had a falling out with Mack.'

Poppy frowned. She wasn't going to get away with not answering, was she? She took a deep breath.

'Because if it wasn't for him breaking Gavin's agreement with Wagging Tails, you'd have had the money to buy a new battery for the van and you wouldn't have...'

She gestured to Flora's leg cast.

Flora shook her head. 'You can't blame this on Mack. The only person to blame for breaking my leg was me. I wasn't concentrating and tripped over the jump lead. That has zero to do with him.'

'No, it doesn't. You probably weren't concentrating because you were worried about the debt.'

'I wasn't worried about the debt.' Flora shifted position on the sofa, gently holding Dougal so as not to disturb him. 'By then I'd decided to remortgage or sell up the cottage. I was worried about Mr Thomas and his animals.'

Poppy frowned. 'But if you'd had the money, you would have had the battery changed already.'

'Maybe. Maybe not. You know me, if something's not completely broken, I won't fix it. Money or no money, I'd have likely kept jump-starting the van for as long as it'd allow me to.'

Poppy fussed Dougal's ears.

'Poppy, lovely, and I mean this in the nicest possible way, but I think you're self-sabotaging your relationship with Mack because you're scared to get into another relationship. Mack isn't like Ben. Mack is one of the good guys.'

Poppy shifted position. Her aunt was right. She knew that. Deep down she knew Mack was one of the good guys but... She shook her head. 'If he is one of the good guys, he'd have given up his time for free to treat the dogs rather than charge full price.'

Flora sighed. 'Mack's had it rough over the last few years. And I mean really rough.'

'I know. He told me about his dad leaving him with Gus and Spencer and how hard it was for him to get through vet school whilst trying to care for them, too.'

Flora patted Poppy's leg. 'It wasn't just hard for him. It nearly damn well broke the lad. Did he tell you that he literally didn't have two pennies to rub together? Did he explain that they lost their home?'

Poppy looked down at her hands. When he'd said it had been

difficult, she'd assumed he'd meant they hadn't been able to afford luxuries.

'No, he didn't.'

'I didn't think he would have. If it weren't for his neighbour at the time, Mrs Moreton, taking them in, he'd have given up and gone back to his old job. He'd been halfway through his vet studies when his dad left.' Flora took Poppy's hand. 'You see, when you've been through losing your home and had the fear of those little kids being taken off you and put into care, you tend to think about things differently. Surely you can understand why he'd be so worried about losing money, can't you, lovely?'

Poppy watched as Dougal jumped down and stretched out on the floor, rolling onto his back, his belly towards the fire.

'But it wasn't about money. He just needed to spare some time to see the dogs.'

'When you're a vet, like him, time is money. He's just trying to protect his little family, his brothers.'

Poppy nodded. 'I guess so. But he's happy to spend his money on expensive things. Things he doesn't need.'

'Yes, but they're one-offs. If he were to sign up to help us free of charge, where would it stop? We might have dogs in which could potentially cost him thousands. Him spending his money on extravagant things is just that, things. If he got into bother with money somehow, he could stop spending out on them or sell them to raise money. Helping out a charity is completely different. It's a commitment. Besides, it's not just the money for the vet bills we've lost. If it had only been that, we would have coped. One of our sponsors has pulled out. Their business is struggling and they've had to cut all the corners they can just to be able to pay the staff.'

'What? When did this happen? Why didn't you say anything?'

'A couple of months ago now. I kept it to myself because I knew you'd worry. That you'd all worry.' Flora fussed Dougal behind the ears. 'Besides I had it under control.'

Poppy sighed. 'You didn't.' If she'd known the debts weren't all down to now having to pay the vet bills, she wouldn't have held Mack as accountable as she had. She'd been so awful to him.

Poppy looked down at her hands. Standing up from the arm of the sofa, she sat back down next to Flora and held her hands over her face. 'I've been so horrible to him, haven't I?'

'No, you haven't, lovely. Nothing of the sort. You've just reacted to what's been put in front of you. The facts you had at the time.'

'What do I do now?'

'Well, I'd ask you how you feel about him, but it's pretty clear to everyone what he means to you, so I'd pop over and pay him a visit. See if you can sort things out.'

Poppy nodded. Yes, she had to. She needed to set things straight. Even though she couldn't expect him to forgive her, she could apologise. She could try.

32

'Next please?'

Poppy stepped towards the reception desk. 'Hi, Kerry.'

'Poppy, isn't it? From Wagging Tails. Who do you have with you?' Kerry looked down at her computer screen. 'I wasn't aware we were seeing any of your dogs today.'

'I'm here to see Mack. For just a moment.' She held her thumb and forefinger a centimetre apart.

Kerry leaned over the counter to look at the floor, checking to see if she had a dog with her. 'You're on your own. Where's the patient?'

'There isn't one. I just need to see Mack. I need to have a quick word with him. Please?' Poppy tucked her hair behind her ear. 'It'll only take five minutes. One minute. Whatever you can spare. Please?'

'I'm afraid even for animal care advice, you need to have made an appointment.'

'But... I only need a couple of minutes.'

'As much as I'd love to let you through, I'd have a riot on my hands if I did.' Kerry indicated the waiting room; two women were chatting amongst themselves whilst stopping every so often to coo into cat carrier; and a man scrolled on his mobile, his dog lying at his feet. The only person who seemed to be aware of the time was a man typing hurriedly into a laptop propped on his knee and he seemed to be busy trying to finish something before his appointment. Besides, his dog seemed happy enough staring and tormenting the cat in the carrier.

'But...' Poppy blinked back the tears which had been threatening to fall ever since Flora had explained everything. She just needed to see him. Whether he forgave her or not, she needed to apologise, tell him she understood.

'Look, the best I can do for you is to let the vet know you're here after his last appointment.' Kerry held her hands up, palms forward.

Glancing at the clock, Poppy sighed. It was only three. She'd have to wait at least three hours until the surgery closed.

'We're closing early today. At four. Mack has an important personal appointment to attend.' Kerry glanced behind Poppy and pointed her pen. 'If you're waiting, please take a seat. I have people with animals to book in.'

'Right, yes. Thanks.' Nodding, Poppy walked towards the far end of the waiting room and sat down on one of the hard plastic chairs. Then she'd wait.

* * *

'He'll be coming through in a moment.' Kerry nodded towards Poppy as she shrugged into her coat, turned off the Christmas music which had been playing and dimmed the waiting room lights.

'Thank you.' Standing up, Poppy moved and sat on the chair closest to the treatment room.

'You're welcome.'

Poppy watched as Kerry wrapped her scarf around her neck and stepped out into the cold. He would be coming out any second now. She looked down at her trainers. Was she ready? After almost an hour and a half of waiting, she was still no closer to knowing what exactly she was going to say to him.

She stood up and walked to the window. Kerry's car had left now, leaving only Mack's and Flora's in the otherwise empty car park. It was almost pitch black already. Strange to think a few short weeks ago, it would still be light at this time of the afternoon.

'Poppy?'

Turning on her heels, she looked towards him.

'Sorry, I didn't know you were waiting. I would have come out sooner.'

Kerry hadn't told him? She understood it wouldn't have been right of Kerry to let her through to speak to him in front of his patients but she'd assumed she would have mentioned she'd been waiting. She blinked. It didn't matter now. He was here, in front of her.

'What can I do for you? Is Dougal okay? The other dogs?' He furrowed his brow.

'Yes, yes, they're fine. All fine. It's me. I wanted to see you. To apologise.' She glanced at the floor.

Mack indicated the chairs. 'Shall we?'

Nodding, Poppy sat down, the hard plastic immediately cutting into the back of her knees.

'You have nothing to apologise for. I do.'

She looked up at him as he sat, placed his rucksack on the floor by his feet and draped his coat over his knees.

'You don't. Flora's just told me that one of the home's sponsors pulled out a while back. The home had money troubles before you'd even taken over Gavin's business.'

'I do. Even if the sponsor had pulled out, I could have lessened the impact. Not added to it. You were right. I as good as put Flora in that hospital.' He leaned his head back against the wall and closed his eyes. 'I did that.'

'No, no, you didn't. I should never have blamed you. That's why I'm here. To apologise.'

'No, you're right. I was selfish. If Flora hadn't been worrying about money, then she would have changed the battery. She wouldn't have needed to jump-start the van.'

'I spoke to her. She wasn't worried about the money. She was distracted thinking about Mr Thomas and his animals. She didn't trip because she was worried about the debt. She'd already decided to remortgage or sell the cottage and buy a caravan by then.' Poppy shifted on the chair. 'And she also said she would have eked out the battery as long as she could have, whether she'd had the money to replace it or not.'

'She was going to sell her home? Because of the vet bills?' Leaning forward, Mack rested his elbows on his knees and dipped his head.

'Flora told me about your past. About what happened after Gus and Spencer were left with you.' She laid her hand on his back. 'She told me about you losing your home.'

Mack rubbed the palm of his hand across his face. 'That's no excuse. I should understand more than anyone then, shouldn't I? How precious money is?'

'No, you were looking out for your brothers. I understand why you felt you couldn't keep Gavin's agreement going.'

'You do? Because from where I'm sitting now, I don't. I've been selfish.' He took a deep breath. 'I guess I just can't seem to move past that fear of having nothing, of struggling to provide for Gus and Spencer. I need to learn that things have changed now, that can afford to give up some of my time. Just as Gavin did.'

Poppy tucked her finger under his chin, gently turning his head towards her. 'Can you forgive me for blaming you? For speaking to you the way I did?'

Mack gave her a quick, small smile. 'Can you forgive *me*?'

Nodding, she looked away and took a deep breath before meeting his gaze once more. 'I really feel something for you, Mack.'

'Same here.' He nodded. 'May I?' He placed his hand at the nape of her neck, his skin warm against hers.

She leaned towards him, until their lips touched...

Mack's mobile pinged, piercing the silence, and he pulled away. He looked at it and frowned.

'I'm so sorry, I'm going to have to go.'

He ran his fingers through his hair, the lines between his eyes deepening. Sighing, he leaned his head back against the wall. He'd said he had to go but it was clearly not an appointment he was looking forward to.

'Don't worry. Is everything okay?'

'I'm not sure. I'm meeting my dad to see what he wants from us.'

Standing up, Poppy held out her hand. 'I'll come with you.'

Mack swallowed. 'You'd do that for me?'

'Of course I will. I'll wait in the car.'

Leaning down, she kissed him before taking his hand and pulling him up.

33

'Again, Flora, I'm so sorry that I've caused so many problems.' Mack looked at Flora, across the kitchen table at Wagging Tails.

'As I've already said, you're not to blame. For any of it. You were never under any obligation to give your expertise away for free and I would never expect it of anyone.'

'Still, I feel to blame. Partly anyway.'

'Mack, you can't control things out of your control. I'm sure Poppy has told you by now but a sponsor recently pulled out. There are so many reasons we're in the mess we're in and that's down to me, not you or the sponsor. No one else. Besides, if you try to apologise again, lovely, I'll make you do all the washing up for the next year.' Flora chuckled.

'I don't blame you.' Looking down into his coffee mug, Mack raked his fingers through his hair. 'I really am sorry. If I hadn't charged you, if I'd just continued with Gavin's agreement, you wouldn't have ended up under so much stress and in debt.'

'Mack, as I've told you a hundred times before, when you bought Gavin out of the surgery, you were under absolutely no obligation to continue treating our dogs without charge. If we' taken them anywhere else, it would have been the same. You were simply doing your job.' Flora took a sip of her coffee. 'This isn't down to you. It's my job to balance the bills.'

'I still feel awful, though. I just struggled to get past everything...' His voice trailed off.

'You've been through a lot with those boys and they deserve the best start in life possible. Don't ever feel guilty for doing just that.' Flora shifted in her chair.

'Do you want another chair to put your leg up on?' Without waiting for an answer, Mack dragged a chair closer to Flora and helped her to settle. 'I won't be charging for treatment any more, though.'

'Thanks, lovely.' Flora picked up her mug again. 'Now, you only offer that if you can, and if you want to. Not because of this.' She indicated her leg. 'That had nothing to do with you.'

'No, I want to.' Mack nodded.

'Okay, lovely. Well, in that case, thank you. But we'll pay for medication and the like, just as we did with Gavin. I won't be a burden to anyone.'

'Yes, thank you.' Poppy leaned across and kissed Mack.

'It's a relief to see you two back together again.' Flora looked from Mack to Poppy and back again. 'You're right for each other.'

'I'm relieved too.' Mack took Poppy's hand and squeezed it.

'And how was everything with your dad?' Flora looked at Mack over her mug. 'Tell me if I'm being too nosey.'

'No, no, it's fine.' Mack chuckled. 'It was... okay. He apologised for leaving the way he did and wants to start seeing Gus and Spencer.' Mack grimaced.

'You don't want him to?' Flora patted his hand.

'I don't know. I think it's important he does, yes, and his apology seemed to be sincere but it's just a lot. How can I trust him again? What if they get to know him and he runs off again?'

'What do you think you'll do?' Poppy looked across at him. He was in an impossible situation, trying to protect his brothers but also wanting them to get to know their father.

'I've agreed he can start visiting them. Slowly. At their pace and at mine. If he's serious about coming back into their lives, I figure he'll respect that.'

'You're right. He will.' Flora nodded and took a sip of her coffee.

The bell above the door into reception tinkled. 'Hello. Anyone about?'

'I'll go and see who it is.' Gulping down the last of the dregs of her coffee, Poppy pushed her chair back and headed out into the reception area. 'Hi. How can I help you?'

'Hi, I'm Nick from the Christmas tree farm over by Penworth Bay. Paige is a friend of mine and she mentioned you didn't have a Christmas tree over here? So, I've brought one over for you. I hope you don't mind?'

'Nick? Is that you?' Flora's voice filtered out from the kitchen. 'Come on through, lovely.'

Poppy indicated Nick to go through.

'Hello, Flora. How are you feeling?' he asked as he bent down and hugged Flora.

'Oh, I'll be as right as rain soon enough. You know Mack, and this is my niece, Poppy.'

'Hello, Nick, mate.' Standing up Mack gave Nick a hug, patting him on the back.

Nick turned to Poppy. 'Lovely to meet you, Poppy.'

'And you.' Poppy smiled back.

'Now, what's all this talk about a Christmas tree?' Flora tapped Nick on the hand.

'I got talking to Paige at the pub quiz yesterday evening and she mentioned you didn't have a Christmas tree, so I thought I'd bring you one over.'

'Oh, you didn't?'

Nick chuckled. 'I did. It's outside.'

'Poppy, lovely, pass me my crutches, would you?' Flora held out her hand.

'Sure.' She and Mack helped Flora to stand before they all followed Nick outside.

And there, sure enough, lying on the bed of his truck was a large Christmas tree.

'It's huge!' Flora paused to catch her breath.

'It is.' Nick nodded and began to unstrap it from the truck. 'Where do you want it?'

'Here, I'll give you a hand.' Mack joined Nick.

Flora looked back towards the reception before scanning their surroundings. 'How about right here, in the middle of the courtyard? I can imagine with a few lights on, it'll look quite spectacular.'

'Great idea.'

With Mack's help, Nick began to drag the tree into position.

'I'll go and get you a chair, Aunt Flora.'

* * *

'Help! I'm tangled! I'm completely tangled.' Alex shrieked with laughter as he attempted to unravel himself from the string of fairy lights.

'Hold still, Alex. You're making it worse.' Susan tutted as she began to unwind the wires from around his middle. 'Here, duck down.'

Doing as he was instructed, he ducked beneath a wire. 'I'm still tangled. I'm going to be here forever. Strung up like some reindeer bauble.'

Poppy laughed as she ran to help. 'You might well be if you don't keep twisting that way.'

'There you go. Free as a bird.' Susan lowered the string of fairy lights, letting him step out.

'Thank you both, you're my saviours.' Alex planted a huge kiss on Poppy's cheek before turning to Susan.

'Don't you even think about it.' Laughing, Susan held up her hand.

'Oh, I do love you lot.' Flora chuckled and tucked her hands under the blanket over her knees.

'Can you take this end, Mack?' Standing on her tiptoes, Poppy took the end of the fairy lights and held them up to Mack, who was standing on the stepladder.

'Wow, it certainly does look festive.' Flora grinned. 'Come and take a look, lovelies.'

Poppy, Mack, Alex, Ginny, Percy, Sally and Susan all gathered around Flora and looked back at the tree.

'It certainly does.' Mack wrapped his arm around Poppy's waist, drawing her towards him and kissing the top of her head.

Smiling, Poppy closed her eyes. With the Christmas music playing from the radio and the Christmas tree in front of them, she almost felt festive herself.

'Oh, I've got an idea! Why don't we have Christmas carols around the tree? We could invite the public and serve hot choco-late? I can make some mince pies, too!' Susan clapped her hands.

'Oh, I love that idea.' Flora smiled.

'Yes, I can ask Darryl to pop something in the paper. When shall we do it?'

'How about Christmas Eve? That'll make sure there're a couple of days for word to get out and us to get organised with the supplies.' Percy stroked his beard.

'Good idea. That's decided then. Christmas carols and hot chocolate around the Christmas tree on Christmas Eve.' Flora beamed.

Poppy watched as everyone else hurried back inside to begin planning for the Christmas carol event and hung back, waiting for her aunt.

'Are you okay, love?' Standing up, Flora slipped her arms through the crutches.

'Yes.' Poppy picked up the chair Aunt Flora had been sitting on before looking across at her. 'I know you don't want to talk about it, but have you thought any more about letting me help out with the debts? I spoke to my friend Melissa earlier and Ben is moving Davina in with him.'

'I'm so sorry, lovely.' Flora paused.

'Oh no, it's a good thing. It means I can accept his offer and because she's buying the other half and she doesn't have a house to sell, I should get my half of the equity pretty soon, hopefully. We can be debt free.'

Aunt Flora set her jaw and looked ahead. 'I'm still not taking your money, Poppy, lovely. It's so very kind of you to offer but I haven't changed my mind. And I won't.'

Poppy sighed as they began walking towards the reception area again. 'But what's the alternative? You give up your home? I won't stand by and let that happen, Aunt Flora. I just won't. I'm happy to give you the money. I don't see the problem.'

'You have a good heart, my lovely. But it would be wrong of me to take it. If I remortgage I can cover the mortgage repayments with Arthur's pension. I will be just fine.'

'Umm.' Poppy shook her head. She wouldn't get her aunt to change her mind, but she could be there to help if things didn't work out the way her aunt hoped they would. She could keep hold of her money. Just in case.

'And don't you go taking some silly low offer just so you get the money quicker.' Flora nodded towards her. 'You insist on going by the estate agent's evaluation. You owe neither of them any favours and you have yourself to look out for. Your future, my lovely.'

'I won't.' Poppy swapped the chair to the other hand. Her aunt was right. She shouldn't accept Ben's silly low offer. She'd put as much into that house as he had.

34

Poppy placed another huge tub of hot chocolate powder next to the two hot water urns Darryl had borrowed from the newspaper office. 'That should be enough, shouldn't it?'

'Yes, I should think so.' Susan unwrapped a large tray full of mince pies.

'Wow, you've been busy.' Poppy grinned.

'Luckily, Malcolm offered to bake some too or else I'd only have half as much.' Susan unwrapped another tray.

'Is he coming tonight?'

'Malcom? Oh, yes.' She smiled. 'Is Mack still coming?'

Poppy nodded as she turned on the urns.

'And Gus and little Spencer?'

'Yes, but we haven't told them we're seeing each other yet.' The urn wasn't turning on. Poppy frowned and clicked the 'on' switch again.

'That's good then. It means there's no pressure on you both.'

'No, we both think it's for the best.' Rolling her eyes at herself, she noticed the plug wasn't in. 'This way we can all get to know each other and then tell them when the time's right.'

They both turned at a new voice in the room. 'Evening.'

Poppy grinned as Mack walked in, followed by Gus and Spencer and an older woman.

Mack introduced everybody, including the woman – his neighbour Mrs Moreton.

'So lovely to meet you all.' Poppy waved before pulling out some takeaway cups. 'Who fancies a hot chocolate?'

'Yes, please,' Gus said, taking some gum out of his mouth.

'How about you, Spencer?'

'Yes, please, but can I have it more milky?' The boy looked behind him. 'And can we turn the music up, please? Mack likes this one.'

Poppy grinned. 'Does he?'

Mack seemed to like every Christmas song going.

'I tell you what, boys,' Susan said. 'Why don't we go and set the radio up outside? That way, when everyone starts to arrive for the carols, they'll be able to hear the music.' And after their enthusiastic grins, she unwrapped the last of the trays of mince pies and led the way out of the kitchen, followed by Mrs Moreton who offered to take the two hot chocolates, now made, with her.

Poppy waited until Mrs Moreton had shut the door behind her before stepping towards Mack. 'I've got to ask; are there any Christmas songs you *don't* like?'

'Umm...' Mack tilted his head before looking at her. 'No, probably not.'

'I didn't think there would be.' Poppy laughed. 'Although, to be fair, most of them are quite catchy.'

Mack grinned as he tucked her hair behind her ear. 'Are you starting to enjoy Christmas now?'

Poppy shrugged and laughed. 'Maybe.' It was true, with family and friends around, maybe there was a little magic in the air. 'I'm looking forward to this, anyway.' She nodded towards the door.

'Me too.'

* * *

Holding the printed song sheet in her hand, Poppy grinned. Mack was standing on one side of her, Ginny and Darryl on the other and Aunt Flora was sitting on a chair in front of the group, Percy by her side. The glow from the fairy lights illuminated the courtyard as a fresh flurry of snow settled, the perfect backdrop for the carol singing.

She didn't remember ever singing in a choir. Apart from one fateful occasion during a school play in primary school, a time she'd much prefer to forget. She'd fallen head first down the stairs leading from the stage and twisted her ankle.

'Are you okay?' Mack whispered in her ear.

'Yes.' Poppy nodded. 'I was just thinking how nice this all is.'

She looked around the crowd of people singing beneath the Christmas tree. Lots of people had made it from West Par and a few from Trestow too. Mr Euston was standing at the front with his dog, Gray, and Nick had brought along his partner, Gabby. Elsie from the bakery in Penworth Bay and Ian were singing at the top of their lungs somewhere too. If this was what Christmas was supposed to be like – coming together to celebrate – then, yes, she was okay. More than okay.

As the song ended, the snowfall grew heavier, large flakes dipping and diving on the breeze around them. A large cheer swept through the crowd as people held their hands out to catch the snowflakes and small children ran across the courtyard, chasing them as they danced their way to the ground.

As another song began, Poppy noticed Percy leaning across to whisper something in Flora's ear before slipping away from the group. She frowned. Where had he gone to?

The snow was even heavier now, quickly covering the branches of the tree – the perfect Christmas Eve.

As the carol came to its final verse, voices became louder, penetrating into the cold, quiet air around them.

A round of applause filled the courtyard as the music faded and people began folding up their song sheets and pulling their scarves up to their chins.

Flora clapped her hands together and stood up with the help of her crutches as the crowds, now settled, looked towards her. 'I just want to say a huge thank you for choosing to spend your Christmas Eve here with us at Wagging Tails. It's a true honour to have you all here on this special day. And, of course, a huge thank you to Nick, who has kindly donated this beautiful tree to us...' Flora paused and looked towards the reception area. 'Did I hear something?'

People looked around the crowd.

Flora held her hand to her ear. 'I'm sure I heard something. Does anyone else hear that?'

A gentle tinkling of bells sounded from behind the building.

'What's that, children? Who do you think could be visiting?' Flora grinned.

The bell tinkled again, louder this time, and a chorus of excited exclamations rose through the group. Children paused; the snow forgotten as they eagerly looked towards the building. As silence fell over the courtyard, the bell tinkled again, this time as Santa stepped out from behind the building, red suit, white beard and a huge black sack behind him.

'Ho ho ho. I wondered if I might find you all here.'

A loud cheer rose as children rushed forward, surrounding Santa.

'Go on, off you go, boys.' Mack pointed towards Santa. 'Gus, why don't you take him?'

'Okay. Come on, Spencer.' Gus held his hand out for hi

younger brother and they both made their way towards the growing crowd.

'He's always been a little scared of the big man.' Mack grinned as he watched Spencer reach Santa, emboldened by the confidence of having his brother by his side.

Poppy smiled as Mack squeezed her hand quickly.

* * *

'You're not?' Poppy laughed as she looked at Alex's guilty-looking face.

'I am. I forgot to buy tape. I only realised this evening before coming back here for the carols.' He shrugged as he pulled red and green tartan wrapping paper over the box on the counter and secured it with some tape.

Laughing, Poppy shook her head as she carried a full bin bag of recycling through the reception area. 'How much have you got to wrap?'

'Not much.' Alex kicked at a collection of bags behind the counter.

'Not much? There're loads there! You'll be here all night. Why don't you take the tape home and do it there?'

'Nah, it's not my wrapping paper either. I forgot that too.' He dropped a now-wrapped gift into a bag and picked up the next, a box of chocolates.

'I'm sure Flora won't mind you taking it. She's probably already done all her presents.' Poppy opened the door out into the courtyard.

'Umm, I might do. I'm happy wrapping here at the moment though.'

Poppy stepped out into the cold courtyard. The snow was still coming down and in the half an hour since the carol singers had left a blanket of fresh snow had already settled adding at least a couple of inches to what had previously been there. She looked towards the tree where Mack, Mrs Moreton, Susan and Malcolm were standing chatting whilst Gus and Spencer helped Percy build a wooden sledge.

'You all right, lovely?' Flora hobbled towards her on her crutches.

'Yep, this is the last bag.' Poppy gestured to the recycling she was carrying, opened the large bin and tipped the bin bag out, the cardboard takeaway cups and lids falling in.

'Thank you for that, lovely.'

'Has everyone else gone home?'

'Yes, Ginny and Darryl left to go and spend the rest of the evening with Darryl's dad, and I think Susan and Malcolm are off soon too.' Flora looked across at the tree. 'It's been a pretty perfect Christmas Eve, hasn't it?'

'The best one I've had.' Poppy grinned.

'Oh, lovely. I'm so glad you've enjoyed yourself.' Flora touched her on the forearm.

'Me too. I can't believe that just a few weeks ago I was stuck in that house miserable with Ben, and now...' She held her arms out, as if to encompass Wagging Tails, Flora, Mack, the boys, everyone. 'It's funny how quickly things can change.'

'It sure is. It really is.'

'Thank you for letting me come down and stay.' Poppy wiped a happy tear from her eye.

'Don't be daft.' Flora batted Poppy's thanks away. 'It should be me thanking you for coming. Now stop before you make me start. Chuckling, she swiped at her eyes with her gloved hand.

'Right, we're off now.' Susan and Malcolm walked towards them 'We'll see you for Christmas dinner tomorrow.' Stepping forward Susan drew first Flora in for a hug and then Poppy.

'Thank you both for coming and helping.' Flora grinned.

'It's been a wonderful evening. The true height of the Christmas spirit.' Malcolm twisted his Christmas bow tie back into position and raised his hand. 'Merry Christmas.'

'Merry Christmas.' Susan waved as they turned and left.

'Flora! Flora! Where's Flora?' Alex's voice was panicked as he ran out of the reception into the courtyard, the cordless reception phone in his hand.

'Over here, lovely.' Flora waved.

When he'd ran over to them, Alex stopped to catch his breath. 'It's Mr Thomas. Paige has just rung. He's been taken into hospital. He's okay, but the dogs are alone.'

'Oh dear, oh dear. And his cats too, I presume?' Flora shifted position.

'No, he agreed to let them be rehomed earlier in the day, apparently.' Alex shook his head.

'Okay, okay.' Flora pinched the bridge of her nose.

'I'll go and get them,' Poppy offered. After all, she'd finished all her tasks taking the bins out.

'What's going on? Where are you going?' Mack reached them, concern etched across his face.

'Mr Thomas has been taken into hospital, so I'm going to drive up and pick up the remaining dogs.'

'I'll come too then.' Mack nodded.

'What about Gus and Spencer?' Poppy looked across the courtyard. Percy and the boys were securing the rope to the newly built sledge.

'They'll be happy playing in the snow with their new sledge for a bit before going back home with Mrs Moreton. If that's okay with you?' Mack turned to Flora.

'Of course it is, lovely, but only if you're sure?' Flora rubbed his arm.

'Yes, I'm sure. It makes sense. If any of them need medical attention, I'll be there to help.'

'Okay, thank you. Both of you.' Flora grimaced. 'I'm afraid the van will need jump-starting before you leave.'

'No, it won't. Percy bought a new battery and installed it.' Alex pulled the van keys from his coat pocket and passed them to Poppy.

'Oh, really?' Flora looked from Alex and then towards Percy.

'Right, I'll go and clear the snow off the van while you tell the boys what's happening.' Poppy walked away.

'You both be careful in this snow, won't you?' Flora called after them.

35

Leaning forward, Poppy flicked the wipers to full power as she squinted out of the windscreen.

'Are you sure you can see properly?' Mack leaned forward, too.

'Enough. It's a lot heavier than before, though.' She turned right down the narrow country lane. With the road covered in so much snow and no visible markings, all she could do was use the grass verges as markers and hope for the best.

'It's a lot heavier. I can hardly see out at all.'

'Same here. I don't think it's too much further, is it?'

'A couple more miles along this road and then down the dirt track across the field to his house, from what I remember.'

'Oh, great.' Poppy lurched as a tyre got caught on something and the van dipped across the bump. She glanced at Mack before focusing on the road ahead again. 'What was that?'

'Umm...' Twisting in his seat, he looked towards the back window. The only light was the pale red glow of the rear lights. Probably the kerb or something.'

Poppy nodded. 'Okay, the kerb is fine.' She turned right again and groaned.

'Ah, I'd forgotten about this bit.' Mack leaned forward in his seat again.

Poppy looked ahead. The road rose uphill a few metres in front of them. From what she remembered from when she'd collected some of the other dogs with Flora, although the hill was steep, it didn't go on for long. And although it seemed impossible, the snow appeared to be getting even heavier. Even with the windscreen wipers on full speed, the time between them clearing the glass and a layer of snow forming again was barely a millisecond.

'Do you think we can make it?'

'There's only one way to find out.' Mack grimaced.

'Okay. Hold on.' Poppy switched to first gear and pumped the accelerator. 'I want to close my eyes.'

'That's not advisable.' Mack chuckled. 'It'll be fine. The worst that'll happen is we get stuck.'

'I hope you're right.' As they approached the bottom of the hill, she tightened her grip on the wheel and gritted her teeth. The van crawled up, the tyres crunching against the newly fallen snow. 'It's working! We're getting there.'

'Yep.' Mack nodded.

Poppy was sure she could see the summit of the hill ahead. Only for a split second before the snow covered the windscreen again, but she was sure she had.

But before she could celebrate, she felt the tyre beneath her hit something in the road. The van stopped abruptly, throwing both her and Mack forward. She pumped the accelerator pad, and the van lurched forward before once more hitting whatever it was. Revving the engine, she willed it to go over whatever was in the road.

'It's stuck. It's stuck on something. What do I do?'

'Let the van roll back a little and then pump the accelerator and turn hard right. Hopefully, we can get around it.' Mack wiped condensation from the windscreen and peered out. The road was dark around them, the snow swallowing the pale light from the headlights.

'Okay, okay.' Poppy took a deep breath and quickly compressed the clutch before pushing the gear stick into neutral. The van inched backwards, slowly at first, before the tyres lost control and the van slipped backwards. 'No, no, don't do this.' Poppy hit the brakes, a seemingly futile attempt to slow the inevitable. 'It's not working. The brakes aren't working.'

Mack twisted in his seat, looking behind him, before turning back around and laying his hand over Poppy's on the gear stick. 'Pop it into first again. Hopefully, we can get some sort of traction going.'

Doing as Mack suggested, she let his hand guide the gear stick into first and pumped the accelerator again. For a moment it felt as though the tyres had found grip and the van moved forwards, but only for a moment, just before it started to roll backwards again.

'We're going to crash.'

Leaning over in front of Poppy, Mack gripped hold of the steering wheel. 'Keep your foot flat on the accelerator and that should slow us down.'

'I hope so.' With her foot flat against the accelerator pad, Poppy gripped the steering wheel, both her and Mack's knuckles turning white.

Twisting in his seat to look behind them. Mack guided the van as it propelled backwards down the hill. 'Almost at the bottom now.'

'Right, okay. That's good.' Poppy swallowed as they finally came to a stop.

'Are you okay?' Mack turned to Poppy as he yanked the hand-brake up.

'No... yes. Yes, I think so. You?' She looked down at her shaking hands before looking across at him. 'I guess we're walking, then.'

'I guess so.' Mack leaned forward for a quick kiss before they braved the cold.

'Right, we'd better do this.'

Mack nodded, reached across and pulled Poppy's hat down lower over her ears before opening his door.

Bracing herself, Poppy opened hers and stepped out, where she immediately sank ankle deep into the snow. This wasn't going to be an easy walk.

* * *

'We should turn back, hole up in the van for the night.' Mack pulled his mobile from his coat pocket, holding it up above his head. 'I've no signal whatsoever.'

'Nor have I.' Slipping her mobile back into her pocket, Poppy turned to him. 'But I don't know if going back to the van will help us, either. We must be nearly halfway to the house by now and Paige said she'd left the front door unlocked for us. If we don't get there someone else might get in. I know it's highly unlikely because of the weather but I'd still feel better if we got to the dogs.' She peered ahead, the light from Mack's torch app on his phone lighting the way. They'd agreed to save her battery for later.

'Yes, you're right.' He glanced behind her. 'We might actually be over halfway by now.'

As she stumbled over something in the snow, Poppy reached out for Mack, gripping his arm as she lurched forward.

'Are you okay?' Mack steadied her. 'Did you get hurt?' He looked her up and down.

'No, I'm okay. I think.' She circled her ankle, testing it out. I hurt, but it wasn't too bad.

After a quick glance at his phone, Mack drew Poppy toward

him, and wrapped his arms around her. 'Merry Christmas,' he said gently.

'What? Has it really gone midnight?' She hugged him back, glad both of the comfort and the heat from his body.

'Yep. Five past.' Grinning, he showed her his phone.

'What about Gus and Spencer? I feel awful that I've dragged you out here and you're not with them.'

'They'll be fine. They'll both be asleep by now and won't even know I'm not back yet.'

'What about Mrs Moreton? Won't she mind?'

'No, she will have made up the spare room. She had asked to stay over anyway so she could see them open their presents in the morning.' Mack grimaced as realisation hit. 'I guess Santa might be a little later than usual dropping those off.'

'Oh no, they'll think he's missed them.'

'Nah, I'll make sure he writes a little note explaining that Rudolph wanted to stop to watch the moose in Alaska or something.'

'I still feel awful.'

'Don't. Besides, I was the one who offered to come. You didn't ask me. And it's not as though Flora could have come with you.'

'No. Although I'd bet she'd have tried if you hadn't offered.' Poppy smiled.

'Yes, I bet she would have done.' He chuckled before taking a deep breath. 'Ready to go again?'

'Not really.' She hugged him a little tighter before pulling away.

36

'I think I can see something. A little light. Are we there? Is that Mr Thomas's house?' Wiping the snow from her face with the back of her drenched glove, Poppy peered through the night. There was definitely a light. It was faint, but it was there.

'Yes, I think so. It must be. There aren't any other houses close by.'

Mack gripped her hand tighter as they made their way closer.

'Thank goodness for that.' Poppy smiled, her cold cheek muscles hurting through the strain. She couldn't feel her feet, hadn't for ages now, and the damp from the snow was seeping higher and higher up her jeans. The snow covered their ankles now and was still falling.

'Here we are. Did you say Paige had left the door unlocked for us?'

'Yes, it should be.' Poppy bit her lip. She'd cry if they couldn't get in, after all the effort it had taken to get here. There was no way they could get back to the van now, and even if they did, the snow was probably deep enough to cover the exhaust and without being able to run the engine, they'd likely freeze, anyway.

Mack reached the door first and placed his hand on the handle, the signs of relief flooding across his face as it gave way and the door opened. A loud raucous of barking met them as at least six pups all bounded over, eager to see their visitors.

Mack ushered Poppy through first before closing the door behind them.

'Hello. It's okay. We're here to help you.' Holding her hands out, Poppy fussed the dogs as they sniffed around them.

'Aw, you're gorgeous pups, aren't you?' Mack knelt down as the dogs came up to him. After fussing them, he stood up again and held out his hands towards Poppy. 'Let me help you with your coat. The sooner we can get warmed up, the better.'

She let Mack help her, clumps of snow falling onto the floor as he did. After helping him with his, she knelt down and pulled her trainers and socks off before wringing the water from her socks. She pulled out her mobile, her heart dropping as she realised there wasn't a signal here either.

'No signal?'

'Nope, nothing.' Poppy turned her screen around to show him.

'Never mind. I'm sure Mr Thomas will have a landline. But first, let's get that fire going and heat up this place.' He walked across to the fire and began to pile kindling and logs onto it.

'I'll go and see if I can find some dog food.' As she turned to the kitchen, she patted the side of her leg. 'Come on, show me where your food is kept.'

* * *

Poppy winced as she held out her hands towards the warmth of the fire, the heat warming her cold fingers.

'Here.' Mack wrapped a blanket around her shoulders before

passing her a mug. 'I couldn't find any tea or coffee or anything, so I'm afraid it's just hot water.'

'Thank you. I have a feeling this will be the best hot drink I've ever had.' She smiled as she wrapped her hands around the mug and took a sip, the hot water immediately warming her throat. 'Yep, best hot drink ever.'

'Ha ha, you're easily pleased.' Mack chuckled as he leaned back against the sofa and pulled the blanket over his knees. He patted his lap and looked at the small spaniel watching him from the kitchen doorway. 'Do you want to come up?'

'Aw.' Poppy held out the blanket as the small dog curled up between them. 'I'm just glad we finally got here.'

'Same here. For a moment there, I was wondering if we'd make it.' Mack grimaced.

'Oi. You didn't tell me that.' Poppy widened her eyes.

Mack shrugged. 'Would it have helped if I had?'

Closing her eyes, she thought back to how far they'd had to trudge through the snow. 'Nope. It definitely wouldn't have.'

'There you go then.' Mack sighed. 'The landline is down. I tried it while you were feeding the dogs, but hopefully it'll be back up and working by the morning.'

Poppy couldn't imagine a lone phone line leading to an almost derelict house on a farm in the middle of nowhere would be particularly high up on the priority list on Christmas Day. But what else could they do but hope?

'At least the dogs are all okay.' She nodded towards the group of dogs huddled by the fire, all clearly glad of the warmth.

'Yes, I've checked them over and they all seem pretty healthy. They just need a good bath and a brush.' He fussed over the spaniel curled up beside them. 'Don't you, buddy?'

'They are gorgeous.' Turning around, she pulled the curtain aside and looked outside. 'I think the snow's stopped.'

'That's a relief.' Mack grinned. 'As much as I love the snow when I've nothing to do but sit inside or take the boys sledging, I don't like it quite so much when we've had to risk our lives driving and traipsing through it to rescue some pups.'

Poppy shook her head and laughed. 'Yes, the rolling down the hill backwards in the van was my least favourite part, I think.'

'Oh, I'm not sure, the half an hour before we spotted the house, when I thought my toes were going to break off from the cold wasn't fun either.' Holding his feet out towards the fire, he wriggled his toes.

'Ha ha, yes, that stretch was tough too.' Sighing, she leaned her head against his shoulder.

Mack wrapped his arm around her shoulders. 'Now, though, even with the aroma of animal poop surrounding us, I'm more than happy.'

Poppy grinned. 'Same here.'

Closing her eyes, she listened to the crackle of the fire and the occasional whimper or yawn as one of the dogs stirred. It certainly wasn't the Christmas Eve she'd imagined, but it couldn't have turned out better. She looked across at Mack, his head leaning against the sofa cushions, his eyes closed. Yes, this was pretty perfect.

37

'Thank you again, Chris. You're literally a lifesaver.' As he shook his hand, Mack also patted Chris on the back.

'Yes, thank you for rescuing us from Mr Thomas's and bringing us all here.' Poppy nodded towards the dogs now being led into Wagging Tails by Percy and Alex and hugged him. 'And Merry Christmas.'

'No worries. Just glad I could help.' Chris looked down at his watch and indicated his tractor behind him. 'Right, I'd best get going. I don't want to miss Elsie's Christmas dinner at the bakery.'

'Thank you again, lovely.' Flora waved before pulling Poppy and Mack in for a hug. 'Don't you two do that to me again. I've been up all night fretting over you both.'

'We won't.' Poppy hugged her back, glad to be home. 'I'm guessing you arranged the rescue?'

'Yes, well, I knew you'd have got stranded there after not hearing back from you. I also knew Chris had a tractor at the farm animal sanctuary.' She shifted on her crutches. 'And being as I didn't have the phone number of the farmer who has taken over for Mr Thomas, I couldn't think of who else to turn to.'

'Well, thank you.' Poppy smiled. 'It's good to be back.'

'Yes, it really is. I'm going to have to run, though.' Mack held up his mobile. 'Mrs Moreton has messaged. Gus and Spencer are waiting until I'm back to open their presents. She found where I'd hidden them and set them out early this morning.'

'Oh, you must rush, then. Off you go.' Flora rubbed his forearm. 'You'll all come for Christmas dinner though, won't you? The boys too and Mrs Moreton, of course.'

'Well, being as I wasn't home to do the meal prep last night, that would be amazing...'

'Oi! Is that the only reason you want to come for dinner?' Poppy tried to keep a straight face. 'Just to eat? Not to spend some time on Christmas Day with me?'

Grinning, Mack shrugged. 'It depends on how good the Yorkshire puds are, I guess.'

Opening her mouth in mock shock, Poppy laughed. 'Fair enough.'

Mack stepped forward and pulled Poppy in for a hug before kissing her on the forehead. 'Of course, to spend time with you.'

Poppy smiled and kissed him on the lips.

'Happy to eat any of your leftover Yorkshires, though.'

'Ha ha, you'll be lucky.'

Poppy watched as he walked across to his car.

'A perfect match, if ever I saw one,' Flora said, linking arms with Poppy as they waved him off.

'Secret Santa time!' Alex called from the open door. 'Come on, you two. Everyone else is ready.'

'Right, you heard him, Secret Santa.' Tapping Poppy's arm, Flora spun them around before leading the way inside.

'Oh, yes, Secret Santa.' Where had she put her gift? 'I think I've left mine over in the cottage.'

'I've already brought it over and popped it in the kitchen.' Flora grinned.

'Come on through and grab a seat. Susan's made hot chocolate in the slow cooker.' Alex held the kitchen door open, ushering them both inside.

'Merry Christmas, Poppy,' Susan said, pulling her in for a hug before turning back to the slow cooker.

Slipping into the chair between Aunt Flora and Ginny, Poppy gratefully took the steaming mug of hot chocolate offered to her.

'Cracker time.' Alex held up a cracker.

Poppy ran the pad of her forefinger across the embossed foil, following the pattern of the holly leaves. She couldn't even remember the last time she'd pulled one of these. Certainly not since she and Ben had stopped going round his parents' house for Christmas dinner.

'Poppy.' Ginny nudged her and pointed at everyone else around the table, who were ready, arms crossed over in front of them, so each person held their own cracker and that of the person to the left, creating a long trail of crackers around the table. 'Like this. It's tradition here.'

Poppy picked up the cracker and looked around the table, copying how they were all doing it.

'After three. One, two, three.'

Bangs and pops echoed around the kitchen as the crackers were pulled, showering paper jokes, tiny gifts and paper hats onto them all. A loud cheer rose as everyone picked up their prizes.

'What did you get?' Flora nodded towards Poppy.

Holding it up, Poppy laughed. 'I think it's supposed to be one o' those spinning top things.' Setting the small plastic spinner on the table, she spun it and tiny pictures of Santa, reindeer and snowflakes merged into one mix of colour. 'How about you?'

'A little padlock!' Flora waved it in the air in front of her. 'Hope fully it'll be strong enough to keep you lot out of the biscuit jar.'

'Oh, it won't be. I can assure you of that.' Darryl laughed as he flexed his arm muscles.

'I was afraid that would be the case.' Chuckling, Flora picked up her hat, and shook it out before placing it on her head. 'Right, Secret Santa time, I believe.'

'Here's yours, Poppy.' Alex passed her a gift bag.

'Ooh, thank you.'

Peering inside, she pulled out a small round present wrapped in green and red paper. She held it to her nose. It was definitely a bath bomb, a Christmassy one at that judging by the smell. She unwrapped it to confirm, before digging into the bag again and pulling out a small tube-shaped gift – a small hand cream. She smiled. She could definitely do with that.

'Oooh.'

Jerking her head, Poppy looked over at Flora, who was holding up a gold necklace, a golden paw print hanging from a delicate chain.

'Wow, that's beautiful.'

'Oh, it's gorgeous, Flora. Shall I?' Susan stood up behind Flora, taking the necklace and fastening it around her neck.

'It is, isn't it?' With the necklace in place, Flora looked down at it and wiped a tear away. 'Thank you to whoever bought me this. I'll treasure it always. And thank you, Susan.'

'And there was me thinking we had a tenner as a limit.' Looking around the table, Alex laughed. 'I wonder who would have bought you that?' He raised his eyebrow.

Poppy glanced at Percy. A fine rash of red flashed beneath his beard and across his face.

'You can't ask that. It's Secret Santa.' Percy cleared his throat.

'You're right, I won't ask.' Flora looked around the table and smiled. 'Whoever it was, thank you.'

38

'Your turn, Poppy.' Spencer pointed his fork at her, a chunk of roast potato dripping gravy down his top, and grinned.

'Really? Do I have to?' Poppy grimaced. Mack and Mrs Moreton had made themselves at home since arriving just as Susan and Percy had begun serving Christmas dinner.

'You do. You know you do.' Alex laughed. 'No one else has been allowed to get away with not doing it.'

'Okay, okay.' Grinning, she straightened her back and took a deep breath, ready to do her best impression of Santa. Laying her palms on the table, she tried her best. 'Here goes... ho ho ho.'

Spencer laughed, the roast potato on his fork forgotten as it lay in a gravy puddle on the tabletop. 'Now you, Mack.'

'Right.' Stretching his arms in front of him, Mack cracked his knuckles. 'Ho ho ho.'

'No way. That was even worse than Alex's.'

'Hey! I thought I was pretty good at Santa impressions.' Mack tickled Spencer under the arm.

'No, don't!' Squealing, Spencer slid across to the other side of his chair, knocking his glass over as he did so.

'Careful.' Mack laid out some napkins, soaking up the orange juice.

'Don't worry. We'll clean that up along with the rest of the after-dinner muck.' Susan waved her hand, dismissing the spillage, and stood up. 'I'll get you another one, love.'

'Thank you.' Spencer looked around the table. 'I think it's just you, Percy. You've not had a turn.'

Percy paused, his fork halfway to his mouth, and blinked. 'Me? Oh, I'm rubbish at impressions. I don't think I'd sound anything like him.'

'You've got the same beard, though.' He pointed to Percy's beard. 'And it's real, isn't it?'

'It sure is.' Percy tugged on it. 'But I don't think I can pull off an impression of the big man himself.'

'Go on, try. Please?' Putting his elbows on the table, Spencer clasped his hands together, in a pleading tone.

'Just this once, then. Because you've asked so nicely.' Percy cleared his throat and holding his tummy, he rocked back and forth. 'Ho ho ho.'

Poppy watched as Spencer pulled Mack closer to him, covered his mouth with his hands and whispered in his ear.

Mack widened his eyes, and as if asking him to keep the secret, he held his finger over his mouth.

Turning to Poppy next, Spencer leaned in close and whispered in her ear. 'It's him. I think Percy is the real Santa.'

Keeping her face serious, she copied Mack and held her finger to her lips.

Spencer nodded seriously before looking sideways at Percy, but Poppy noticed him sit up a bit straighter as he began to cut up his potatoes.

'Do you know what Santa's favourite thing to do is on Christmas Day after spending all night travelling the world delivering presents?' Flora asked in a hushed tone, leaning across the table towards Spencer.

'No. What? Sleep in front of the fire?'

'Nope. Guess again.'

'Umm, eat mince pies?' Spencer grinned.

'Nope. He likes to play a game of Monopoly.' Flora raised her eyebrows.

'Really?' Spencer looked from Flora to Percy and back again before lowering his voice. 'Do you think he'll let me play?'

Sitting back in her seat, Flora shrugged. 'Ask him.'

But it was his eldest brother the little boy turned to. Spencer pulled Mack towards him and whispered in his ear again, at which, straightening his back, Mack looked at Percy and grinned.

'So who's up for a game of Monopoly this afternoon?'

'Absolutely. There's nothing I like to play more after a good Christmas dinner.' Percy smiled.

'Great!' Mack looked at Gus and then around the table. 'Before we play, Gus, do you want to tell everyone what you've done.'

Gus shrugged nonchalantly before mumbling, 'I've set up a fundraising page online.'

Mack shook his head and chuckled. 'He's raising money to pay off your debts, Flora.'

'What?' Flora laid her cutlery down. 'A fundraising page? Online?'

'That's right. And he's emailed all of my customers asking them to donate.' Mack looked at Gus and grinned, pride flooding his face 'You've raised quite a large amount already, haven't you, Gus?'

Gus shrugged again, a deep blush flooding his face. 'Most of it.'

'Oh, sweetheart. That's amazing! Thank you so much, lovely. Flora picked up a napkin and dabbed at her eyes.

'You kept that quiet.' Poppy looked over at Mack and raised he eyebrows.

'We wanted it to be a surprise. A Christmas gift if you like.' Mack nodded towards Gus.

'Thank you. Thank you so much, Gus.' Poppy grinned at him.

'It doesn't hurt having all these rich celebrities as customers, does it?' Alex picked up his glass. 'Let's raise a toast for Gus and his genius fundraising idea.'

'Oh yes. What a good idea.' Flora held her glass high in the air. 'To Gus.'

'To Gus.'

* * *

'Poppy, love.'

Poppy looked up from where she was kneeling on the floor of Dougal's kennel fussing over the small dog. She'd left everyone to set up the board game whilst she went to give the dogs some meat from their Christmas dinner. 'Sorry, Aunt Flora. Dougal was whimpering so I just wanted to spend a bit of time with him.'

'Oh, poor little love.' Flora leaned against the door to the kennel, her crutches dangling from her arms.

'I know. I don't think it was such a great idea of mine to bring him over to the cottage for those few days. I think it's made him even more homesick for a family.' She sighed. She'd thought she'd been doing the right thing, for Dougal and for her aunt whilst she had been forced to rest after coming out of hospital.

'Well, you know one way to fix the problem, don't you?'

'No? How?'

Flora shifted on her good leg, balancing her weight on her crutches again.

'Are you okay?'

'I'm fine.' Flora waved away Poppy's concerns. 'I have one question for you before I offer up a solution for Dougal's troubles.'

'Oh, right?' Poppy rummaged in her pocket for a treat and held it out for Dougal. 'What's the question?'

'Were you serious when you said you were thinking about moving down here?'

Standing up, Poppy watched as Dougal pawed at her leg for another treat. She couldn't imagine moving back home now. Not away from her new-found friends, the dogs, Aunt Flora, Dougal. And, of course, Mack. 'Yes. Yes, I am.'

Flora beamed. 'Good. I was hoping you'd say that. In that case, why don't you adopt Dougal? He loves you and it's clear you love him. When you get a teaching job, you can drop him off here or back at the cottage and I'll wander over and walk him.'

'Adopt him?' Poppy fed him another treat. She could. She could adopt him.

'Yes. Of course, it goes without saying that you're more than welcome to stay on at the cottage for as long as you like. With Dougal, of course.'

'I don't know what to say.' Poppy wiped her eyes. This could actually be her reality. Living down here, with Dougal, being in a relationship with Mack.

Flora chuckled as she hobbled across to her niece and drew her in for a hug. 'Yes?'

'Yes. Yes, I'd love to adopt Dougal and I'd love to move down here. Permanently.'

39

'Are you sure you're okay? You don't need a hand?' Mack looked across at Flora and Percy. Flora was hobbling along with her crutches, Percy hovering next to her, ready to catch her if she stumbled.

'Honestly, you two. I'm fine. Perfectly capable of swinging myself along with these. How do you think I get from the cottage to Wagging Tails each day?' Flora paused, balancing on her good leg, and held up the two crutches.

'I told you she wouldn't accept any help.' Poppy hugged the pile of board games to her chest. After playing Monopoly, they'd decided a board game marathon was in order so the four of them had wandered across to the cottage to raid Flora's understairs cupboard of board games whilst everyone else fed the dogs.

'Ah, that is where you're wrong, Poppy, lovely.' Flora placed her crutches back on the ground and carried on. 'Now, Mack and Percy, if you really want to help, why don't you go ahead and get the kettle on?'

Percy looked from Flora to Mack and back again and tugged on his beard.

'I'll run ahead and turn the kettle on. Why don't you hang back and close the gate behind everyone, Percy?'

'Good idea. Yes, I'll do that.' Percy nodded, relief flooding his face.

'I'll walk ahead with you.' Poppy quickened her step in time with Mack's.

'Do you want me to take some of those?' Mack shifted the pile of games he was holding under his arm and held out his free hand.

'Thanks.' Poppy passed a couple across to him. 'I really don't know if we're going to get through this many games.'

'Ha ha, no, probably not.' Mack chuckled as he took the games. 'Thank you for having us over today. The boys are really enjoying it and Spencer is truly convinced Percy is the real Santa.'

'He is, isn't he?' Poppy grinned. 'You do realise he'll be doing all his homework and chores on time until next Christmas, don't you?'

'Oh yes.' Mack grinned back. 'I'll have to buy Percy a pint to thank him.'

Shaking her head, Poppy laughed.

'So, are those two an item or what?' Mack nodded behind them towards Flora and Percy.

Poppy shook her head. 'No. Although apparently, he's liked her in that way for a while, but she has no idea.' She paused. 'Unless everyone's just teasing me.'

'Oh, I don't think they were teasing you.' Mack chuckled. 'You can see how much he dotes on her.'

'Maybe.' Poppy shrugged. 'Have you heard any more from your dad?'

'Yes, he's coming over tomorrow for dinner.' Mack swallowed.

'That's good, isn't it?'

'Yes, yes, it is. He's told me he's bringing presents for the boy and wants to treat it as an extra Christmas Day dinner.' Mack shrugged. 'It's good.'

'I'm pleased things are working out with him.'

'Me too.' Mack smiled. 'It's early days but if he continues to keep his word and visits when he says he will then I think things might just be okay.'

As they neared the gate, the courtyard came into view and in it, a van Poppy didn't recognise. 'Huh, I wonder whose van that is.'

'I don't think it's a van.' Mack squinted his eyes. 'It's one of those ambulances that takes people places.'

'You mean the non-emergency ones? The ones that take people to appointments and things?' She glanced back at Flora. 'I'm sure Flora would have remembered if she had an appointment today. Besides, she would have just asked me to take her rather than arranging a lift. Not to mention it would be strange to have one on Christmas Day. I don't understand.'

'I guess we'll find out in a moment.'

'I guess we will.' Poppy watched as Ginny and Darryl appeared from the reception area and walked up to the ambulance. 'Is that Paige?'

'I'm pretty sure it is.' Mack pointed as Paige helped someone out of the ambulance. 'Oh, and that's Mr Thomas, isn't it?'

'Yes, I think so.'

Quickening her step, Poppy rushed over and paused behind Ginny and Darryl as they waited while Paige and Pat helped Mr Thomas out of the back of the ambulance. He looked better than when she'd last seen him when they'd collected Eden and the other four dogs he had surrendered.

Ginny smiled at Poppy. 'Mr Thomas is on his way home and has come to pop by and wish his dogs a Merry Christmas.'

Poppy swallowed. It must be so hard for him not being able to take them home. At least they'd spoken about him keeping one of them.

'Oh, that's a lovely idea. How are you feeling, Mr Thomas?'

'As though I've been on twenty fairground rides without any safety belts.' Mr Thomas grimaced. 'But I'll get there, I will.'

Poppy nodded.

'Come on then, let's get inside out of this cold.' Paige held her arm out towards him.

Turning again, he looked at Poppy and Mack. 'I believe I owe you two a thank you.' He nodded at them. 'Thank you for collecting my dogs after I was taken to hospital.'

'You're very welcome.' Poppy smiled. It must be such a bitter-sweet moment for him. He knew his dogs were now safe, but he also knew he wouldn't be taking them home. Apart from the one and that wouldn't be today.

'Come on then, let's get you inside into the warmth.' Paige supported Mr Thomas as they all made their way into Wagging Tails.

* * *

'Mr Thomas, you're looking much better than when I saw you last,' Flora said, when she and Percy had caught up. 'Do you want to come through and see your dogs?'

'Yes, I'd like that very much.' Mr Thomas nodded and stood up where he was now sitting at the table.

'Right, let's go through to the kennels then.' Flora turned to Gus and Spencer. 'Are you two coming to help?'

'Okay.' Gus nodded as he and Spencer held the door to the kennels open.

'Why don't you two go and put that kettle on?' Flora nodded towards Poppy and Mack.

'Good idea. I'm parched.' Nodding, Mack waited for everyone to follow Flora and Mr Thomas through to the kennels before opening the kitchen door.

Walking inside, Poppy placed the board games she was carrying onto the table before turning and helping Mack with his. She looked across at the slow cooker, the rich aroma of chocolate filling the kitchen. 'Umm, that hot chocolate smells so good.'

'It sure does.' She watched as Mack turned the radio on, Christmas tunes quickly filling the room. 'Here, let me.' Holding out his hands, Mack helped her out of her coat.

'Thanks.'

'Care to dance?' Mack held his hand towards her and raised an eyebrow.

Poppy grimaced. 'I couldn't dance to save my life.'

'Ah, but I can. Come on, I'll teach you. I took lessons in school. I may be more than a little rusty, but I can still hold my own. I think.'

'Okay.' Poppy laughed as he placed one hand on the small of her back and held her hand with his other one.

Looking down at her feet, she tried to copy Mack as he led her around the room.

'Do you trust me?' Mack paused.

'Of course.'

It was true. She may not have known him for very long, but she felt as though she knew him deep down, knew his soul, and could trust him.

Mack grinned and tucked his finger beneath her chin, gently lifting her face until their eyes met. 'Don't look down. Let me lead.'

'Okay.' She nodded; her eyes fixed on his as he moved to the music. She smiled as he spun her around the room. She was doing it. She was dancing.

The song changed, a slower beat filling the kitchen.

Pulling her closer, he wrapped his arms around her as she leaned her head against his shoulder. 'I'm so glad I met you, Poppy.'

'Me too.' She laughed. 'I mean, I'm glad I met you.'

'I know what you meant.' Chuckling, he gently tucked her hair behind her ears and leaned towards her.

As their lips touched, Poppy closed her eyes. She hadn't felt like this in a very long time. If at all. Had she felt this deeply for Ben? She wasn't sure she ever had.

'Oh, I've got something for you.' Pulling away, he rummaged in his coat pocket and pulled out a small present.

'Oh, thank you.' Taking the gift, she looked at it. The gold wrapping paper was finished with a red bow and a small cardboard tag in the shape of a heart bore the words, '*Merry Christmas xxx*'. 'Shall I open it now?'

Mack nodded, rubbing the back of his neck.

She smiled as she carefully untied the ribbon. As the wrapping paper fell to the floor, she gasped and held up the small snow globe. It was smaller than the one he'd won for her at the ice rink. Small enough to fit in her palm, but the metal casing around the globe was so intricate and delicate. Tiny silver snowflakes were etched across branches that weaved around the sphere. Inside the glass was a woodland scene, four beautiful silver reindeer standing in a copse, looking right at her.

Standing behind her, Mack wrapped his arms around her. She leaned her head against his chest and he enclosed her hands with his so they were both holding the small snow globe.

Together they tipped it upside down before setting it right again and watching the almost impossibly delicate snowflakes flutter gently down, covering the reindeer and the ground in a dusting of snow.

'Mack, it's so beautiful.' Twisting in his arms, she looped her arms around his neck and pulled him closer, their lips touching. 'I have a present for you too.' Stepping back, she opened the top cupboard by the door and pulled out a present. 'It's not much though.'

'Thank you. I didn't think you'd have had time to get me anything.' He rubbed his palm across his face before taking the small gift. He squeezed it and grinned. 'It's squishy.'

'It is.' Laughing, she went to go stand next to him. 'Go on, open it.'

Ripping the paper off, Mack grinned as he held up the keyring – a small reindeer teddy holding a tiny banner with the words 'Merry Christmas' in a cursive font.

'Thank you.'

'Sorry, it's only small and nothing like what you've given me.' She looked down at the snow globe, still in her hand, and shook her head. She still couldn't believe he'd bought her something so special.

'Oh, it is. It's brilliant. Thank you, and it seems as though we both had the same idea.' He chuckled.

'Yes! Both our gifts are similar to the ones we won at the lucky dip.'

'A reminder of a wonderful date together. The perfect Christmas gifts.'

EPILOGUE

Poppy lowered the large plastic storage box in front of the Christmas tree and stood, hands on hips, looking up at it.

'You're going to miss it, aren't you?' Mack opened the stepladder next to her.

Poppy nodded. 'I am actually.'

Mack shrugged. 'At least it's less than a full year to next Christmas.'

'Ha ha, yes, I suppose it is.' Poppy shook her head. 'I've enjoyed this Christmas more than any other. It's strange to think that when I arrived at the beginning of December I hated the festivities, everything to do with Christmas, but now...'

'You're no longer a Scrooge wannabe?' Mack leaned against the stepladder and grinned.

'Oi!' Poppy glared at him before laughing. 'I guess you're right I hated Christmas. I guess I dreaded having to pretend to be happy.'

'And now?'

'And now, I don't need to pretend.' She tilted her head back looking up at the top of the tree. The pine needles were falling, and some branches looked a little bare, but she felt hope. Hope for the year ahead. Hope for her and Mack's relationship.

'You're happy?'

'I'm happy. After making the decision to move down here permanently, I just...' She glanced at him. 'I see my future here. Here with Flora, Alex, Percy, Ginny, Sally and Susan. Here with Dougal and Ralph and all the other dogs. Here with the beach a short stroll away and... with you.' She looked at him, their eyes meeting.

Mack stepped towards her, clasping her hands in his. 'I for one am glad you've decided to stay. In fact, I wanted to say...'

'Watch out, Dougal's out. Is the gate shut?' Ginny called across the courtyard.

Mack glanced down before looking across the courtyard towards the gate. 'Yep, the gate's closed. He's safe.'

'Hello, you. Have you come to help?' Bending down, Poppy waited as Dougal barrelled towards her and fussed him behind the ears, his favourite spot.

'Right, let's get this done and then I'll make everyone a nice cuppa. I'm parched.' Susan unplugged the fairy lights.

Picking Dougal up and cradling him in her arms, Poppy watched the small bulbs flicker off. Christmas was well and truly over now.

'Spring next!' Ginny said as she began to unravel the string of fairy lights. 'My all-time favourite season of the year.'

'Oh, yes. I do love spring. It's full of hope, isn't it? Hope of things to come in the new year.' Sally smiled as she helped Ginny with the lights. 'I love planning out my year, what I want to achieve, places I want to visit.'

Poppy nodded. 'I like that idea.'

When she'd been with Ben, she'd just seen spring as the start of another year, another year doing the same things, going to the same places. Now, though, she felt free. According to Melissa he was apparently happy with Davina, and she was definitely happy their relationship was over. And she had Mack. She grinned as she watched him help with the tree. She felt as though she'd stepped into a new chapter in her life. Yes, she liked Sally's way of thinking.

'Well, you lot can take your spring. Now Christmas is over, I'll be waiting for summer.' Alex moved the stepladder closer to the tree. 'Pub garden weather, shorts, holidays. They're my idea of fun.'

'Are you taking the lights off from the top?' Ginny crossed her arms and tilted her head, her eyes fixed on the stepladder in Alex's hands.

'I was going to, yes. Why?'

'No reason, just try not to get quite so tangled up again.' Ginny laughed. 'Getting in a tangle on the ground is one thing, doing it halfway up a ladder is another.'

'Don't worry. I know one broken leg in the Wagging Tails family is quite enough.' Alex grinned as he climbed the ladder.

'Have you heard back from that supply agency yet, Poppy?' Susan dropped a length of the fairy lights and bent to pick them up.

'Yes, they contacted me yesterday. They've invited me for an informal chat. So, all being well, I should get hired. The woman said they have loads of supply work going at the moment too.'

Dougal fidgeted in her arms.

'You want to get down?' Lowering him to the ground, she grinned as he ran across towards Mack.

'That's great then. It sounds very promising.'

'Yes, hopefully. I'll miss working at this place, though.' Poppy looked across the courtyard towards the reception building and dog kennels.

'Well, you'll be living with Flora for the time being, so you won't get away from us that easily.' Ginny grinned. 'I bet you're looking forward to getting back into the classroom and doing what you love, aren't you?'

'Yes, I am.' Poppy nodded.

And it was true. She was.

'That's all we can reach. Alex, you've got the rest, okay?'

Susan helped Sally and Ginny place the lights into the plastic box, leaving a trail of fairy lights trailing upwards towards Alex.

'I do indeed. In fact, here's the last of the lights.' Alex nodded towards the mound of fairy lights in his arms.

'I'll take them.' Reaching up, Poppy took the lights from him and packed them away. Bending her knees, she picked up the box and grimaced. It was heavier than she'd thought it would be.

'Hold up, I'll help you carry it.' Mack placed Dougal back on the ground and ran towards her, grabbing the end of the box and taking half the weight.

'Thanks.' Poppy straightened her back a little and led the way towards the storage shed at the back of the courtyard.

Inside, they lowered the box and pushed it across the floor under the shelf.

'All done for the year.' Poppy wiped her hands down the front of her jeans.

As they walked back, Mack turned to her. 'There was something I wanted to tell you earlier.'

'Oh, yes?' Poppy smiled as she watched Dougal tugging on the low branches of the tree as Susan, Ginny, Sally and Alex tried to carefully lower it to the ground. She looked back at him and frowned. 'Is everything okay?'

He shifted from foot to foot before running his fingers through his hair. 'What I was going to say was...' He cleared his throat. 'I love you.'

Poppy opened her mouth and then closed it, not knowing what

to say. Had he actually said that? Those three words, small but powerful?

'Did you just say what I think you did?'

Chuckling, Mack stepped towards her, taking her hands in his. 'I did. I love you, Poppy. I never thought I'd find love again, not until the boys were older, anyway. I wasn't looking for anyone to come into my life. I was focused on my job and on raising Gus and Spencer as best I can, but then you...'

He grinned and glanced away.

'What? Then I what?' She smiled sweetly.

Shaking his head, he met her eyes again. 'You came into my life and I know we've not known each other long but, I love you. I really do.'

Poppy laughed. 'Good, because I love you too, Mack.'

A NOTE FROM THE AUTHOR

Very few rescue centres are as lucky as Wagging Tails to find a vet who is able to give such a discount to treat the animals in the rescue's care. The majority rely on donations from the public to cover vet bills as they do with food, shelter etc. Some may receive a small discount such as ten or twenty percent off vet care and fundraise to cover the rest of the costs.

ACKNOWLEDGMENTS

Thank you, readers, so much for reading *Chasing Dreams at Wagging Tails Dogs' Home*. I hope you've enjoyed reading Poppy and Mack's story as well as catching up with Flora, Ralph and all of the Wagging Tails family, humans and dogs alike, as much as I have enjoyed writing this book.

A huge thank you to my wonderful children, Ciara and Leon, who motivate me to keep writing and working towards 'changing our stars' each and every day. Also to my lovely family for always being there, through the good times and the trickier ones.

I'd like to thank Vicki and Lynn at Wellidogs (Wellingborough Dog Welfare – www.wellidog.org) for allowing me to come along to meet the wonderful dogs they have at Wellidogs and for letting me volunteer. Thank you to Jasmine, Aidan, Amy and Ash for giving me more of an insight to volunteering at a dogs' home.

I'd also like to take this opportunity to thank each and every person who works or volunteers at a dogs' home or rescue centre. Thank you for caring for the dogs in your care, and for relentlessly fighting for their future and happiness. You are wonderful beyond words.

And a massive thank you to my amazing editor, Emily Yau, who reached out and believed in me – thank you. Thank you also to Sandra Ferguson for copyediting Wagging Tails, and Shirley Khan for proofreading. And, of course, Clare Stacey for creating the beautiful cover. Thank you to all at Team Boldwood!

ABOUT THE AUTHOR

Sarah Hope is the author of many successful romance novels, including the bestselling Cornish Bakery series. She lives in Central England with her two children and an array of pets, and enjoys escaping to the seaside at any opportunity.

Sign up to Sarah Hope's mailing list for news, competitions and updates on future books.

Follow Sarah on social media here:

[f] facebook.com/HappinessHopeDreams

[twitter] twitter.com/sarahhope35

[instagram] instagram.com/sarah_hope_writes

[BB] bookbub.com/authors/sarah-hope

ALSO BY SARAH HOPE

The Wagging Tails Dogs' Home Series

The Wagging Tails Dogs' Home

Chasing Dreams at Wagging Tails Dogs' Home

Escape to... Series

The Seaside Ice-Cream Parlour

The Little Beach Café

Christmas at Corner Cottage

Boldw∞d

Boldwood Books is an award-winning fiction publishing company seeking out the best stories from around the world.

Find out more at www.boldwoodbooks.com

Join our reader community for brilliant books, competitions and offers!

Follow us
@BoldwoodBooks
@TheBoldBookClub

Sign up to our weekly deals newsletter

https://bit.ly/BoldwoodBNewsletter

Printed in Great Britain
by Amazon

29917663R00152